D0349173

014461268 X

The Askham Accusation

The Askham Accusation

REBECCA TOPE

Allison & Busby Limited
11 Wardour Mews
London W1F 8AN
allisonandbusby.com

First published in Great Britain by Allison & Busby in 2023.

A CIP catalogue record for this book is available
from the British Library.

First Edition

ISBN 978-0-7490-2971-5

Typeset in 11/16 pt Sabon LT Pro by
Allison & Busby Ltd

FSC
www.fsc.org
MIX
Paper | Supporting
responsible forestry
FSC® C171272

Printed and bound by
CPI Group (UK) Ltd, Croydon, CR0 4YY

*Dedicated to all five of my grandchildren,
Morgan, Leia, Luke, Leonie and Caitlin*

Author's Note

As with other titles in this series, the action is set in a real village. The pub, church and Askham Hall are actual places, but the other properties have been changed or invented.

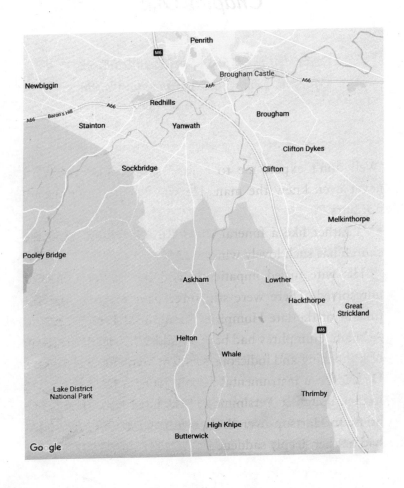

Chapter One

'Well don't expect me to come,' said Angie crossly. 'I never even knew the man. He was Persimmon's friend, not ours.'

'I rather like a funeral,' said Russell mildly. 'And the church has such lovely windows.'

His wife tutted impatiently and the matter remained unresolved. There were still three days to go before the funeral of the late Humphrey Craig in St Peter's Church, Askham. Humphrey had been a builder, his death the result of a shocking and ludicrous accident involving a chainsaw. He had been instrumental in converting a barn belonging to their daughter, Persimmon Henderson, into a handsome house in Hartsop over the previous winter and his death had left her deeply saddened.

'Besides,' said Russell, ten minutes later, 'Simmy could do with some company.'

'What?' said Angie, who had forgotten all about the dead builder by then. Her attention had been diverted by a very black cloud looming over Blencathra. 'Surely it can't be going to snow? It's only October.'

'Don't be silly,' said Russell. 'The forecast is for gales at the end of the week.'

'Could be a blizzard.'

'I doubt it. We haven't had a good blizzard for decades now. I'm not sure there's ever been one in October.'

'We missed the one in the eighties. People are still talking about it. There was a woman in the shop only yesterday—'

'You'll be able to mind the baby, then. When I go to the funeral,' he interrupted. 'Simmy and I, that is.'

'So I will,' Angie agreed with neither enthusiasm nor reluctance. Baby Robin was not yet able to crawl or engage in conversation or clearly express his wishes. Angie was not-very-patiently waiting for him to grow up a bit. She did, however, like the sense of being an influence in his development and there were activities the two of them enjoyed very much. Singing and playing with water were top of the list.

'It's a terrible thing about poor Humphrey, though.' Russell heaved a deep sigh. 'All that blood.'

The accident had made headline news in the local media, and earned a mention nationally. The man had been lopping a large branch off a dying ash tree, twelve feet above the ground, when he had somehow inadvertently leant over the whizzing blades and cut his own chest open. 'Just as if he was doing his own post-mortem,' said Angie. Nobody did black humour like Mrs Straw. Humphrey had no qualifications as a tree surgeon, but as some tooth-sucking wise-after-the-event commentators remarked, there were no restrictions on who could buy and wield a chainsaw.

He left a wife and two teenaged daughters. It was a genuine tragedy, everybody said.

Russell was upset not only by the ghastly accident, but by words he had just had with a local woman. She had heard him saying 'Threkkled' as the correct pronunciation of Threlkeld, where he and Angie now lived. 'It's not said like that,' she accused him. 'You're obviously an incomer. It should be "Threlkkled". You have to say the first L.'

'Really?' He had not been able to believe her. 'Are you sure?'

She had merely given him a withering look and walked away. For the following hour he had rehearsed both pronunciations and wished the darn place had been called something else.

Christopher Henderson, son-in-law to Angie and Russell, felt the death far more acutely than anyone might have anticipated, including himself. It literally made him shake. When nobody was looking, he permitted himself to shed tears about it. Humphrey had been so full of life – a capable, plain-speaking, hard-working human being. He and Christopher had argued a few times, got in each other's way, caused a degree of mutual irritation, in the process of turning a barn into a house where the Hendersons could live. But all that had been perfectly normal; part of the process where each man knew his role. With a new baby to worry about, Humphrey had been a reassuring presence for the Hendersons. Merely visualising his open smiling face made Christopher cry again.

Simmy, his wife, was equally affected. 'I still can't believe it,' she said, after four days. 'I know it's a cliché, but it's true. I can't persuade myself there's a world going on without Humphrey.'

'Yeah,' sniffed Christopher. 'You know the way you can usually find something to hang on to. I mean, you dredge up little memories that make it less awful that they're dead. All a sort of magical thinking, I suppose, or self-delusion, but it helps. This time, it's not working at all. Sorry, that sounds like gibberish, doesn't it.'

'I think you're saying there are sometimes signs, when you look back. Or the person had it coming in some way. Or they had a miserable future ahead of them and they're better off out of it.'

'Sort of. Not as definite as that. All unconscious, really. But this time . . .'

'I know,' said Simmy. She was careful not to voice her relief that her husband's feelings chimed so well with hers. There had been moments over the past months when she had not been sure that they were as well matched as they'd thought. Now his grief was making him a better person in her eyes. The old Christopher, who she'd known all her life, was still there. But what a pity it took a truly tragic death to expose it to view.

The funeral was likely to be extremely well attended. 'How big is the church?' Simmy wondered.

Christopher shrugged. 'No idea. But I'm told the pub is just next door. Good business for them.'

'Askham won't know what's hit it – where's everyone going to park?'

He shrugged again. 'We'd better offer your father a lift, if he's serious about coming.'

'Good idea,' she sighed. Until that day she had assumed that baby Robin would also go to the funeral, which had been a worry, but his grandmother's offer to mind him had come as a welcome surprise.

'Any excuse to get out of the funeral,' said Angie with a frown. 'I have a feeling it's going to be mawkish.'

'And we all know you wouldn't like that,' said Simmy.

Angie opened her mouth to defend herself, but then shut it again and nodded. 'Ought to by now,' she agreed.

The church was down a hill, outside the centre of the village, with a river running close by. The Punchbowl Inn was slightly further up the hill. Across the road was the entrance to Askham Hall, which was all Simmy had known about the village until today. The pub's car park had been given over to the use of mourners, and a steady stream of people were walking from it to the church, as well as appearing from other points in the village. The Hendersons parked in the roadway alongside a grassy bank, under a massive tree. All normal rules had evidently been suspended, and vehicles were crammed into every available space.

'What a lovely spot,' said Russell, admiringly. 'It must be ten years since I was last here. I'd rather like to be buried in this churchyard myself.'

'You'd have to move into the Askham parish, then,' said Christopher.

11

'I doubt that,' said Russell airily. 'There are ways and means.'

'We're late,' said Simmy for the third time. 'We'll never find anywhere to sit.'

They were met by two men belonging to the undertaker, who asked them to sign their names on the list of mourners and pointed out a scattering of spare seats. 'Sorry there aren't three together anywhere,' said one of the men.

Inside, the organ was softly playing, and the distinctive church windows were admitting more daylight than one found in most churches. Plain glass was arranged in regular lozenge-shaped panes, bounded by dark pewter fixings. The panes were small and looked ancient. Simmy found them soothing, with none of the puzzling or threatening depictions of biblical scenes in bright stained glass that often assailed her when visiting a church. There was no distraction in these simple designs. If anything, they seemed to invite a quiet meditation – entirely suitable for a funeral. She sat with her father, while Christopher gallantly took himself to the end of a pew two rows back. Was it gallantry, though, she wondered. Perhaps he just wanted to be amongst strangers, who would ignore him if he wept.

Simmy sat quietly, wondering what it was that made this death so special. The waste; the suddenness; the fact that Humphrey had been such a thoroughly nice man? There were none of the softening veils that usually blurred the worst of the grief and shock. If it was like this for her, she thought, what must the poor wife and daughters be suffering? It was impossible to imagine, or contemplate.

As the hymns and eulogies and prayers rolled by, the usual comforting detachment began to make itself felt. The service was doing its necessary work far better than could have been reasonably hoped. Perhaps it was merely achieved through the sheer numbers present. People were standing at the back; some were even outside. When it was over, a lengthy line of mourners waited to speak to the widow, as she took up a place near the church door, once the interment was accomplished.

When everybody began to drift out of the churchyard, having expressed their condolences or decided to head straight for the pub without doing that, Simmy saw that there was a knot of villagers in the road beyond. People who felt they might be intruding, or who had noisy toddlers with them, or simply wanted to be where the big event was happening – they gathered and watched and witnessed the disappearance of a man they perhaps only knew by reputation, or casual recognition due to living near him. A man who had wantonly ended his own life by a momentary lapse of good sense. It could happen to anybody, they decided. Simmy had not heard a word of criticism of Humphrey's own carelessness – not even from her mother.

'Come on,' said Christopher. 'I think we can go now.'

'Aren't we staying for the bunfight?' asked Russell. 'It feels a bit previous to go so soon.'

'It'll be bedlam,' said Simmy. 'And we really don't know any of these people. We ought to get back to Cornelia soon, as well. She still can't be left on her own for long.'

'Your mother would have had her, along with the baby,' said Russell unconvincingly. Angie could see the merits of the new member of the Henderson family in theory – indeed she had acquired the animal – but she preferred to keep it at arm's length.

'Too late now,' said Simmy. 'Though it does seem a

bit bad to leave so early.' She lingered on the pavement outside the church where there were numerous other people, watching mourners talk to Humphrey's widow and daughters, wishing she had not let Christopher hustle her away from the long line of sympathisers. 'Poor woman,' she said. 'And what must it be like for those girls? They're so young.' Humphrey had spoken of his children a few times when working in Simmy's house. The older one had a few problems, she remembered. *Usual teenage stuff*, the baffled father had shrugged. The girl had apparently fallen out with all her friends and stopped going to Girl Guides, which she had always loved. Looking at her now, seeing a tall adolescent wearing a black jacket slightly too tight for her, brown hair tied back severely, Simmy thought how wrong it all was. Without her father, the girl was bound to take life even harder than before.

Christopher had also been keeping an eye on the family, especially Sophie. 'She looks so young and lost. Don't you think she's a bit like Bonnie? Same pale frizzy hair,' he said. 'Her girls aren't anything like her, either of them. How old are they, do we know?'

Simmy shrugged. 'Teens. Thirteen and fifteen, something like that. They're tall, like Humphrey, aren't they? And you're right – Sophie's hair is just like Bonnie's.'

Bonnie Lawson's parentage was no great mystery, but neither was it ever discussed. Whether she looked like her mother or father was of no apparent interest. Both had let her down disastrously, leaving the Social Services to patch her up as best they could. To Bonnie's great good fortune, they had found her a woman who was quite possibly the best foster parent in the country.

14

Bonnie's biological mother was now and then mentioned, but never her father. Simmy could not remember ever having given him a thought. But now it occurred to her that he could be living somewhere in the area, with siblings, other offspring, the whole works. Perhaps Sophie Craig was connected somehow.

Russell snorted at this remark. 'You sound like your mother,' he told Christopher. 'She was always looking for likenesses. It'll get you into trouble one of these days.' Christopher's late mother had been a close friend to the Straws in years gone by. Russell especially remembered her fondly and often talked about her. How was it that funerals always seemed to direct one's thoughts to earlier generations and remote family connections, wondered Simmy.

She tapped her father's arm and laughed. 'That's true,' she said and followed her menfolk as they started up the hill to where they'd left the car. There were other people all around, going the same way. 'I might come back tomorrow for a proper look at the flowers, if they're still here,' she said. 'It'll be nice to see the grave when it's gone quiet.'

'It's a wake, not a bunfight,' said Christopher pedantically, referring to Russell's remark three minutes ago.

Russell raised his chin. 'Technically, you're wrong. I grant you the definition has shifted in recent times, but the wake was always *before* the burial and prayers and so forth. Not afterwards. But in the absence of a word for the food and chatter that follows the main event, it became usual to call it the wake. Erroneously, in my opinion.'

'Trust you, Dad,' said Simmy. 'Pedantic to the end.'

'It's always been the wake in my experience,' Christopher insisted.

'Well, you're only young,' said his father-in-law tolerantly.

A young woman was walking just behind them. She leant forward and said, 'It's right, though. The wake was always a vigil, held before the funeral, sitting around the coffin to keep the dead person safe. Not many people seem to know that these days.'

Russell stopped and turned, his face beaming. 'Well said, my dear. How refreshing to have your support.'

The newcomer gave a fleeting smile. She was short, with spectacles and a long face. 'I shouldn't have intruded, but I just couldn't resist. They get it right in America, oddly enough. Most of the time, anyway.'

Simmy was examining the face, wondering who this might be. There was nothing distinctive or memorable about it. 'Do I know you?' she asked.

The reply was diffident, uttered with a small shrug. 'I don't think so. My name's Lindsay. I live just up the road. Are you local?'

'Not very. I live in Hartsop, and my father's in Threlkeld, near Keswick.'

'Well, it was nice to meet you,' said Lindsay, with a special nod at Russell. 'Perhaps I'll see you again sometime.'

'And perhaps not,' said Russell in a whisper, as they parted company with the woman. 'That was a very funny look she just gave us.'

Chapter Two

There were a hundred things in the house to remind them of Humphrey. Every door had been hung by him; the staircase and several walls had been his handiwork. Simmy vividly remembered the way she had colluded with him to hide the slight bodge on the bottom stair from Christopher, who could be picky about small things. There had been a few millimetres of empty space where the floor dipped under the riser. 'I could just pop a bit of filler in?' Humphrey had suggested. 'Otherwise, I'll have to take the whole section out and start again.'

'Do it,' Simmy had advised with a smile.

Humphrey had first met them when Simmy was seven months pregnant, following the arrival and early months of little Robin with keen interest. More than once he had offered comforting words when the baby was unsettled. He had even acted as unofficial babysitter once or twice when Simmy dashed off to a shop.

But it was irrational to miss him, because he had finished the building work and gone, months ago. 'We never invited him to the wedding,' Simmy said now, in deep remorse. 'Why didn't we?'

'It was a working day.'

'We forgot about him.'

'We probably did,' Christopher conceded. 'Let's hope he didn't notice.'

And so it went on, all over the weekend following the funeral. Neither of them could shake the man and his untimely death out of their minds, despite the major distractions provided by their son – and their new pet.

Cornelia had arrived only three weeks earlier, her acquisition finally orchestrated by Angie Straw, who had had enough of talk and took unilateral action. 'A boy should have a dog,' she said, looking at the infant Robin. 'A *man* should have a dog. The dog has been too long coming. So I've found one. She's four months old, and completely perfect for you.'

It took everyone by surprise, including the dog, who had been born in a house on a busy street in Workington. 'By rights, she would have been drowned at birth,' said Angie. 'That's what my mother would have done. She's the unplanned offspring of a pedigree golden retriever and a springer spaniel. As far as I can understand, both breeds are excellent with children, but she might grow rather large.'

'How did you find her?' wondered Simmy.

'There's a website called Pets Are Us, or something. I was browsing and there she was.'

'You should have consulted us first. You can't just go and get a dog for other people and dump it on them like this.' Despite its yellow parent, the animal was jet-black. It was sitting in the middle of their kitchen floor looking from face to face, but reserving a special smile for Christopher. The tongue lolled; the tail wagged; the ears flickered every time he caught its eye. Simmy pretended not to notice.

But Angie was implacable. 'Look at that! You know that dogs smile with their ears, don't you?'

'Yes, Mum. You've told me that a thousand times.' Angie and Russell had an ageing Patterdale terrier with expressive ears and minimal personality. Simmy sighed, knowing she had little ground for objection. She had actually promised Christopher a dog as a wedding present, and then disgracefully defaulted.

'Cornelia,' he said. 'That's what I'll call her.'

'Too many syllables,' said Angie firmly. 'You'll sound ridiculous, calling her across the fells.'

'Cor-NEE-lia,' Christopher warbled at the puppy. 'Come here!' Nothing happened, apart from another tentative ear-smile. He picked it up and rubbed his chin across the top of the soft black head. 'I actually wanted a *yellow* dog,' he said, as if it didn't matter a bit.

'Her mother was yellow,' said Angie daftly. 'She might have yellow puppies if you ever bred from her.'

Simmy yelped, sounding rather like a dog herself. 'No way! They'd be *mongrels*.'

Everyone looked at her, even little Robin.

'I don't think that word is allowed these days,' said

Angie. 'They're designer dogs, and the wilder the mix the better. This is a mongrel already, come to that. And all the better for it. Widens the gene pool and so forth.'

Simmy found herself in shameful isolation. 'I expect you're right,' she muttered. It was a rare experience to be chastised by her outspoken mother for using a forbidden word. In general, Angie fought hard for freedom of speech. 'I haven't got used to the idea yet.'

Her husband was clearly in love. The puppy licked his face, and he accepted the gesture as his rightful due. He murmured into the floppy spaniel ears. He held the robust little body high in the air and laughed. 'She's beautiful. I can never thank you enough,' he told his mother-in-law. 'Just what I've always wanted.'

'Except for the colour,' growled Simmy.

'Look, Robin!' Christopher lowered the dog to his son's level – which was a blanket on the floor. 'See your new friend. She'll be like your sister. You'll grow up together. It'll be like something out of a story.'

'Famous Five,' Angie suggested. 'That dog was a retriever, I think.'

'Where did "Cornelia" come from?' asked Simmy. 'What's wrong with Hetty or Buffy or even Sally? Cornelia's awfully pretentious.'

'It just *came*,' said Christopher airily. 'The moment I looked at her. Although I did also toy with "Zenobia" for a minute.' Again he sang out the name: 'Cor-NEEL-ia,' giving it a warm inviting tone that made everyone smile.

The puppy settled in with minimal fuss, although bedtime was never easy. 'It seems so *mean*,' said Christopher, as he shut his new darling into the kitchen. 'Leaving her all by herself.'

'What's the alternative?' asked Simmy darkly, knowing she was going to have to stand her ground unwaveringly if the dog was not to spend every night on her bed. 'We could get one of those cages that people seem to favour nowadays.'

'Perish the thought,' exclaimed Christopher. 'That's a horrible idea.'

'Apparently most dogs like them,' she said mildly. 'Makes them feel secure.'

'Rubbish!' said Christopher.

Robin wasted no time in taking his father's side. On the first day he grabbed the puppy's ears and pulled. He then seized hold of her tail. They rolled over together and squealed in unison. Simmy was paralysed with horror. 'She'll bite him!' she cried.

'She won't,' Christopher argued. And she didn't. Instead, she licked him lavishly and Simmy winced. It was one thing to be relaxed about ordinary household germs and quite another to see her infant exchanging saliva with a dog.

'She's got to stop licking his mouth,' she protested. 'It can't be healthy.'

'It's *fantastically* healthy,' came the implausible reply. 'It'll boost his immunity brilliantly.' And he proceeded to recount some memories of his time in Central America where children and animals played gloriously together with no ill effects at all. There were moments when Simmy wished her husband had remained in Bowness-on-Windermere all his life and shared the same perfectly reasonable attitude to viruses and bacteria that most British people adopted.

To Simmy's relief, Cornelia soon learnt that licking the baby's mouth earned disapproval, and she stopped of her own accord. It became apparent, a week after the pup arrived, that both she and Robin were cutting teeth – a second lot in the canine case, and first for the little human. Neither seemed unduly perturbed by the process, but Simmy rather liked the coincidence. The dog was also growing at an amazing rate. 'She gets taller every day,' said Simmy. 'And heavier.' Christopher pointed out the large paws, which suggested there was still a lot of growing to come.

The day after Humphrey's funeral was one of Christopher's working Saturdays. He performed as an auctioneer of assorted antiques and collectables every other weekend, taking a day off midweek as compensation. Simmy was left in charge on a blustery autumn day, unsure what to do with the time. Her Windermere florist shop was amply covered by Bonnie Lawson, her young colleague-cum-employee, assisted by an even younger girl, Tanya Harkness. Simmy's parents had very recently moved to a bungalow near Keswick, having spent twenty years or more running a busy bed and breakfast in Windermere. The whole family had shifted northwards, ostensibly because of Christopher Henderson's workplace. Even Bonnie's boyfriend Ben had temporary lodgings in the area, so he could continue working for the auction house. Something that had begun as a fill-in summer job was rapidly becoming permanent, to widespread adult concern. Ben was only nineteen, officially genius-level in his intelligence quotient and still reeling from having failed as an undergraduate. The university ethos had defeated him, as he repeatedly fell foul of the plethora of rules as to what it was permissible to say or think. The no-nonsense vigour of the auction business fitted much better with his nature.

'Surely it can't have been as bad as all that?' his parents

kept saying, perpetually distressed and baffled by his failure.

'It was,' Ben assured them. 'Worse, if anything.'

And still Simmy's thoughts returned to Humphrey. She and Christopher and Russell had hung back from the interment, with the majority of the mourners. They had not spoken to Mrs Craig or her daughters. At the time it had felt like enough to hear the eulogies and register their names on the undertaker's list. They had dropped a ten-pound note into the collecting box, destined for the Air Ambulance people. Just such a rescue had been attempted following the man's ghastly accident, summoned by the owner of the tree he was lopping in the village of Tirril. It arrived too late, albeit faster than a motor vehicle obstructed by stone walls, crowds of tourists and a ploughed field would have managed.

By a rather opaque process, she made the decision to go back to Askham for another look. It was no great distance from her home in Hartsop. In essence they were at opposite ends of Ullswater, in the same north-east corner of the Lake District. But there was no direct connecting route and the drive could easily take half an hour. Longer on a Saturday that was still on British Summer Time – just. The clocks would go back the following weekend. The sudden urge to go and look at the grave felt unreliable, as if her instincts were leading in quite the wrong direction. There would be no headstone for many months yet; the pile of raw earth would look violent and unnatural. But there would be flowers and Simmy was a florist and she had acquired an eye for nuance when it came to funeral tributes. Humphrey's wife had stipulated family flowers only, but there would always be those who insisted on sending them, either from an adherence to tradition or a failure to find any other satisfactory way of expressing their sympathy. Simmy knew a lot about these motives and the force with which they were manifested. She had learnt from hard experience just how central a simple bunch of flowers could be to some of life's largest moments.

The arrival of the dog had greatly increased the sense of pent-up energy in the house if there was no outdoor activity that day. The favourite option for some time had been a short walk through the little village to the end of the road and up the nearest fell, which was Hartsop Dodd. From the car park it was a mile to the top. With a baby in a back carrier it was possible but not especially enjoyable to do it in an hour or so. The first part was uncomfortably steep and whoever had Robin was in constant fear of slipping over or getting the centre of gravity wrong. The child would wobble or cry and the whole exercise had soon been set aside for a time when Robin could scramble up the path by himself. Now the habit was to stroll along beside the little river that flowed into Ullswater – officially entitled the Goldrill Beck – ending up in Patterdale and one of its pubs.

But that felt too strenuous as well. Cornelia had to be kept on a lead until Christopher could convince her that sheep were not to be chased and orders were to be obeyed. Simmy had rejected any suggestion that she should share in this training, but she could not realistically avoid frequent outings for the creature. Christopher was at work all day, and she was already committed to giving their child fresh air and stimulation. The dog was inevitably included. 'Surely it's no hardship?' said Christopher and it wasn't, exactly. It was just one more thing to be factored in, along with giving the pup its food, washing its bedding, tidying up its toys and monitoring its toilet arrangements.

Cornelia very much liked the car. She associated it with days out in interesting places, encounters with other dogs, and the company on the back seat of her young master. Simmy felt bad at not inviting her father and his dog to join her on this return trip to Askham, especially as he would know the best places to walk – as well as all the local points of interest. Russell Straw had an encyclopaedic knowledge of the whole region, and never tired of exploring. But, Simmy reminded herself, she was really only planning to visit the church again, and perhaps a short stroll along the river if there was a handy path.

There was a very small parking area across the road from St Peter's, with a sign insisting that it was exclusive to people on church business. 'That's us,' Simmy muttered, feeling unsure. She spent two long minutes extracting child and dog from the back seat, putting Robin in a buggy and keeping firm hold of Cornelia's lead. The outing was not going to be of much interest to either of them, she feared.

Before crossing the road, she paused to ·assess the immediate setting. A large square house was perched on rising ground above the church, intriguing in the way it both dominated and yet remained detached. It looked old and slightly weather-beaten and had probably once been the vicarage. Perhaps it still was, come to that. The church had clung on to at least a few handsome old mansions for their clergy to inhabit, where the temptation to sell them off had been resisted.

To her left the river flowed serenely under a bridge and away to the north. She had a feeling it must be the River

Lowther, which meandered all across the north-east Lakes, past Penrith and off to join the Eden, which was a really serious waterway. Lowther was a name to be found all over Askham and its surroundings. There was a Lowther Castle, Lowther Park as well as a tiny Lowther village. Simmy had heard the word uttered with something like reverence by local people, but she was very hazy as to the history and origins of it all. Another reason to have included her father in the outing.

The church claimed her attention, at last. Its unusual windows were as effective from the outside as they were to worshippers inside, unlike stained glass. There was something plain and Quakerish about them, despite the obvious skill required in their construction. Again, there had to be a history behind the decision to choose such a distinctive design. There was a lively breeze, flicking at the few dead leaves and toying with Simmy's hair.

Humphrey's grave was at the back, easily located. Simmy pushed the buggy along the path, with Cornelia twisting and dragging at the lead, still refusing to conform to the usual procedure demanded of dogs. 'Come on, you fool,' Simmy told her crossly. 'If you can't behave, you'll have to stay in the car.' She was already wishing she'd thought of that before.

There were two other people examining the funeral flowers, which almost made Simmy turn back. But one of them looked familiar and she hesitated. Cornelia uttered a wholly unnecessary squeal, which drew two pairs of eyes her way. One pair was old, behind glasses, bordered with wrinkles. The other belonged to a young woman who had introduced herself as 'Lindsay' the previous day.

26

'Oh, hello!' the latter chirped. 'We meet again. What an adorable puppy!'

'She's a pest,' said Simmy, offended that the dog had elicited more admiration than her beautiful little son. 'And she's actually my husband's, not mine,' she added treacherously.

'Got enough on your hands already, I dare say,' chimed in the other woman, with a quick laugh that was more of a cackle. 'Is this your first?'

'Yes, he is,' said Simmy, not quite truthfully. There was no way she was going to explain that her first child had been stillborn. 'And he's really not much trouble.'

'Come to look at the grave, have you?' the old woman went on. 'They've left the flowers on it for once. I've no patience with the way they whisk them off to some old folks' home these days. Everything always in such a rush.'

Simmy smiled. Here was a living embodiment of what her own mother would be like in another thirty years or so, any residual inhibitions long dispersed to the winds, prejudices aired with impunity. Or would the thought police have gained so much ground that even ancient crones would be silenced by them?

'Did you send flowers?' the younger woman asked Simmy.

'No. Did you?'

Lindsay shook her head. 'I'm only a cousin-in-law. I didn't think I'd qualify as family. Sophie and I are good enough friends, all the same. Or I thought we were.' Her expression turned wistful for a moment.

'Daft business that,' came the aged commentator. 'People ought to be free to send what they want to. There

27

were never all these requests and such in my time. Specially when it was such a tragedy as this. We're all going to miss 'im and no mistake.'

'That's very true,' said Simmy, with a sigh. She looked from one to the other, wondering about the connection. Lindsay seemed to be under thirty, her companion well over eighty. Grandmother and granddaughter perhaps?

'Do you both live here in Askham?'

'Practically next door to each other,' said the old woman. 'How about you?'

'Oh – I live in Hartsop, actually. Humphrey did our barn conversion. We got to know him quite well.'

'Hartsop – fair way off, that'll be. Must have time on your hands, coming all over here like this.'

'Not really.' Simmy was growing tired of having to defend herself against something that felt at best disapproving. She looked to the other woman for rescue.

'You'd best be getting back,' Lindsay said to her aged companion. 'Unless you want me to come with you? Wait for me over the road, if so. I'm staying here a bit longer yet.'

'Nay, I won't keep you. I'm not helpless yet. You youngsters can have a bit of baby talk without me chipping in. Never did like babies much, to tell you the truth.' She turned away and began trudging through the graveyard to the road. She seemed fairly steady on her feet, her legs somewhat swollen but perfectly vigorous. In Simmy's experience, old women were generally too fat or too thin, but this one seemed a reasonable shape on the whole. Her shoulders were very slightly bowed and her face extremely wrinkled; her knees bowed outwards and her hair was white. She turned left when she reached the road and began to walk up the long incline towards the village centre.

'Will she be all right?' Simmy asked.

'Not my problem if she isn't – but yes, she'll be fine. She's at least ninety and never known a day's illness, or so she says. Awful old bat. Nobody likes her. You saw the best of her just now. She's a JW, you know.'

'Pardon?'

'Jehovah's Witness. A dying breed, these days. That's why she wasn't at the funeral – wouldn't set foot inside a Christian church.'

'Are they not Christians, then?' Simmy inwardly acknowledged her ignorance of the matter.

'Very much not. No Christmas or Easter for them. No birthday parties, either. They've got their own skewed version of the Bible. Though I have to admit she doesn't push it down people's throats like some do. I sometimes wonder if she's a bit lapsed these days. And she's the only one in the village, which must be lonely.'

'Hasn't she got a family to share it?'

'She's got a family all right, but hardly any of them are really signed up to it. One or two of them still stick to the basic rules, apparently. As I say, the whole thing is fizzling out in this country.'

'She's rather like my mother,' said Simmy thoughtfully. 'Doesn't seem to notice when she's being rude.'

'Oh, she notices all right. She just doesn't care. She's like something out of Grimm. A nasty old witch.'

'And you live next door to her?'

'Not quite, but close enough.' The young woman sighed, and then gave a little laugh. 'As neighbours go, she could be a lot worse.'

Chapter Three

The two of them stayed in the churchyard for another fifteen minutes, talking about Humphrey and debating whether or not Cornelia would be safe off the lead. Lindsay trotted down and closed the gate onto the road, and then offered to take the dog for a romp at the top part of the modest graveyard while Simmy wheeled Robin up and down behind her. They talked in snatches, managing to convey all the usual basics.

Lindsay lived on the left-hand stalk of the Y-shaped rows of houses at the upper end of Askham. She was renting it while she completed a doctorate. She had a cousin whose husband was related to Humphrey Craig, who had worked regularly for the owner of the rented house. 'He spent weeks shoring up the chimney only recently. That's how I know him,' she explained. 'They all know each other in these villages, of course. The cousin connection only occurred to me recently. And I've seen Sophie once or twice to chat to.'

Simmy shared items of her own information – the florist shop and Christopher's auction house. Then she asked, 'What's the subject of your doctorate? Do you have to write a thesis?'

'Very much so. It's on cruelty in *Dombey and Son*, believe it or not.'

'Gosh!' said Simmy weakly.

'I'm not the first, of course. But I'm looking at how typical of the time his characters are in the way they behave, which is harder than you might think. It's slow going.'

'Are you enjoying it?' Simmy had never been a big reader, and had avoided Dickens since she'd done *A Tale of Two Cities* at school. 'What happens after you've finished? You'll be a PhD – is that right?'

'Right. I'll be Doctor Lindsay Wilson. I like the discipline and the challenge and the "thought experiments", as my supervisor calls them. I have to do some teaching as well, mostly in Lancaster. I cram all that into one day a week – Fridays, would you believe? It's murder. When I finally get the doctorate I'll go full-time there, I suppose. I must admit I shudder a bit at the prospect of a life spent on campus.'

Simmy thought of Ben Harkness and his failure to integrate into university life, and wondered what he would make of this person. She made a bigger effort to listen, wondering if she should ask more about contemporary university life. 'You said "mostly in Lancaster"?'

'Oh, well, I do a bit of ad hoc tutoring locally. School

31

kids falling behind with English. Just a few hours in the evenings here and there.'

Something clicked in Simmy's head. 'Fridays are in Lancaster, are they? But you were here yesterday. That was a Friday.'

Lindsay raised her eyebrows at the stream of questions, but answered readily enough. 'By the skin of my teeth. I juggled the timetable mercilessly to be here. I had to go back for two more sessions in the afternoon.'

But why? Simmy wanted to ask. Lindsay had appeared entirely peripheral to the funeral. But perhaps that was a wrong impression. For all Simmy knew, the woman had been down at the front of the church, actively engaged in consoling poor Sophie Craig. And she must have skipped the socialising afterwards in order to rush back to her students. 'Very noble of you,' she said.

'You only get one chance with a funeral,' was the slightly obscure response.

Simmy changed the subject, in a vague attempt to offer up some personal information. She said a few sentences about her shop and the need to get back to it and what a wrench it would be to leave her baby. 'He still seems so tiny,' she sighed. 'And my mother's not terribly good with them when they're small. Actually, she's not great with kids of any age. It's mostly down to my poor old dad.'

'Mm,' said Lindsay, still devoting the bulk of her attention to the dog. Simmy watched her, with only the mildest of interest. She had no reason to think she would have any reason to meet this woman again. She had grey-blue eyes behind a pair of serious-looking spectacles and light brown hair. She was of short stature and had no noticeable accent. Her skin glowed with a nice tan that had to be recent. She wore a short coat in a colour that Angie would term 'camel'. It looked expensive.

'So she's not your granny, then? The old lady.' It was spoken idly, simply for something to say, the answer already obvious. But she was sure to be somebody's granny, if not Lindsay's.

'Who? Pauline? Perish the thought! I told you – she's an old witch. Loves a funeral more than anything. Gossips mercilessly. She knows absolutely everyone for miles around. I must admit some of her stories are pretty amazing. She's over ninety, you know. I said that before, didn't I? Remembers the war as if it was last week.' The woman grinned. 'In fact, you could say she's straight out of the pages of Dickens. The only way I can cope with her is to hold that thought. I've been trying to work out a way of putting her into my thesis. She could be Good Mrs Brown. And I keep wondering what Dickens would have made of the JWs. He didn't have a lot of time for anything churchy. He seldom mentions religion, you know.'

The reference to Good Mrs Brown was lost on Simmy, who had begun to admit to herself that she really didn't like this Lindsay person very much. Despite being in need of a local friend or two, this was clearly not a candidate for the post. Too young. Too clever. And oddly unpleasant in the way she ignored poor Robin. And not really very local, come to that. 'I actually came to see the flowers,' she said, rather late in the proceedings. 'And to have a little moment with Humphrey. There were too many people here yesterday.'

'Is that a hint for me to get out of your way?' Lindsay uttered a very forced laugh.

33

'Not at all. I was assuming you were here for much the same reason.'

'I suppose I was, in a way. I generally go out for an hour or so at some point. Mostly I walk up to the Cockpit, but it's very blowy up there today. Wind gives me a headache.'

'The Cockpit?'

'It's right up on the fell – all very ancient and mysterious, if you get it to yourself. A good place for thinking – but not today.'

'It seems quite sheltered down here, anyway. Just a nice little breeze.'

'Right,' said Lindsay vaguely. 'That's why I came this way.'

There was a pause in which Simmy looked up at the solid pale-coloured house standing sentinel over the church. 'Is that the vicarage?' she asked after a long moment.

'What? Oh, no, not any more. It was originally, of course. Now it's famous for being the most valuable property in the village. Not counting Askham Hall, obviously.'

'It's very . . . distinctive,' said Simmy, feeling slightly ashamed of her interest. She was staring hungrily at somebody's house, imagining herself living there and wondering about its history. 'I must ask my father if he knows anything about it. He's full of local stories about places like that.'

Lindsay cleared her throat. 'Actually, you can find out quite a lot online. There are photos of the interior – painted blue and all terribly tasteful.'

'Do you know the people?'

'No, not at all. I suspect they don't live in it much of the time. I don't think I've ever seen them. There's a lot of that sort of thing round here, obviously.'

The way she kept repeating the word *obviously* was irritating. It made Simmy feel dim, which led to a growing resentment. 'Well . . .' she said, spinning the buggy around rather violently. 'Come on, Cornelia. We'd better get moving. Soon be time for lunch.'

Robin had been showing an intent interest in the skittering leaves and the swaying branches, as well as a pair of fearless sparrows hopping around on the grass. The excursion had been worthwhile if only for this new bit of stimulation. The child was smiling and chirruping, gladdening his mother's soft heart. The dog was still pulling at the lead, wanting to chase the birds and probably run across the road and dive into the river for good measure. This was much less gratifying. 'Dratted dog,' Simmy muttered.

'She's adorable,' Lindsay corrected her. 'All she wants is to run free.'

'Which is out of the question here – obviously,' said Simmy.

Simmy put the child and dog back into the car and sat for a moment, trying to settle her thoughts onto Humphrey, as originally intended. But Robin was hungry and Cornelia confused and their needs were impossibly distracting. There was little choice but to drive home and rustle up something to eat. She had vaguely assumed there would be an alternative route back to Hartsop, but a glance at the tattered road atlas she kept in the car showed that there was little option but to follow the wiggly roads to Pooley Bridge and straight down the A592, which bordered Ullswater the whole way. She gave a thought to Pauline, the old lady who would be hard-pressed to get out of her home village without a car. No wonder she thought Hartsop was such a distance away.

It was unknown territory and she had left her phone at home deliberately. Even if she got slightly lost, she knew the main points along the way and trusted to the signposts to keep her on track. Once at the pub and shop in the middle of Askham, she simply had to turn right and then follow her nose – or preferably fingerposts saying 'Pooley Bridge'.

It worked, more or less, although it seemed to take longer than the outward trip had done. She passed through a fair-sized village called Tirril, which she was sure had not featured the first time. The name rang a bell, and she recalled that it was the place where Humphrey Craig had died. The twists and turns had quickly obscured any sense of east or west, and the overhead sun was no help. 'We're not lost,' she told her passengers, who seemed prepared to trust her. 'But I think we missed a turn somewhere.'

It was twenty past one when they got back to the house, which still very much resembled a barn on the outside. Simmy was every bit as hungry as Robin, so she mashed two bananas instead of one, and shared his lunch with him. 'You'll sleep well this afternoon,' she told him. He had been too hungry to fall asleep in the car. Only by the means of some loud singing had Simmy managed to keep him from screaming. Cornelia had been no help at all.

The rest of the day had an aimless quality to it that had become increasingly familiar in recent months. The Windermere shop felt remote and irrelevant at times like this. Bonnie and Verity – Simmy's weekday stand-in – handled the business with little difficulty and there had been no disasters or loss of custom. The move to Threlkeld had always threatened to be bad news for Persimmon Petals, since while Angie and Russell had lived in Windermere, it had been fairly easy for Simmy to work a regular day or two each week, dropping Robin off with his grandparents. Now that safety net had gone, and the dog had arrived, and everything was infinitely more complicated. Christopher had his own work commitments and was seldom available for proper baby care. It had been simpler for Simmy to let him off the hook and just stay at home almost all the time. Bonnie was readily contacted by phone, and Simmy could monitor most of the business online.

The only saving grace was that Ben Harkness now had a car of his own and could drive down to see Bonnie any evening he liked. The young couple had suffered from enforced separation for much of the year, but had reached a place where nobody doubted that they were united in perpetuity. There was not a soul in the Lake District who did not wish them well.

Now, as Angie kept saying, Christmas was just around the corner, and Robin would be old enough to enjoy all the excitement. Russell and Simmy did their best to restrain her enthusiasm, fearful that the baby would be disappointing. 'He'll probably just want to scrumple up the wrapping paper,' said Simmy.

It was not as if she *wanted* something to happen, she reminded herself now. It was more a case of knowing that something was *going* to. It always did. There had been crimes of violence in Ambleside, Grasmere, Coniston, Staveley and several other places close by. Simmy had become good friends with the local detective inspector, and often managed to be of assistance, if only obliquely. Ben and Bonnie had thrown themselves into amateur investigating, earning grudging respect and affection from Detective Inspector Moxon. Christopher had watched, alternately appalled and admiring. He himself had been dragged into the heart of the matter more than once. A colleague at the auction house had been killed earlier that year, and another victim had breathed his last in the very week he and Simmy had got married. Until moving back to Cumbria after ten years wandering around the world, he had believed himself to be quite adventurous. Now he suspected that he might be something of a wimp.

Perhaps the awful death of Humphrey Craig was enough to distract the fates for a while, Simmy thought. Perhaps life would continue calm and contented and uneventful for the foreseeable future. Decisions about the shop would make themselves, somehow or other – and there was even the prospect of a second child if things worked out as she hoped.

Christopher got home at the usual time, which was close to half past six. The last auction lot generally went under the hammer between five and six. Ben had told Simmy that her husband had implemented a little game at the start of the day, where he predicted to the minute when the sale would finish. 'He's almost always within five minutes,' said Ben wonderingly.

'He can probably control it more than you think,' said Simmy. 'Speeding up or slowing down as required.'

'Maybe,' said Ben with a frown.

Simmy had regretted her cynicism and agreed that Christopher was very clever.

'Good day?' they asked each other now, with the slight wariness that experience had taught them. Christopher knew that the dog was something of a trial, and Simmy had learnt to take nothing for granted.

She told him about her outing to Askham in some detail, while they were giving Robin his supper and getting him into his sleeping suit. Christopher did most of this, in an unspoken acknowledgement that the world took it for granted that having total charge of an infant all day long was more arduous than sitting on a rostrum watching bidders wave their numbers. Simmy was axiomatically more exhausted than her husband.

He was interested in her report of the day and mildly reproachful that she had done it without him. 'It was a nice thing to do,' he said wistfully. 'You never told me you were planning to do that.'

'I think I did mention it yesterday, actually, in a vague sort of way. Cornelia didn't like it much. I couldn't let her off the lead.'

'You should have taken her up on the fell.'

'What if she'd run away? She doesn't come when I call her, and I'd have been hampered with the buggy. It could have been disastrous. There's bound to be sheep up there.' The fact that the idea had never occurred to her was withheld.

'She's all right with sheep now. I told you.'

'With you, perhaps. She has a lot more respect for you.'

Christopher had been firm in his training methods, brooking no disobedience from the dog. In some mysterious way, he knew just what to do, despite never having lived with a pet of any kind. 'It's not rocket science,' he said, when Simmy asked how he did it. 'She wants my approval and will do almost anything to earn it.'

Pathetic, thought Simmy guiltily. There was something about dogs that she was never going to entirely like. She was also aware of a thread of jealousy whenever the animal and its master engaged in one of their lavish cuddles or frenzied garden games. It didn't help that Robin was very much on his father's side, adoring Cornelia with no reservations whatever.

She went on to describe the people she had met in the churchyard, as well as the snippets she had gleaned about Glebe House. 'It's the most valuable property in the area, apparently.'

'I never even noticed it,' he admitted.

'I came back through a place called Tirril. Do you know it?'

'Vaguely. As far as I can recall, its main claim to fame is the filling station. The fuel is always cheaper there. And it's where Humphrey died, so I suppose that'll add something to its local celebrity.'

Simmy sighed. 'I remembered that, as well. It's not a nice reason to be famous, is it?'

'I don't imagine they'll do anything to deliberately keep the memory alive. Like putting up a memorial.'

'No.' She tried to visualise what such an object might be like. 'So what about Sockbridge?' she added.

'What about it?'

'I saw a sign and thought it must be a misprint for Stockbridge. I've never even heard of it – have you?'

He shook his head. 'Probably just a tiny little hamlet,' he shrugged.

Only a few days earlier, Simmy had pinned the large-scale Ordnance Survey map on the wall of their main room. She went over to it now, and tried to trace the route she had taken that morning. 'Here it is!' she proclaimed. 'It's stuck to Tirril – they're just one conglomerate. About halfway between Stainton and the M6. Unexplored territory, as far as I'm concerned.'

'Great,' said Christopher inattentively. Robin was energetically bouncing on his lap, wanting another game of 'Down into a ditch'. Christopher had invented several unorthodox characters to add to the usual list, building the tension until they got to the old man and his ditch. The child shrieked gratifyingly every time.

'The clocks go back next weekend,' said Simmy wistfully. 'It'll be dark at five o'clock.'

'But lighter in the mornings. Much better than now.'

'Bare trees. Fog. Gales. Mud,' Simmy listed gloomily. 'We haven't had a whole winter here yet. It might be dreadful.'

'Sparkling snow. Frozen puddles. Blazing log fires. It'll be lovely.'

They laughed at the role reversal. It was generally Christopher who took the less positive line.

Chapter Four

They had no plans for Sunday, other than the usual routine of Angie and Russell coming over for lunch. This would often be followed by a walk carefully chosen by Russell to suit a pushchair and two dogs, now that Robin had started objecting to the back carrier. They would all pile into Christopher's big Volvo and head for a spot where they could be sure of finding somewhere to park. Russell had the task of researching gateways, lay-bys and abandoned tracks where nobody would move them on or charge them a fee. In September this had been a major challenge, but tourist numbers dwindled in October and everything was easier.

But it was too windy for a decent walk. Yesterday's breeze had turned into something much stronger, snatching leaves prematurely off the branches while they were still green. 'We'll have to play a game,' said Russell hopefully. 'I could fancy a bit of Scrabble. Haven't played it for ages.'

Nobody else expressed enthusiasm for that idea. Gradually they drifted into talking about Friday's funeral and how it had probably been of some consolation to Humphrey's wife that so many people had shown up. 'I wish we'd spoken to her,' said Simmy. 'We should have waited around a bit longer.'

'She wouldn't remember us in that great crowd,' said Russell. 'I think it's just nice to know she's got so much support. It was all rather old-style, when you think about it. Villagers rallying and all that.'

'I saw people I recognised from Keswick and Ambleside and all sorts of places,' said Christopher. 'The man must have operated across a pretty wide area.'

'It was because of the way he died,' said Angie with a hint of impatience. 'And because it hit the national news. Half those people you're talking about came because they wanted to feel part of some big story. They probably never knew Humphrey at all.'

'Oh, such cynicism!' sighed her husband.

Simmy and Christopher laughed uneasily, aware that Angie was probably right.

It was half past two when Simmy's phone chirruped. 'Ben,' she said, glancing at the screen. Angie made a loud sound of irritation, which was comprehensively ignored. At some point in recent months, Simmy's mother had formed an antipathy towards the boy that was upsetting. It had to do with his abandonment of his education and his decision to work for Christopher.

Simmy listened quietly for a few seconds. 'I was there yesterday,' she said then, and 'No, I didn't . . . Honestly, Ben, I really don't want to get involved . . . it's got nothing to do with any of us.'

It took Simmy's husband and parents no time at all to deduce that something familiar had happened. Ben had read a fresh item of news concerning a violent death and was thereby excited. His excitement was overflowing onto them, as it always did. But his dependence on them for transport had ended since he passed his driving test and acquired a car. Christopher had performed some trick with the insurance, putting it through the auction house books. Nobody thought there was anything wrong with that, since insurance companies were universally understood to be the work of the devil.

Simmy ended the call. 'He's in Windermere now, so he's bringing Bonnie up here,' she reported. 'Somebody's been killed in Askham.'

'So why come here?' asked Christopher.

'Why do you think?' said Simmy.

The youngsters often spent Sundays driving around on visits to friends and relations. Bonnie lived in Windermere, an hour's drive from Ben's accommodation in Keswick. His parents were in Bowness. The triangle created by Hartsop as a third regular destination was a well-used route already. None of it could be accomplished quickly. There were very few unimpeded stretches of road and a constant mass of tourist traffic to negotiate. Windermere to Hartsop was, however, a relatively straightforward business, usually taking less than half an hour. So Simmy had the kettle on at three o'clock, just in time to offer tea to her visitors.

Bonnie astutely won a general welcome and approbation by grabbing little Robin and tickling him the moment she was in the house. She was one of his favourite people and he clutched tightly to her cloud of pale hair as she manhandled him. 'Oof, he's getting heavy!' she said.

Bonnie herself was small and slight, never putting on any weight, despite eating more than ever before – which was still not a lot, starting as she did from a very low base. Nobody understood where her energy came from. Russell said she was a fairy child, and even Angie half-believed it to be so.

Cornelia nudged jealously at Bonnie's legs, wanting her share of adoration. It had soon dawned on the dog that her young master took priority in the general scheme of things, but that there was often plenty of overflowing adoration to come her way if she pressed the right buttons. 'Oh, look at you!' Bonnie obligingly squealed. 'You've grown, you beautiful thing.' Bonnie was very fond of dogs.

'So who died?' asked Simmy, aware that the sooner they got onto the main subject, the better.

'An old woman. They found her this morning in the Cockpit above Askham. That's all I know. Except that foul play is suspected.'

'People keep talking about the Cockpit. Even the Lindsay woman yesterday said something about it. What is it exactly?' Simmy asked. 'Something ancient and mysterious, apparently.'

Ben answered very willingly. 'It's a stone circle. Like Castlerigg and Long Meg. There are paths connecting them, actually. It's on Askham Fell. I went up there about three years ago.'

'How far is it from the village?'

Ben and Simmy automatically moved to the map on the wall as they spoke. The fell was west of Askham, overlooking Ullswater. 'Quite a walk from where I was yesterday,' Simmy concluded.

'So?'

'I don't know. What would an old woman be doing up there? How did she get there?'

'No idea. There are dozens of questions like that. The main one is – how concerned do we want to be? It won't be Moxon's case – again. We might never have any more to do with him. We've moved out of his area.'

'I haven't,' Bonnie reminded him.

'And he doesn't seem too bothered about that,' Simmy said. 'If he thinks we're involved, he'll probably find a way to muscle in at Penrith. He did it last time, after all.'

Ben looked doubtful. 'Well, we're not involved, are we? There's no way. Even if you were there on Friday at the funeral, you were among hundreds of other people. Moxon's only used us before because we've been genuinely involved. This one is just a poor old lady dead on the fell. She might have fallen over. Or she might have been killed a hundred miles away and been dumped up there.'

'Unlikely.' It was Russell joining in. 'It's a pretty obscure point on the map. If you were a nasty greedy grandson bumping off the old dear in Glasgow, you'd hardly drive her to Askham of all places to dispose of her.'

'No,' said Simmy, without really thinking.

'So we have to find out who she was,' said Ben firmly.

Christopher made a moaning sound. 'What's the betting

we saw her on Friday? If she's local, she will have been at the funeral, like as not.'

Simmy stared at him, suddenly full of foreboding. 'Or perhaps I met her yesterday,' she said.

Everyone looked at her. Variations of *'What?'* and *'How?'* and *'When?'* were uttered by five people.

Simmy explained about Pauline and Lindsay and the Askham churchyard. Russell interposed with his own comments on the way Lindsay had struck him at the funeral. 'So you saw her again next day?' he queried. 'That's a coincidence.'

'Let's hope the old woman you met isn't the one that's dead,' said Ben lightly. The heavy silence that followed made him blink. 'Come on – it's hardly likely. The place must have dozens of old women.'

'Probably not more than two or three as old as that one,' said Simmy, feeling very cold and shivery all at once. 'Why do I feel so worried? Why do I instantly assume it was the same person I met yesterday?'

A barrage of questions and speculations ensued, until they all realised there was nothing to be gained until they at the very least had a name for the dead woman. Ben worked hard on his phone, trying to find more detail, but it was firmly withheld. 'Perhaps they don't know who she was,' said Christopher.

Nobody disagreed, but one or two people pulled faces.

'Are there any CCTV cameras in Askham?' Bonnie said suddenly. She had been very quiet up to then.

No answer was forthcoming for half a minute or so. Russell and Simmy both shrugged and said they hadn't seen any. Christopher frowned and finally said he thought there must be, with so many of the houses being used for holiday lets. 'They'd want to keep an eye on what their customers get up to,' he said.

Angie rolled her eyes at that, having very recently been in the business of providing holidays for people from all over the world, never once thinking to record their activities.

Ben looked at Bonnie with a little frown. 'Why did you ask that?' he said.

'Well, I thought the police might be scanning through any film, back to Friday and the funeral. I mean – there could be some sort of connection. There's usually a connection, you know,' she finished with a little laugh.

Simmy recalled at least one occasion when her detective friend DI Moxon had looked right at her and said, 'It's you. *You're* the connection,' when she had stumbled into trouble by the simple act of delivering flowers. Flowers had a way of getting themselves entangled in high emotion of every sort. 'Well, I don't think it has anything to do with me this time,' she said with more conviction than she actually felt. 'There must be lots of old ladies living there. It won't be the one I met.'

As if on cue there was a sudden knock on the door. Robin and Cornelia both jumped. The dog barked and the child gave a brief wail.

Christopher went to the door, glancing back at the room full of people. Simmy met his eye and could see that he was worried. Hard experience had taught him that there were generally good grounds for anxiety when Ben, Bonnie and murder all came together.

A uniformed policeman was revealed on the doorstep.

'Mr Henderson?' he said, the moment the door was opened.

Christopher nodded.

'Is Mrs Henderson at home? We have a few questions for her.'

Simmy pushed forward, carrying Robin as if he was a shield. 'That's me. What do you want?'

The newcomer looked around the room. The door opened directly into it, so that the entire gathering was visible. Cornelia sidled up to him, wagging slowly. He ignored her.

'We understand that you were in Askham yesterday, in conversation with a lady by the name of Mrs Pauline Parsons. Is that correct?'

'I suppose so. I didn't know her surname.' Already it was obvious to everyone in the room where things were heading. 'She's the woman who was killed, is she? I mean – was she?'

Ben gave a small sound like a hiss, making it all too clear that he disapproved of her naivety. Bonnie nudged him and smiled vaguely at the policeman.

'We need to ask you some questions,' the man repeated.

'All right. Come in, then. We can go in the kitchen.'

'I'm sorry, Madam, but it'll have to be done at the station. If you could just come with me, it probably won't take too long.'

Simmy gazed at him, uncomprehending. She looked first at her baby, then at her husband. Finally, she faced her father, as the most likely to give the desired response. It flashed through her mind that all her menfolk were gathered there together, plus Ben Harkness, who was a different matter entirely. Ben was almost certainly enjoying himself.

'But why?' she said. 'What about the baby? How long will it take?'

'Do you have the legal right to insist?' Russell asked in a calm pedantic tone. 'Are you arresting her?'

'Just asking her to help with our enquiries, sir, that's all. But I can promise you that it would be in everybody's best interests if she complied with the request. We believe she may have some very pertinent information that's relevant to our investigation. It shouldn't take too long.'

'But where's Moxon?' Bonnie suddenly cried. 'He wouldn't let you do this. Get Moxon from Windermere and let him sort it out.'

'Detective Inspector Moxon is already at the station in Penrith,' came the reply. 'And he's waiting for us.'

Chapter Five

Simmy repeatedly assured herself that there was nothing to worry about. She had a totally clear conscience. Somebody had drawn a completely wrong conclusion based on a bit of fuzzy film or a simple mistake made in a witness statement.

The drive to Penrith took about half an hour, following the edge of Ullswater along the A592. The very familiarity of it made Simmy uneasy. She had never done it in a police car before. She agonised about how her parents and Christopher would be feeling after her sudden removal. She worried that Ben would somehow make everything worse, with his shaky grasp of empathy. He would be throwing out wild hypotheses in a misguided attempt to make light of it all.

There were two male police officers in the front, while

Simmy had the back seat to herself. This also felt wrong. She never sat in the back of a car. They told her to strap herself in and not to ask them any questions. There was nothing aggressive or hostile in their manner, but they were far from friendly. Once or twice she caught them exchanging glances, as if they too were uneasy. Did they have private reservations about what they had been asked to do? Did they know her by reputation, as a friend of DI Moxon, and an accidental participant in several murder investigations? If so, what were they thinking now?

The police station was a large brick building on two floors. The constables walked her in, pausing briefly at the front desk. The woman there gave her a long look, starting just above her eyes, as if searching for meaning in her hairline. Then she flashed a fake smile and indicated with her chin that it was all right for the group to proceed down a corridor to a room intended for interviews.

There were voices coming from a number of directions. A woman came out of a room further down the corridor, releasing the sound of keyboards being clattered inside the room. 'We're usually closed on a Sunday,' said one of the men, as if feeling a need to explain.

The sight of Nolan Moxon sitting behind a plain table took Simmy back to her very first encounter with him, three or four years ago. He had been sitting behind a very similar table in Windermere, interviewing her as a witness to a murder during a big wedding in Storrs. She had instantly liked and trusted him and had found no cause to change her judgement of him since then.

'Sorry about this,' he said, looking more than sorry. He seemed almost tragic. 'But there wasn't any choice.'

There was a young woman in uniform sitting a few feet away, apparently in the role of some kind of chaperone. A machine was squatting near Moxon's elbow that could only be a recording device.

'I hope it won't take long.' A dawning sense of injustice was squeezing out her natural inclination to be meek and accommodating. 'What's it all about?'

'There has been an accusation,' he said heavily.

'What? Against me? What am I supposed to have done?'

'Let's start at the beginning, shall we? You will be aware that there was an unlawful killing of an elderly woman by the name of Pauline Parsons this weekend.'

'As it happens, Ben told us this afternoon. He found it online – as usual. Although we couldn't find her name.'

Moxon ignored this attempt to arouse old friendships and associations. 'I see,' he said.

'But we had no idea who she was. I met a woman called Pauline in Askham yesterday. She was quite old – well, very old, actually. I assume she's the one who died. Is somebody saying I killed her?' It was uttered lightly, almost as a joke. The idea was so impossibly ridiculous that it felt safe to laugh at it.

'I'm afraid so,' said Moxon, with grooves etched around his eyes and mouth, deepening as she watched. 'Which is why we've had to bring you here.'

Simmy swallowed back the surge of panic that rose in her throat and forced herself to speak calmly. 'That's absolutely ridiculous. Am I allowed to know who it is who said that? Can I confront him – or her? Is it someone I know?'

'Not at this stage, I'm afraid.'

'You mean not until I'm in court being prosecuted for

murder?' Her voice rose to a squeal. 'And stop saying you're afraid, like a reproachful headmaster.'

He flinched. But Simmy's mind was not on his discomfort now. 'It's that Lindsay person, isn't it!' she flashed, as the realisation hit her. 'She set me up somehow. Good God – she even told me how much she disliked the old lady. She must have done it herself.' She blinked. 'So is it her word against mine? Or what?'

'Slow down. Stop talking.' He looked alarmed, glancing at the recording machine on the table and then at the silent woman in the background. 'Just answer the questions I put to you, okay?'

She sat back, her vision disrupted by sparks and swirls that reflected her thoughts. 'Go on, then,' she said.

'Where were you yesterday between 4 p.m. and midnight?'

'At home.'

'Can anyone corroborate that?'

'Christopher got back soon after six, as he always does on a Saturday. I was on my own with the baby until then. We were both in all evening. Don't you know the time of death?'

He gave her another headmasterly look. 'Let me ask the questions, all right?'

The stark difference between this interview and every other encounter she had ever had with him was disorienting. He was a different person here in Penrith. She gave a thought to Ben and Bonnie and how frustrated they were going to be if he treated them in the same way.

'Were you acquainted with Mrs Parsons?' came the next question.

'Absolutely not. I spent a maximum of ten minutes with her yesterday in the churchyard in Askham, with another woman. I know nothing whatever about her.'

'And this other woman?'

'Lindsay something. She talked a bit about herself. She told me where she lives and how she knew Humphrey slightly, because there's a family connection. *Dombey and Son*,' she added distractedly.

'Sorry?'

'She's doing a PhD thesis about *Dombey and Son*. Cruelty in fiction or something. She's related to several local people.'

'And who might Humphrey be?'

She stared at him in disbelief. '*Humphrey* – you know, the man who died in that awful accident with the chainsaw. His funeral was on Friday. You must know about that. He was related to Lindsay. Or maybe his wife was – is, I mean. I didn't take much notice of the precise connection. She was at the funeral. I saw her then, as well.' She sat back, listening to her own words and the muddle she had made of them. 'The trouble is, I can't remember everything she said. On Friday she barged in when Christopher and I were arguing about wakes – my dad was there as well.'

Moxon rolled his eyes and wrote something on a pad in front of him, glancing again at the recorder. For a mad moment, Simmy expected him to show her his writing, a secret message not to be picked up by the machine or the watchful WPC. But that did not happen. *Just a little note to himself, then*, she thought, disappointed. Whilst her trust in this man was unshaken, the same could not be said for the system in which he worked. He himself was steady, fair, well-intentioned, and inescapably fond of Simmy. But the law would make no allowance for that, and he was going to have to tread very carefully. She felt a flood of overwhelming pity for him. This was a lot worse for him than it was for her.

A silence fell in the room, but the inside of Simmy's head was noisy with questions. How had the old woman died? Gunshot? Cudgel? Knife? Pushed over a cliff or into a mere? The possibilities were legion, and Simmy spent a moment trying to imagine herself using any of the methods she could imagine to kill an old woman she had never known. Was it possible she'd gone into some fugue state at teatime and driven back to Askham, located Mrs Parsons and savagely slaughtered her? Ben had talked about the Cockpit stone circle, which Simmy had never seen, but was starting to understand was significant. She was desperate for more information, and knew that Moxon understood this. 'This is a nightmare,' she said flatly. 'Perhaps literally. I might be going to wake up in a minute.'

He shook his head miserably. 'How well do you know Askham?'

'Not at all. I'd never been there before Friday. Christopher might have been once or twice. He seemed to know where the church was, at least. Of course, everybody knows of Askham Hall. And Lowther, which is close by.'

'But you'd never been there? Not to a wedding to do flowers – anything like that?'

'No. I nearly did, once. Those people in Staveley were going to have a party there, but they changed their minds.'

Moxon obviously remembered 'those people in Staveley'. He smiled briefly, and directed his gaze at the eerily silent female constable seated behind Simmy. She turned round for a look, but the woman evaded her gaze.

'Well, I think that will suffice for now,' said Moxon, looking up at a clock on the wall. 'Interview terminated at 5.10 p.m. They'll just take your fingerprints and then you're free to go.'

'I assume you'll be taking me home again?'

He sighed. 'Oh yes. We're not that barbaric, you know.'

'Thank goodness for that,' she said, feeling angry for the first time. 'This is all completely ridiculous, you know.'

The detective sighed again and said nothing.

At home again, Simmy was bombarded with questions. Her parents had stayed on, as well as Ben and Bonnie, all of them anxious to hear first-hand what was going on. Christopher made a pot of tea and tried to quieten everyone down. 'Let her tell it in her own way,' he ordered.

Instead of complying with this suggestion, Simmy simply broke down in tears and buried her face in her husband's chest. Cornelia pushed between them, eager to understand this new game.

'It's all so *insane*,' Simmy wailed. 'It doesn't make any sense at all. What have I done to her that she thinks it's all right to accuse me of murder? I actually thought she liked me and wanted me to be her friend. She kept me talking yesterday when I was wanting to go.'

Christopher gently pushed her off, keeping his hands around her upper arms. 'Someone accused you of murder? Really?'

'That Lindsay woman we walked up the hill with on Friday, who talked about wakes. Remember? I saw her again yesterday. She says I killed the old lady.'

'She's mad,' said Christopher.

'Stark raving,' said Russell.

'Must have escaped from a secure mental health facility,' said Ben.

'But that's *awful!*' said Bonnie. 'Surely Moxon can't be taking it seriously?'

Angie didn't say anything.

Simmy sniffed and tried to smile her appreciation. 'Moxon was horribly upset about it. He knows it's mad, but he has to follow the proper process. He wouldn't tell me what she said, exactly. He probably shouldn't have told me it was her – well, he didn't really, but I guessed it had to be her and he didn't deny it. After all, it was pretty obvious, because nobody else knows me there. He didn't say what she said about me. It can only be complete lies. I didn't do anything remotely suspicious. I never went near the Cockpit. I don't know how she was killed.' Her voice was rising as all the implications hit her at once. 'What if they come to arrest me?'

'They won't,' said Russell. 'That's obvious. The rational thing to do would be to just sit back and let them try and make a case against you, if that's what they want. You're innocent until they can prove you guilty. And they can't. There's no shadow of a doubt about that. The woman can't mean it seriously.'

'Just what I was going to say,' Ben beamed. 'Precisely. It's some kind of game she's playing.'

'But who *is* she?' Bonnie asked. 'Does she know you from somewhere? Flowers or something? What's her surname? Where does she live?'

Simmy put her hands over her face, trying to think

straight. 'She did tell me her surname yesterday. Talking about her PhD. Something quite ordinary. I didn't even try to remember it. I don't think I have ever seen her before.'

'Think,' said Ben. 'We need her name. It's important.'

'Didn't Moxon mention it?' asked Russell.

Simmy shook her head. 'I don't think he said her name at all. It was probably stupid of me, the way I said "It's that Lindsay person, isn't it?". It just came to me that it must have been her.' She looked round at them all. 'I shouldn't have done that – introduced her into the conversation. But how could I possibly know?'

'Don't worry about that,' Christopher soothed her. 'It can't really matter too much.'

But Simmy felt increasingly as if she was caught in a very sticky cobweb. Sticky and unwholesome, tainting her with a covering of malice, madness or mendacity. Or all three. Ben's instruction to *think* was impossible to follow. Coherent thought was a distant goal. Had she somehow said or done something that made Lindsay genuinely believe she meant harm to Pauline Parsons? Did someone else, who looked like Simmy, kill her? 'I wish we knew more about how she died,' she said. 'And where? After all, she was over ninety. How would she get all the way up to the stone circle place? It looks a long way on the map.'

'Who gains?' said Ben portentously. 'Or *cui bono?* as the Latin says.'

They all ignored him, since the answer was far beyond anyone's knowledge.

'So we go and see her, this Lindsay woman,' he continued. 'Not all of us, of course,' he amended, looking round, as Simmy had just done. 'There are rather a lot of us.'

Angie was holding Robin on her lap, where he had fallen asleep, slumped against her front. She had been unconsciously rocking him throughout the conversation. 'Not me,' she said softly. 'I'm opting out of this nonsense. You're all quite capable of sorting it out without me. I didn't go to the funeral and I'm not going to rush around Askham trying to solve one of your murders. I'll be the babysitter and nothing more than that.'

'No problem,' said Simmy. 'You can be excused.' There was no need for her to add *I just wish I could be as well.*

'We do need her surname,' Ben persisted.

'All right. Let me think.' Simmy reran all she could recall of the conversation the previous day. 'We were talking about her PhD. She said she'd be known as "Doctor Lindsay hm-hm." Two syllables. Something ordinary. Gosh – I'll never remember. I wasn't even trying to keep it in my head. You know how it is with names. It didn't connect with anybody I know.' She sighed helplessly. 'It isn't going to work. I might not even recognise it if you said it.'

'Okay,' Ben said. 'What else did she say about herself? We might find her through the place she's doing the studies. I mean – she must have tutors and so forth. Funding. Is she doing some teaching, even?'

'Yes!' Simmy slumped with relief as her memory began to function again. 'Lancaster. She teaches there one day a week. English literature, presumably. Thanks, Ben. I don't know how you do it.'

'She'll be listed on their website as being on the staff, then. But what about where she lives? If we can locate the house, we won't need anything else.'

'Renting in Askham. Humphrey repaired the chimney.

Her cousin's husband is his nephew – no, not literally, but there's a family connection somewhere involving cousins and in-laws. That's why she was at the funeral.'

'Cousins are complicated,' said Ben. 'As I know from experience.'

'We should go,' said Bonnie suddenly. 'It's going to be dark and you know how you don't like night driving.'

Nobody asked whether Bonnie was spending the night in Keswick with Ben, in his cramped little lodgings, or whether he would just deliver her back to Windermere, where she lived with her former foster mother. Corinne had defied the usual rules and kept Bonnie with her past her eighteenth birthday, when the girl was officially meant to be thrown to the wolves. The relationship was gently mutating into one of two friendly adults living their own lives. If Ben stayed the night, there would be no complaints from Corinne. Ben's own parents were less accommodating, half a mile down the road in Bowness.

In any case, both youngsters were due to report for work bright and early next day.

'There's no time to do anything now,' Bonnie went on. 'It'll have to wait.' She looked from Russell to Christopher. 'Maybe one of you could do something tomorrow? You could go to Askham and see what's happening, couldn't you?'

'Not me,' said Christopher. 'I'm at work all day.'

'And I'm a pretty poor detective,' said Russell. 'I wouldn't spot a clue if it bit me.'

'We'll have to wait for Moxon,' Simmy summarised. 'Which suits me perfectly well. It was always what I thought I should do. We can all carry on as normal tomorrow.' She felt braver already. Surrounded by people who loved her, trusting Moxon to fend off the worst eventualities, and far enough away from Askham to put it out of her mind – surely it couldn't be as bad as she first feared?

Nobody pointed out that 'carrying on as normal' would be a lot easier said than done – for Simmy more than any of them. Russell and Angie had a new house to play with and everyone else had work to go to. Bonnie was first to speak. 'Why don't you come down to the shop tomorrow? It's been over a week since you were there, and it needs your eye casting over it. Verity keeps fiddling with the cards and the dried things and some of the customers have been asking after you. Tanya thinks we should start planning a Christmas display.'

It was a brave effort. Simmy smiled weakly. 'I could, I suppose. It would feel like running away, though. And I might drive the customers away if I can't pull myself together. And I'd have to bring Robin.' She glanced at the baby, still dozing on his grandmother's lap. 'And Cornelia, if I'm going to be out for long. She'll pee in the house if she's left all day.'

'See how you feel in the morning,' said Bonnie easily. 'I'll see you if I see you.'

Ten minutes later everyone had dispersed, leaving three Hendersons and a dog to get through the evening as best they could.

Chapter Six

Christopher was relentlessly solicitous throughout the evening meal, Robin's bedtime and an hour or two watching television. On Monday morning he was visibly reluctant to leave Simmy on her own. 'You should follow Bonnie's advice and go down to the shop,' he urged.

'I know,' she said. 'Or maybe I'll just go back to bed for the morning.'

'Don't you dare.' He seemed alarmed. 'Then I'd think you'd sunk into hopeless depression, and I'm no good with depressed people.'

'I've got good reason, don't you think?'

'Not really. Confusion. Anger. That sort of thing, yes. But there's nothing to be depressed about.'

'There will be if I'm sent to prison for twenty years.

Miscarriages of justice do happen, you know.'

'Not to people like us they don't,' he said with reassuring certainty. 'Now, keep your phone on and I'll call you at coffee time. And don't forget I've got tomorrow free.'

A braver woman would go back to Askham and confront the unconscionable wickedness of the Lindsay woman, demanding to know what she thought she was playing at. Simmy tried to boost her courage by composing a ferocious speech in her head, throwing back accusations in the creature's face. Rage did not come easily, but when it did, it flamed and burnt red hot. But she knew it would never find the emotional outlet she imagined. What would she do with Robin while she went onto the attack? What would Moxon say? And where, in the end, would it get her? Lindsay was unlikely to want to talk to her and explain what in the world she thought she was doing, however much Simmy might threaten or plead for enlightenment. There had to be an explanation, perhaps tucked away in something the woman had said on Saturday, which Simmy had wantonly failed to register. She had not listened very well, she had to admit. Had she missed a message, or warning, or appeal for help? Every time she ran through her recollection of the encounter, she got stuck in the same fog of forgetfulness.

Her best hope was that Ben would be ferreting out helpful details with the aid of the Internet. He and Christopher might well be hatching a plan of action in any quiet moments at work – which would probably be few. After Saturday's sale, the place would be busy with buyers collecting their purchases after bidding for them online. Everything had to be gone by the end of the day, so that all the workers could take a breather on Tuesday. Anyone who had worked on Saturday had earned a day off, including Christopher. Entries for the next sale would start to arrive on Wednesday. It was a predictable and efficient two-week cycle, which Christopher had honed and polished until the entire staff felt happy with it. His standard riposte to any objections was, 'If you're not careful, I'll start weekly auctions. Then you'll really know what hard work means.' The fact that such a system existed in auction houses all across the land was enough to scare everyone into compliance.

Outside it was windy again and not very inviting. The dog had to have some sort of exercise, though, and the baby could do with a bit of outdoor stimulation. Short walks were readily available in a number of directions, but the baby buggy was a handicap on all of them. It seemed that every stage of the child's development brought new frustrations. The sling they had used early on was now rather tight and constricting. The backpack was almost impossible to get right without assistance, and Simmy disliked not being able to see Robin as she walked. Almost for the first time since living there she felt trapped. Winter was coming, the dog was growing bigger and bouncier by the day and life felt dangerously unpredictable. And all that was before she remembered that she had been accused of committing murder.

She ought to go and see somebody. Christopher and Bonnie had both understood that and tried to persuade her. She was still getting used to the dramatic relocation of her parents from Windermere to Threlkeld, near Keswick. That had skewed the balance between the two parts of the

Lake District, so that Windermere now felt further away and less relevant. All of which left Bonnie and Persimmon Petals in danger of being neglected. Meanwhile Robin had dropped off on an unscheduled nap at ten o'clock, which solved the dilemma for a while. She took him up to his cot and gently put him down. Before he woke up, a person came to the door.

The knock was peremptory and Simmy went rather nervously to answer it. Cornelia was of no help as a guard or protector, but she did soften the anxiety with her eagerness to greet a newcomer. Even an axe murderer might be seduced, Simmy thought foolishly.

A man she had never seen before stood on the threshold. 'Mrs Henderson?' he asked in a deep voice. He had a substantial moustache and beard and looked to be in his early fifties.

'That's me,' she said, sounding as confident as she could manage. It could yet turn out that he was merely delivering a parcel, after all. 'Get back, Cornelia, for heaven's sake.' She had to bar the dog's exit with her leg. 'She'll run off if we're not careful,' she told the man.

'I'd better come in, then,' he said. 'It's rather blowy out here,' he added.

I asked for that, Simmy reproached herself. 'All right,' she said, aware that almost everybody who knew her would be screaming at her to have more sense. In the reality of the situation, with dog and wind and a basic trust in humanity all urging her the same way, she let him in. 'Who are you?' she said, too late. Perhaps he was a plain-clothes policeman. Or an insurance salesman. Or even a disoriented hiker.

The man smiled and Simmy remembered that she rather liked a man with a beard. He had dark eyes, shadowed in their deep setting, and bushy eyebrows. He looked a bit like a pirate. Somebody well travelled and world-weary. His nose was large and his lips fleshy.

'My name is Howard Isaacs. It won't mean anything to you, but I did see you at Humphrey's funeral on Friday.'

'Did you? I didn't see you.'

'It was crowded, and I don't think you stayed for the pub part.'

'No.' She waited for further explanation.

'The thing is, I'm taking over the business, in a manner of speaking. Humph and I worked together now and then, on really big jobs. I'm based in Carlisle. It's quite a big enterprise these days. Sophie asked me to take all the books and see if I can keep it going. She's worried about the boys who worked for him, and the outstanding jobs.'

'But he finished up here months ago.' She was bemused. The man did not look at all like a builder. 'And we paid the bill in full, if that's what you're worried about.'

'Ah. Of course. No – I haven't made myself clear. I was hoping we might take a few pictures of what he did here – for the website.' He had been gazing around ever since Simmy had let him in. 'That staircase is magnificent. Superb workmanship.'

Suspicion dawned. The staircase was perfectly ordinary and it had a mistake on the bottom step. What sort of nonsense was the man spouting at her? Was he a cunning burglar, casing the joint? It seemed horribly likely. 'I don't think so,' she said. 'Humphrey was a lovely man, who did a perfectly adequate job on our conversion. But it's hardly

Homes and Gardens, is it? Your story seems a bit flimsy to me.'

The man laughed, showing the inside of his mouth. He stroked his beard, still smiling. 'Well said! But I assure you I'm not up to anything shady. We really are gathering material for a website, with the story of poor old Humph's ghastly accident. This was his last big job and we thought it would help to have some pictures.'

She pressed her point. 'You don't look like a builder.'

He pulled a mock-hurt face. 'I'm sorry about that. I'm not sure whether or not to be offended on behalf of builders, actually. I can show you certificates if it helps.'

'Show me your website,' she challenged. 'We can get it on my laptop.'

He cocked his head. 'Why are you so suspicious? What's the matter? I thought you'd be pleased to help keep the thing going. Humphrey worked hard to get himself established, and those boys depended on him for work. I'm just trying to find ways to get them local jobs before some cowboy muscles in. There's a sympathy vote out there, but it won't last for long. You and your husband are respected local residents – your endorsement would go a long way.'

'The staircase is not at all magnificent,' she muttered stubbornly. 'Why did you say it was?'

'Hyperbole,' he shrugged. 'They tell me it's one of my failings.'

She wondered whether such exaggerations helped or hindered him in his work. Did customers really swallow flowery language and exuberant promises? Some of them probably did, she concluded. 'Did you know a woman was murdered in Askham this weekend?' she asked suddenly.

He blinked. 'Sorry? What?'

'An old lady called Pauline. It's been on the news.'

He rubbed his forehead, breathing slowly. She could see him thinking he should tread carefully. 'You knew her, did you? That's why you're upset?'

From upstairs, right on cue, Robin began to wail. 'That's my baby. I'll have to go.' She took a step towards the stairs, but the man didn't move. They had been standing in the main living room since he arrived, not far from the door, where he could readily examine the staircase. 'What?' she demanded, conveying a lengthy interrogation in a single word.

'Well – can I take some photos?'

'I told you no already. It feels like an intrusion, you doing that. My father would tell you it's unacceptable surveillance.' She remembered that there were interior shots of the former vicarage in Askham on the Internet, and thought it wrong. 'The inside of a person's house is private,' she finished.

'Tell that to anyone with an Alexa,' he said crossly. 'It hears everything you say, you know.'

Simmy only vaguely knew what he was talking about. A thing that played the music of your choice and turned the cooker on. It had never occurred to her to wonder how it worked.

'And electric cars,' he persisted. 'They track every move you make and report back to the big boss computer. Sometimes they override what you want them to do.'

'And you approve of that, do you?' She was on the

bottom stair, listening for Robin, who was now chirruping contentedly to himself.

He shrugged. 'It's the way things are. Not much anyone can do about it.'

Suddenly she rather liked him. He had nice eyes and a manner that carried no threat. But his mere presence was unsettling. 'I don't understand why you're here,' she said. 'It feels as if you're spying on me just like Alexa.'

He laughed, a peal of genuine surprised delight. 'A spy!' he chuckled. 'I've always wanted to be a spy.'

'Don't be silly. Now you'll have to go. I'm bringing the baby down and giving him a drink and then we're going out. The dog needs a walk.'

The dog had been sitting close by, watching the human faces with fascination.

'Okay. Don't panic. I like you, Mrs Henderson, let me just say that. I can see what Humphrey meant. He thought you were the real thing – and he was crazy about the baby.'

'Oh!' Tears flooded her eyes without warning, as the dead builder was so deftly conjured. Humphrey had been wonderful with little Robin, keeping Simmy calm in the face of unexplained screams, and admiring the speed of the baby's growth. 'Poor Humphrey!' she wept. 'I still can't stop thinking about him.'

'And why should you? But believe me, I have a real commitment to keeping things going, for Sophie and the girls. I came to you because I thought you might feel the same way.'

'Oh,' she said again.

He turned to go at last, without saying anything more.

Simmy closed the door behind him and went upstairs, muttering to herself, 'But what about the old woman in Askham? What about me being accused of murder?'

She dawdled over giving Robin some mashed vegetables and apple juice, and herself some coffee. What had that man really wanted? Hadn't she been rather horrid to him, when he seemed so innocent of any malice? Was he in any way connected to the death of Pauline Parsons? He had more or less ignored Simmy's mention of her, and the subject had changed of its own accord. After all, there was no way she could blurt out that she was under suspicion of killing somebody. The shame alone would prevent that. Beneath that was a sense that it had to be a dream, anyway. Such a thing could not happen in the real world. Could it?

She had to get out and talk to people. She needed connection and reassurance. She found herself more and more angry with Moxon, as well as Lindsay Hm-Hm, whatever her name was. Again, she felt tangled in a sinister sticky web of other people's making, a helpless fly unable to understand what had happened.

Bonnie had been persuasive in her suggestion that Simmy go down to the shop, but the dog and baby made it too complicated, the way she was feeling. Instead, she decided to go to Threlkeld and see if she could help her parents with their decorating, or whatever they might be doing. There was something soothing about that idea. Practical work, a scratch lunch, even a little walk up Blencathra if it wasn't too windy. The route lay north-westwards, far from Askham and all its dreadful associations. Nobody would find her in Threlkeld – she could pretend that everything was perfectly normal.

Except that Christopher had told her to keep her phone on, which meant that anybody could call her with disturbing information or demands. Even a call from Ben would not be particularly welcome. So she sent her husband a text: 'Going to Threlkeld. Turning the phone off. See you later.' It felt liberating to silence the thing and toss it onto the back seat next to Robin. She dithered about Cornelia, and in the end decided not to take her. The animal would have to get used to being left alone at times, and Simmy wanted to make the point that she was not going to automatically take it everywhere with her.

It was nearly half past eleven when she finally got to Threlkeld. Angie came out to greet her, wearing rubber gloves. 'You might have warned us,' she said. 'We're stripping wallpaper in the spare room.'

The bungalow only had two bedrooms, which seemed minute after their large detached house in Windermere, which they had run as a B&B. The new home was perched halfway up a hill, looking down over the small settlement that was Threlkeld. Angie had seen Simmy's car from the moment it first turned into her road. The bland face of Blencathra rose behind the house, inviting hikers from far and wide.

'Sorry,' said Simmy, insincerely. 'I thought we could take Robin for a bit of a walk. I didn't bring the dog.'

Angie shook her head. 'Too windy,' she said.

'We can go round the garden, at least.'

The garden sloped uncomfortably and was not very big. Her parents' dog was old and stiff and did minimal amounts of running about. Russell had begun to talk of getting a replacement for him from a rescue place.

Russell now came in on the conversation – just too late to grasp the gist. 'Why don't we go over to the Cockpit this afternoon?' he said brightly. 'Take the bull by the horns, as it were.'

'God no!' said Simmy without pausing to think. 'Won't that look as if I'm the killer returning to the scene of the crime?'

Both her parents stared at her. 'Rubbish,' said Angie. 'It would give you a better ground for defending yourself.'

'All I really want is to crawl into a hole and pretend it's all a dream. Sorry, Dad, but it's an awful idea.'

'You're probably right,' he said easily. 'But I do suggest we have a look at the local TV news at lunchtime and see what we can glean. They're sure to have a few details by now.'

'If they can be bothered,' sniffed Angie. 'The death of an obscure old woman isn't very compelling news.'

Russell got his way and the four of them all lined up to watch the television in the bungalow's main room. Robin sat on his grandfather's knee and tried to instigate the same game his father often played with him. Russell was uncooperative, saying, 'Keep still, now. There's a good boy.' Simmy watched the two of them, trying not to think of the effect on her baby's development if she was sent to prison for most of his childhood.

Fortunately for Russell's credibility, there was a substantial item about the death of Pauline Parsons.

Police are asking for anybody who was in the vicinity of the Cockpit stone circle near Askham at any time on Saturday to please come forward. They are investigating the death of 90-year-old Mrs Pauline Parsons, which

73

is believed to have been the result of a violent attack at some time between mid-afternoon and late evening on Saturday last. A walker found the body on Sunday morning. Anyone who saw the victim recently is also asked to come forward, so that her last hours can be established. Neighbours say that she was a remarkable old lady, in good health and the source of countless local stories. She remembered in particular a great snowstorm in 1940, which coincided with her eighth birthday. Her young brother almost died falling into a snowdrift and remaining undiscovered until Pauline found him. Many more such stories of Cumbrian life emanated from her fertile memory. Her first great-great-grandchild was born only two weeks ago.

'"Emanated from her fertile memory"?' Russell expostulated. 'Who writes this stuff?'

'It's right that she was in good health,' said Simmy. 'I saw her walk all the way up the hill from the church. She was slow, but didn't seem to find it very difficult. That's awful about the new baby. Fancy being a great-great-grandmother.'

Angie ignored the implication that such an honour would never be hers. Mere grandmotherhood had been a long time coming and the very most she could hope for seemed to be one more generation. 'No mention of your accuser,' she said.

'Well, there wouldn't be, would there? They're not going to give the names of key witnesses.'

'Nice legacy to have, though,' mused Russell, who was rather proud of his own ability to recount innumerable local legends, anecdotes and events. 'Remembering so much from nearly a century ago. I bet she pushed the little brother into the snowdrift herself, though. Isn't that what big sisters always do?'

Simmy gave this some thought. 'She didn't strike me as particularly nice,' she said. 'I wonder if people actually liked her.'

'Somebody obviously didn't,' said Angie tartly. 'Given how unusual it is for such an old woman to be "violently attacked", there must surely have been a specific reason for it.'

'Somebody who didn't want her splurging the facts about something they did in 1955, perhaps?' said Russell. 'Don't you think that might tie in with the accuser woman and her studies? Something to do with *Dombey and Son* and how awful people can be?'

Simmy closed her eyes and rubbed her forehead. 'I can't think straight. There seems to be nothing remotely credible about any of it. Just a lot of mad ideas that don't make any sense. But I keep thinking that Lindsay did quite like me. More than I liked her. Maybe she's punishing me for disappointing her, when all she wanted was a friend.' She looked from one parent to another. 'That's the most *normal* idea I've had so far.'

'You would have to have been extraordinarily nasty to her to justify doing what she did,' said Angie. 'Which I don't expect you were, were you?'

'Not deliberately. But I wasn't showing much interest in what she was telling me. She might have found that offensive.'

Angie made a scoffing sound. 'Pooh! If this is all about some fool being offended, we might as well give up hope now. You'll be persecuted for the rest of your life.'

'Be quiet, woman,' said Russell. 'She might take you seriously.'

The afternoon added rain to the blustery wind and any lingering thoughts of a fellside walk were finally abandoned. 'I feel a bit bad about leaving poor Cornelia at home,' said Simmy, who could not escape the complicated set of emotions she felt towards the dog. It was well-intentioned, appealing to look at, excused from all responsibility, and a major commitment. Christopher readily accepted that the dog was his, its welfare down to him. But Simmy had all day with it, factoring it into every move and attending to its needs. 'She's not going to get a run today.'

'I wouldn't have minded taking her up to the car park and back,' said Russell. 'I could have taken them both.' Of the whole Straw family, only Russell really enjoyed the company of dogs.

'Another time, Dad.'

He gave her a long scrutiny, hearing something like defeat in her voice. 'Look, love – nobody thinks you killed that woman. Absolutely nobody at all. Somebody's playing a very nasty cruel game with you for some twisted reason of their own. It'll all get sorted out, so keep smiling, eh?'

That would make anybody cry, Simmy thought, as she wiped her eyes. 'I know,' she whispered.

She was home again soon after four, her phone and the heating system both switched on. Christopher texted to say Ben would be spending the evening with them. 'He has plenty to tell us,' he elaborated.

If only we could ignore the whole thing Simmy thought wistfully. Instead of that her mind was obsessively running through every conceivable reason why she might find herself accused of murder. Did the Lindsay woman know of her involvement with previous murders and decide that she must do something to ensure Simmy's involvement with this killing? If so, why? The simple answer had to be that Lindsay herself had killed Pauline Parsons and had then done her best to implicate someone else. But there had been a clear implication from Moxon that this was not the case. Or if it was, they were nowhere near to proving it. Lindsay must have an excellent alibi if she were to avert any suspicion falling on her. What would the police make of one woman accusing another, in the first place? Would there be lingering assumptions about female hysteria and irrationality? A variation on the Victorian habit of administering poison to annoying rivals – poisoning a reputation instead? Or was it all much more complicated than that? Other people must be involved as well; not least the actual killer. Was it someone in Askham who needed Pauline out of the way and who had recruited Lindsay to divert police attention? Or what? The longer Simmy thought about it, the more abstruse the theories became. And that was *before* Ben Harkness showed up with a whole new lot of ideas of his own.

Christopher was early, and every bit as solicitous as he had been the day before. He pulled Simmy close to him and hugged her hard. It felt wonderful. There had been times over the past months when he had threatened to be a fragile support in times of stress. He had hang-ups and phobias of his own, which Simmy had not realised when she married him. As a father he could be tentative and not entirely dependable. Yet here he was, stepping up unreservedly. The psychology was easy to read – this crisis was in no way his fault. He had nothing to feel bad about; nothing to prevent him and Simmy sticking firmly to the same side, them against the world. He was free to be a brick, a stalwart protector. She rested her head on his shoulder and felt thankful.

'Is Ben eating with us?' she asked a little while later.

'No, I don't think so. He said he'd come about seven – after Robin's in bed.'

'Okay. Actually, you might want to take Cornelia out for twenty minutes while I get supper. She didn't have much exercise today.'

'Good idea,' he said and disappeared towards Hartsop Dodd. By mutual consent they had steered off the subject of Askham until Ben arrived.

'Wilson,' was the boy's first word when he was in the house. 'She's called Miss Lindsay Wilson. Aged twenty-nine. Born in Workington, eldest of three. Father a teacher.' He grimaced slightly, presumably because his own father taught maths at a big comprehensive. 'I've got her address in Askham as well.'

'Wilson,' Simmy echoed. 'I would never have remembered that. I did say it was two syllables, though.'

'You did.'

'So everything she told me checks out. She really is doing a PhD about *Dombey and Son*.'

Ben nodded. 'Looks like it.'

'We should read it,' said Christopher. 'It might have some clues.'

'I saw the film about twenty years ago,' said Simmy vaguely. 'There's a girl called Florence in it, I think.'

'I never read it,' said Ben regretfully. 'I'm not too keen on Dickens. *A Tale of Two Cities* isn't too bad. We did that at school. But I was never tempted to try any more of them.' He was tapping his phone as he spoke.

'I did it at school too,' said Simmy.

'I never even got that far,' said Christopher.

'My father would be horrified,' said Simmy with a smile.

'It's 700 pages, in the unabridged edition,' Ben reported. 'Bags I'm not the one to read it.'

'Must have plenty of material for a doctorate then,' said Christopher.

'It can't possibly have anything to do with anything,' said Simmy firmly. 'That would just be silly.'

'You're probably right,' said Ben. 'So did anything happen today?'

Simmy was about to shake her head when she remembered her morning visitor. 'A man came,' she said. 'Howard Isaacs. He said he was a builder, trying to carry on Humphrey's business as he would have wanted. It sounded a bit odd, and he wanted to take photos. I wouldn't let him. He's got a beard and a moustache.' She laughed. 'That's not why I wouldn't let him take photos. He was actually quite pleasant, really, but I didn't think I should be too trusting.'

'Photos of what?' demanded Christopher.

'The house. To show off Humphrey's excellent work. He said the staircase was magnificent, and I said it really wasn't.'

'So he was just pretending to be a builder, was he?' said Ben. 'Is that what you think?'

'More likely he was trying to butter me up, or say nice

things about Humphrey because he's dead. People do that a lot.'

Christopher grunted sceptically. 'You should never have let him in.'

'Too late for that now,' said Ben. 'He's got to fit somewhere in the picture. Does he know you're a florist, do you think? That makes you unusual when it comes to funerals and so forth.' This led him to a connected thought. 'Bonnie was sorry you didn't go down to the shop today, by the way.'

'Oh dear. I thought I'd explained it would be tricky with Robin and the dog. I'll work something out later in the week.'

Christopher was frowning. 'What did you mean about the Isaacs man and funerals?' he asked Ben.

'Nothing specific. Just trying to spot all the possible connections. I admit it might turn out that the murder has nothing at all to do with Humphrey and this other builder bloke, but you can't assume that.'

Christopher sighed. 'I expect you're right,' he said.

They spent a few minutes settling down with coffee and a tin of biscuits in the main room. Christopher remarked that it was time they started having log fires, which was cheaper than using the central heating. Ben pointed out that burning wood was deemed almost criminal, on account of apparent air pollution. His elders ignored him.

'So nothing from Moxo, then?' the boy went on.

'Not a word.'

'No news is good news, I guess. Basically, all he wanted yesterday was to ask you where you were at the relevant time. He hadn't any choice but to do that. Nice, really, that they brought him in on it so quickly, when it's out of his area.'

'They all know we're connected, after what happened in Threlkeld,' said Christopher. 'The moment Simmy's name came up, they'd have the sense to bring him in.'

'Yes,' said Ben patiently. 'That's what I meant.'

'It was on the news at lunchtime,' said Simmy. 'They've got a very vague time of death, sometime on Saturday. I could easily have gone there before Christopher got home and done the deed. And even after that, my only alibi is my husband. I don't think that counts, does it?'

'You can't drive all the way to the Cockpit. You have to walk the last bit. They'd have to say you took Robin with you when you committed murder – or else left him in the car, way out of sight. Nobody's going to believe that.'

'They might say Christopher was in on it, and watched the baby while I went off and bashed poor Pauline.'

Ben nodded. 'If we only knew what the Wilson person says she saw, it would help a lot. Without that, there are just too many possible scenarios.'

'It will become clear eventually, if she sticks to her story,' said Simmy.

'We can't wait. We need to go and face her and find out what she thinks she's playing at,' said Christopher.

'You'd think Moxon would have told me not to do that – but he didn't.'

'Maybe because you doing that is exactly what he wants,' said Ben. 'Only he wasn't allowed to say so.'

Chapter Seven

'We'll go tomorrow, you and me,' said Christopher, brooking no argument. They were in bed at the end of the day. 'It's my free day, so it'll work out perfectly. We can even go and have a look at the Cockpit. And have lunch at that pub by the church after we've done the important stuff.'

'Oh,' said Simmy, her insides fluttering. 'You mean, go and talk to Lindsay Wilson?'

'I do. Confront her with her lies and see what she has to say for herself.'

'Surely we're not allowed to do that?' She rummaged through countless memories of films and books involving murder, as well as her own personal experience, and could come up with no instances where such a thing had been done. 'Isn't it tampering with a witness or something?'

'Who's going to stop us? What can they do to us?'

She had a confused notion of games and rules and proper procedures. 'It might get Moxon into trouble. He wasn't supposed to tell me who'd made the accusation against me.'

'Did he say that?'

'Not exactly. He just left me to work it out for myself.'

Christopher eyed her sternly. 'Did he actually say in so many words that she was your accuser?'

'I don't remember. I think not. I guessed it must be her and he didn't contradict me.'

'There you are, then! He had to ask those questions and you were obviously going to draw the right conclusion. Nobody broke any rules.'

She shook her head. 'It all feels like a ghastly game, with me as one of the pawns to be sacrificed.'

'I know. Ben makes it feel like that, don't you think? But the thing is, he's very often right.'

Simmy tried to think. 'Can it be possible that Lindsay might even *want* to talk to me? That she's expecting me to track her down and demand to know what she's doing? What if she knows the real killer and is terrified for her own life, and thought up this accusation against me as a way of dragging me – and you and Ben – into it? After all, people do know we've been involved in crimes before and have a hotline to the police.'

Christopher gazed at her, a little smile on his lips. 'That would never have occurred to me in a thousand years. Isn't it rather . . . convoluted? Do real people ever do that sort of thing?'

'I expect they do. Didn't somebody say that anything that can be imagined can be translated into action? Or something.'

'Did they? I never heard it before. What about dragons and elves and time travel and . . .'

'All right. Even so, people can be tremendously ingenious when they try.'

He was clearly struggling to makes sense of this line of thought. 'So – that would imply at least some sort of connection between Lindsay and the killer. Right?'

'Yes, I suppose. She might be scared of whoever it is.'

'Which doesn't actually get us very far. The police will be thinking the same thing, assuming they know the accusation against you is garbage. They might be following her, to see who she contacts. Monitoring her phone and email and stuff. But maybe she'd expect that, after what she did.'

'Don't get carried away. We have no idea why she went to the police in the first place, or what she told them. There must be a dozen possible explanations. More than that.' She sighed. 'I'm not at all sure it's a good idea to go and find her. I don't know that she likes me. Although . . .' She tried for the hundredth time to think back to the Saturday morning conversation, 'she did seem to want to be friendly. She told me quite a lot about herself. I hardly said anything about me or you or work or our lives. She did most of the talking.'

'That sounds as if she did quite like you – not that it matters. She just needs to explain why she slandered you the way she did.' He laughed. 'Hey – maybe we can sue her for defamation of character! Wouldn't that be fun!'

'I imagine there's some sort of immunity from anything like that given to witnesses to a murder. We'll have to ask

Ben.' She had another thought. 'He's off work tomorrow as well, isn't he? Are we taking him with us?'

Christopher gave a small moan. 'I was hoping you weren't going to ask that. I was hoping, in fact, that you and I could just have a nice day out by ourselves.'

'Not to mention Robin and your dog. We're never going to be on our own again. You must realise that?'

'Yes, dear. And I don't expect it'll be a very nice day tomorrow, anyway. We can phone Ben in the morning and see what he says.'

When Simmy did phone Ben at nine o'clock on the Tuesday morning, he gave her the startling news that he would not be able to accompany them to Askham because he had broken his wrist and couldn't drive. 'And I've got to go back to the hospital this afternoon for a closer look at it. It was too swollen to do a proper plaster cast this morning.'

'But how did you do it?' Simmy wanted to know. Sudden accidents frightened her more than they did most people. They reminded her that nothing could ever be taken for granted. A stupid accident with a placenta had killed her perfectly healthy first baby, so she ought to know.

'Fell down the step into the house, last night, when I got back from seeing you. The landlady's cat was winding itself round my legs, and I stepped back into the void. Landed right on my hand and it couldn't take the strain. I heard it snap, although I thought it might just be a ligament. It didn't really hurt much at first.'

'Why didn't you call us?'

'I called my mother instead,' he said, sounding very young. 'At four o'clock this morning, actually. I couldn't sleep and it got horribly swollen and started hurting and I remembered that an unstable fracture can cut off blood supply and other bad things, so I decided I should go to hospital. I had hoped to leave it until a more civilised time.'

'Honestly, Ben.'

'Anyway, Mum came and took me to Penrith and she's still here now, so she can take me back later today. I think they might want to do an operation, depending on what the X-rays say.'

'So you've been and come back already?' She was following the story painfully slowly. 'Which arm is it?'

'The left. So I can't change gear. I've never broken a bone before,' he added proudly, still sounding like a young boy.

'You can manage to work a phone, though,' she remarked.

'Oh yes,' he laughed. 'It'd take more than this to stop me doing that.'

'What about your job?'

'I was going to call Chris this morning and suggest he pick me up tomorrow on the way to work. I can probably find something useful to do, even with only one arm.'

'I'll tell him. He can speak to you later today, after you've got your new plaster.' She tried not to contemplate the possibility of surgery. Surely, they would never have let him go home if that was likely to be needed?

'Right,' said Ben. 'Okay.'

He was scared, Simmy realised. For the first time in his life his body had betrayed him. *They do that*, she thought wryly.

* * *

Christopher was surprisingly concerned. 'He'll be out of action for *weeks*,' he said. 'Which arm is it?'

'The left. He can still write, and probably check things on the computer, if a bit slowly. Are you worried about him for himself, or for his usefulness to you?'

'Both,' came the frank reply. 'Have I got to add fifteen minutes to my journey twice a day, to go and collect him from his digs and take him back again?'

'Probably. But it won't be nearly that long. It's all in Keswick, after all.' The auction house was a mile or so outside the town. Christopher would almost pass Ben's current home on his way there.

'He could walk it, come to that.'

'I suppose he could. But I don't think you'd be so mean as to make him do that.'

'You flatter me. Really, Sim, it's nothing like as quick and simple as you think. He'd have to be standing on the pavement waiting for me, because there's never anywhere to park in that street. And in the morning there's always a jam at the top end, where I'd have to try to get out. Though maybe he could go up to the corner and save me having to go into his road at all.'

Simmy lost patience. 'Just work it out with him, okay? It's not rocket science, as my father would never say.'

'Huh!' said Christopher.

There had been no mention of Askham in the conversation with Ben. He had evidently pushed it out of his mind, quite understandably. 'Lucky he gave us her address,' said Christopher, referring to Lindsay Wilson. 'It's probably going to be easier without him, anyway.'

Reluctantly, Simmy agreed with him. A delegation of three showing up at the woman's door was hardly likely to earn much of a welcome. Four, with Robin, she reminded herself.

'Are we really sure this is a good idea?' she worried. 'She's bound to be on the defensive.'

'We'll be very meek and mild, just asking her if she really does believe you . . .' He floundered, unable to voice the unthinkable.

'Killed someone,' Simmy finished for him. 'I still think we'd be breaking a whole lot of rules. Not to mention getting Moxon into trouble.' Again she racked her brains for any matching situation, where accused confronted accuser. There had to be something somewhere to offer a bit of guidance. 'What are we actually going to *say* to her?'

'How about – we've been asked by the police to account for our movements on Saturday, thanks to a person making an accusation, and we think it must have been her? Nice and vague and unthreatening. However she reacts to that will go a long way to showing us where she stands.'

'Will it? You mean she'll either slam the door in our faces, or burst into tears and beg forgiveness. I like the plural, by the way.'

'Sorry?'

'You've included yourself in the police questioning, which is very supportive of you, even if completely inaccurate. What's she going to think about that?'

'That she's got more than just you to reckon with,' he said, putting an arm round her shoulders. 'Strength in numbers.'

A crazy thought shot through Simmy's head. 'Do you

think she knows you? Has she been to an auction and fallen in love with your charismatic performance? And now she wants me out of the way so she can have you to herself?'

He laughed. 'I can see about eight things wrong with that idea. For a start, she can't possibly be mad enough to think you'd be charged with the murder just on her say-so. There'd have to be a whole lot more evidence against you than that.'

Simmy heaved a deep sigh. 'I know – but evidence can be fabricated. She was close enough to me on Saturday to have taken a hair off my coat, recorded things I said and edited them to sound sinister. All kinds of things are possible if a person's clever enough. And if the other person is so hopelessly naive as to make it all feasible.'

'Fantasy,' he scoffed. 'Real life doesn't work like that.'

'Except sometimes it does,' she disagreed. 'Just ask Ben.'

They decided that a first move might be to have a look at the Cockpit, where Pauline Parsons' body had been found. Simmy peeled the Ordnance Survey map off the wall and took it with her in the car. Before they were out of Hartsop she had spread it out on her lap and when they reached Askham, she directed Christopher through the upper part of the village, right at the fork and on until the road petered out. They then left the car and walked on with Robin and Cornelia. Simmy held the dog firmly on a lead, because there were sheep, cattle and ponies scattered across the fellside, ripe for the chasing. Ullswater lay ahead of them, not yet visible. The sky was heavy with pale grey cloud. 'How in the world would that old woman get up here?' Christopher asked. 'If she didn't drive, it must be a mile and a half from the nearest house. At least.'

'Maybe she did drive. Old people often do. If she had a Land Rover or something, she could get nearly all the way.' The improbability of this was blatant. 'Although I doubt if that's right. They'd have found her vehicle abandoned, wouldn't they?'

'Perhaps they did,' he said generously, and not very sincerely. 'They haven't told you anything much, after all.' He looked all around, the sky huge above them, with fells stretching away into the distance. 'It's amazing how quickly it feels as if we're on another planet,' he marvelled. 'Just piles of stones to show any human presence.'

The map was marked with the phrase 'pile of stones' in several places, along with 'cairns' and 'circles'. 'This must be absolutely ancient,' said Simmy. 'And there was a Roman road running through at one time.' She peered even more closely at the map. 'I suppose Pauline knew all the old legends and so forth. That's what they said on the news.'

'I get the impression that we know less than nothing about how or why she died. Look at this place! I can imagine coming here to kill yourself, if you've always lived here and know the stories and feel it's in your blood. You can almost see the ghosts. But it's the last place you'd choose to do a murder. Wouldn't you be scared you'd be haunted for ever after?' He waved his arms at the wide, open hilltops. 'I mean – it's got nothing to suggest it was a place of violence or sacrifice. I've seen some of those, and you can't miss the sense of cruelty and horror. This has something benign about it.'

* * *

Simmy was gazing at him in rapture. Such flashes of a sensitive interior life were all too rare. It reminded her of the teenaged Christopher she had known, who read poems and watched birds with no shadow of self-consciousness. His travels, she feared, had somehow hardened him, so that he could be quick to go on the defensive at times.

'I remember when you used to talk about atmospheres,' she said. 'That castle in North Wales – where you said you could feel people from a thousand years ago.'

'Beaumaris, on Anglesey,' he nodded. 'Fancy you remembering that. I have a nasty feeling I was teasing you, to be honest. It's nowhere near a thousand years old, for one thing.'

'Don't spoil it,' she begged.

Robin was in the rucksack on his father's back, dozing and floppy. Simmy wondered whether he was picking up the strange empty atmosphere all around them or was he totally oblivious to his surroundings. She forced her attention back to the main issue. 'We have to assume they've ruled out suicide,' she said.

'Yes,' said Christopher inattentively. 'Although . . .'

'What?'

'People sometimes arrange their own death in complicated ways. Wasn't there something like that in Coniston that time?'

'Not really.' She waved the reference aside, as too much of a distraction. 'So what do we think happened to Pauline, then? Are you thinking she arranged the whole thing to look like murder to get someone into trouble?'

'Sounds daft put like that. It's sure to be something much simpler than that.'

Belatedly she realised there was no police tape or any sign of Sunday's discovery. 'Shouldn't there be some sort of police presence?'

'Maybe it wasn't exactly here that they found her – when they said it was the Cockpit, they might have meant somewhere half a mile away. There are fells and moors all over this area.'

'I know,' she said, again consulting the map. 'Barton Fell. Tarn Moor. Something with an unpronounceable name. Hewscer, Hawscar – I've never heard of it before.' She spelt it out 'H-e-u-g-h-s-c-a-r. How would you say that?'

'No idea,' he said. 'And I've noticed that names on maps are often different from names the locals use.'

'Not very helpful.'

'I wish we could let Cornelia have a run. Don't you think we could risk it? She's got to learn to come back when she's called. I can't see any livestock up here.'

'It might be better without Robin. I warn you I won't go running after her if she makes a bolt for it,' said Simmy. Christopher bent over his dog, almost tipping Robin out of his carrier. He showed her a treat he had in his pocket and tried to convey to her that she was to stay close. Then he unclipped the lead and started to walk back towards Askham. 'Walkies,' he said fatuously.

Everything worked perfectly for ten minutes or so. The dog ran in a zigzag, staying within close range of her people. But then some sort of bird rose squawking into the air from under a clump of bracken and Cornelia gave chase.

Christopher immediately made things worse by shouting the dog's name in a harsh angry voice. 'That won't help,' said Simmy impatiently. 'You have to make it sound as if it's in her best interest to come back. If she thinks you're angry with her, she'll just keep running. I thought you knew all that.'

'Since when were you such an expert?' he snarled.

'I think it's just basic common sense. Look at it from her point of view.'

Two people were walking along a track towards them – as well as towards Cornelia. 'Stop her!' yelled Christopher.

The whole drama was over within three minutes. Even before the people could react, the dog had paused in her flight to greet them. The woman showed signs of admiration and Cornelia jumped up at her legs. Simmy and Christopher hurried to join them, and Cornelia was swiftly reattached to her lead. 'Thanks!' panted Christopher. 'I thought I might never see her again.'

'She wouldn't have gone far,' said the woman. 'She's hardly more than a puppy, as far as I can see.'

'Nearly five months now. I'm trying to train her.'

'Shouldn't be very difficult. Just make sure she knows you love her. But she's still very young. She won't understand the rules for a while yet.'

Simmy giggled. 'Just what I was trying to tell him,' she said.

'Don't even try to fight it, mate,' said the man, who was watching Christopher's face. His gaze then fell on Robin who had clearly been enjoying the bumpy ride. His eyes were bright with excitement. 'Somebody thinks it was fun, anyway.'

The couple looked to be in their mid sixties. Lean and fit, intent on maintaining a level of physical activity that belied their age, if Simmy's first assessment was correct.

They represented a very common subsection of humanity in that part of the world. The Hendersons were about to walk on, the exchange already over, when the woman spoke again. 'Did you know there was a murder up here at the weekend?'

Simmy said nothing, but pretended to be putting Robin straighter in his carrier. Christopher swiftly picked up the message and acted dumb. 'Oh?' he said.

'Yes. An old lady. Just past that cairn.' The woman pointed northwards, to a spot which Simmy and Christopher had ignored. 'We saw the place yesterday, actually. It's in a bit of a dip beside the beck.'

'And you came for another look today, did you?' said Simmy, suddenly angry. What did such people think they were doing?

'No, no, not at all. We come up here three or four times a week for the birds. We're doing a survey of kites and other raptors. We knew the old lady, as it happens. She was called Pauline and was a very fine person.' The reproach was painfully mild. A snappy response would have felt more deserved.

'There hasn't been much publicity about it,' said the man. 'You might not have heard.'

It was too late to confess. 'Well . . .' said Simmy hesitantly. 'I'm sorry I got you wrong. These things make people behave strangely sometimes.'

'Indeed,' said the man, giving her a look. He obviously knew that she really wanted to go and view the scene of the crime but had managed to prevent that being an option by what she had said. 'There really isn't anything much to see, of course,' he added kindly.

'Such an awful thing to happen,' said Simmy, hoping she sounded as if it had come as fresh news.

'At least it was in a place that she loved,' said the woman fatuously. To Simmy's mind, that just made it worse.

Robin obligingly started to whimper, which meant forward progress was required. The woman patted Cornelia again and they all went their separate ways.

When they were safely out of earshot, Simmy said, 'What if I am arrested and my face is all over the news? Those two are going to recognise me.'

Christopher laughed. 'That'll be the least of your worries,' he said.

'Don't be so mean.'

'It isn't going to happen, Sim. You know it isn't. Now let's go and find that woman. This boy and I are both going to be hungry soon.'

They found Lindsay Wilson's house along the left-hand fork at the upper end of Askham. 'She said it was here,' Simmy remembered. 'I could probably have found it for myself if I'd thought about it.' Ben had comprehensively identified the property on Google Earth, down to the colour of the front door and the number of chimneys.

'Quicker with Ben's help,' said Christopher.

'I still don't know what we're going to say to her,' Simmy worried. 'And even without Ben this feels like something of an invasion.' They had put Cornelia in the car, but Robin inevitably went with them.

'Serves her right,' said Christopher.

'Let's try and keep things nice and calm. I feel quite scared. What if she's got a gun or something?'

95

'Stay behind me if that makes you feel better. Don't forget I saw her as well on Friday. She must know she's going to have to reckon with us both. She's probably expecting us.'

But she wasn't. For a long minute there was no reply to the doorbell and the little family stood foolishly on the path, wondering what to do next. Then a window above their heads was pushed open and a voice came from it: 'Who's that? What do you want?'

Simmy stepped back until she and Lindsay could see each other. 'It's me,' she said.

'So it is. What do you want?'

'What do you think we want?'

'Who's with you?'

'Husband and baby. The dog's in the car.'

'That's a shame. I liked your dog.'

'So did Pauline,' said Simmy, not entirely accurately, but determined to get to the main point from the start. As far as she could recall, the old lady had pretty much ignored Cornelia.

'Nonsense,' Lindsay Wilson said lightly. 'Pauline never had any time for gushing over puppies – or babies, come to that.'

Christopher stepped into her line of sight. 'Are you going to let us in, then?'

Lindsay shook her head. 'Oddly enough, I am not. I wouldn't be such a fool. You must know you aren't supposed to talk to me. This is intimidation, technically speaking. I can call the cops and have you removed. Harassment as well, I shouldn't wonder.' Her tone was casual, as if she was thinking about something else and was only half attending to the visitors. 'Not that I care about that, to be honest. It's just that I have nothing whatever to say to you.'

'But why did you tell such lies about me?' Simmy burst out, loudly enough to be heard by any inquisitive neighbours. 'Never mind harassment. What about slander?'

The woman was just too far away to detect any subtleties in her expression. Simmy saw no scowl or angry reddening. But the words were not encouraging. 'Oh, go away. And don't come here again. You must know I can't talk to you. Have some sense.' And she disappeared into the room behind her.

The Henderson family slunk back to the car acutely aware of potential watching eyes. Five or six houses at least could have people inside who were eagerly viewing the little drama. Some of them might step forward as witnesses if things got nasty. Except there had been no sign of nastiness. The whole exchange had been quite calm.

'That did not go well, did it?' said Simmy, when they were in the car again. 'Although I don't know why I'm surprised.'

'Are you surprised? Wouldn't you have done the same in her position?'

She blinked at him. 'I'm never likely to be in her position, am I? I don't go round making false accusations against people.'

'The whole thing was very peculiar,' he said. 'Don't you think she was over-egging it a bit? As if she was just making another move in a game? I didn't get any sense of much real emotion.'

'I know. That's what I'm thinking. And that's a surprise in itself. I was bracing myself for a vat of boiling oil over my head.'

'She wasn't angry. She was being careful about what she said. But the bit about liking our dog – that wasn't in the script. That was her trying to make human contact. You spoilt it by mentioning Pauline.'

'Oh.' Simmy tried to rerun the exchange. 'Did I?' Again, she blinked at her husband, who seemed to be morphing into a kind of cross between Ben and Moxon.

The morphing did not stop there, either. 'There's got to be something else going on, just below the surface, that we're not getting. Do you think there's any chance that *Humphrey* has something to do with it all? After all, it does seem to have started on Friday, somehow. Don't you think? Or am I trying to channel Ben and getting it all wrong?'

'Anything's possible,' she said faintly, 'I suppose. But she can't have known she'd see me again on Saturday, can she?'

'No, but listen. She saw us – you and me but not Robin – after the funeral. She seemed quite friendly and forthcoming then, didn't she? All that about wakes. Then on Saturday she said something about being related to Humphrey, or his wife, or someone. A family connection, anyway. Could be that something happened later on Friday, which changed her mind about you – us, and then when she saw you again it fitted with some kind of plan.'

'So where do we go with that?'

'I don't know. It's probably completely wrong. But I bet there's something important we should know. What if Pauline is related as well? Old grudges and feuds that got stirred up when Humphrey died.'

'Can we go to the pub first and talk about it there?' she begged. She felt exposed, parked outside Lindsay's house under the probable gaze of the whole village. Robin was strapped into his seat and Cornelia was eyeing everything as a potential game. 'You said you were hungry.'

'Yes. It's barely a minute's drive. Don't fret. We ought to walk really, but I'm not keen on leaving the car here.'

I have every reason to fret, she thought mutinously, but said, 'Nor am I. Lindsay might come out and slash the tyres.'

Chapter Eight

The pub was busy, but there were still one or two free tables. Some men were playing billiards in a bar off to the side. A few people gave Robin a rueful look as the Hendersons walked in. Babies in pubs were anathema to some committed drinkers. Two or three others smiled, first at Cornelia and then at the child. There was nobody that Simmy recognised.

'We can't talk freely here,' Christopher muttered. 'What if the murderer is at the bar and hears everything we say?'

She laughed, not taking him a bit seriously. Being in a pub always felt like a little holiday: someone else doing the cooking, other people generally in a good mood. 'I want a whole pint of beer,' she said. 'Whatever their local ale is.'

'Me too,' he agreed. 'And shucks to the driving police.'

'I think even they would allow you one beer. I hope.' She remembered how people had fussed if she imbibed a single small glass of wine when pregnant, and sighed.

Cornelia was persuaded to lie down under the table and Robin perched unsteadily on his mother's lap, deliberately swaying from side to side. 'Keep still,' she told him and rummaged for the cup of milk she had somewhere in her bag. Between them, they got him contentedly sucking at the spout of the cleverly made container. 'Look!' she said to Christopher. 'He's holding it by himself.'

'Remarkable,' said the unimpressed father.

Food came quickly, to their relief, and they settled down to eat. Robin was handed a chip, and then a few forkfuls of fish from Simmy's plate were consumed. 'This is nice,' she said.

'Er . . .' warned Christopher, slightly too late. A man was approaching them, unsmiling, his head tilted to one side. Simmy realised she had forgotten all about her invidious position in Askham. How was it that she had stupidly assumed that nobody but Moxon knew of Lindsay Wilson's accusation?

'You're that florist,' said the man. 'They're saying you had something to do with the attack on poor old Pauline.'

Run away! thought Simmy, half a second before becoming aware that with baby, dog, bag and food, this was not just ridiculous but impossible. 'Pardon?' she said, avoiding the man's face and meeting her husband's eye instead. He gave a little nod of encouragement.

'Don't act daft,' said the man. 'You were here on Saturday. That's when she was killed. You were seen talking to her. You know what I'm getting at.'

He was in early middle age, somewhat crumpled and unshaven. Unsteady, too. Simmy's brain was swiftly examining each of his phrases and tossing them aside as lacking all logic. Robin was gurgling in a wholly misjudged welcome. Cornelia was asleep.

'I think perhaps you're a trifle drunk,' said Christopher, sitting up very straight and speaking with pure BBC diction. 'I'm sure the landlord would be very upset if you caused a disturbance.'

'Eldon! Come back here, you fool,' called another man who was standing at the bar. He took a few steps towards the table. 'Sorry, folks. He's not been himself lately. Good mate to poor old Humphrey Craig. You'll know who I mean. And now with Pauline as well – with her being one of the family, well . . .' He spread his hands eloquently. 'He's fine as a rule. Just having a bad day.'

Simmy forced a smile. 'Yes,' she said, meaninglessly. Anything to defuse the situation.

The second man went on. 'Village all at sixes and sevens this week, the way things are going. Nobody knows what to think. All sorts of stories flying about. Might be an idea for you to keep clear for a bit, know what I mean?'

Eldon's friend was sober and less unpleasant, but the subtext was not so different. It had been rash of them to expect to be able to eat at the same pub that had hosted Humphrey's wake, without some sort of recognition or reference to recent events. Even without Pauline Parsons, there would be talk of the funeral and probable questions as to how they came into the picture. As it was, with a murder to contemplate, there had never been much hope of a peaceful meal.

'Can we finish our food before you throw us out?' said

Christopher, still in the same clipped voice. His work as an auctioneer had taught him how to project, as well as conferring a degree of authority – all of which worked effectively now.

'Nobody's going to throw you out,' came a third voice. 'Don't worry about Eldon. He's been listening to all kinds of rubbish. People like him should never be allowed to look at Facebook and all that stuff. He's always getting the wrong idea.'

Somebody laughed; somebody else said something rude. Simmy glanced around at the whole room and saw that everyone was watching her. There was no overt hostility, but neither was there any noticeable friendliness. 'Facebook?' she said, suddenly jumping to a worrying conclusion.

'Not seen it? Have a look, then, if you want to know why Eldon recognised you.'

'What?'

'You'll see,' was all the answer she got.

The word *invidious* came to her again. She and Christopher were not locals. Nor were they tourists, hikers or day trippers. They fell between all the accepted stools and were accordingly to be treated with suspicion – especially if the fact of Lindsay's accusation was on social media for all to see. All appetite evaporated and she pushed her plate away. 'We'll go,' she said.

Christopher waved at her to stay still. 'I haven't finished,' he said.

In the car, they talked it over obsessively. Christopher insisted that they had gleaned a great deal and were a lot further forward than before. Simmy was unconvinced. 'All I can think about is the way they knew who we were as soon as we walked in. That's horrible. They know I'm a florist, for heaven's sake. Somebody's put it on the Internet. We'll have to find out what it says. Why didn't Moxon warn me? I feel awful now.'

'People talk even without the Internet. They'd have known about us before the murder, because of Humphrey. He was working on the house for *months*. Everybody who knew him would probably have heard stories about our door frames and staircases and new baby. We'll have been "the Hartsop barn conversion people".'

'It's worse than that. What about that man who came yesterday? Isaacs. That felt sinister at the time – now it's got to have something to do with Pauline and all this. He must have been some sort of spy. I actually said that to him and he just laughed it off.'

'Of course he did,' said Christopher. 'What else was he going to do? But the thing is, Sim, you have to hang onto the knowledge that you haven't done anything wrong. You're completely innocent. Whatever's going on, they've put you in the middle of it for reasons of their own. The fact that it's you is probably just a random accident. You're useful somehow. Most likely because of being friends with Moxon. Can't you see how it's all coming together? Coming into focus. Those men in the pub are irrelevant, other than to show how it's all turning out.'

'If it's because I'm friends with Moxon, then it's not random, is it? You're not doing a very good job of making me feel better, to be honest. The way you're talking, I've walked into a ghastly stretch of quicksand and there's no way I can get out of it.'

'You're not in quicksand. You're . . . let me think . . . maybe crossing a road that turned out to get busier while you were halfway across.' He laughed. 'That's very feeble. And not really right. How about you've been pushed onto a stage without any script, the spotlight's shining on you and everybody's watching? You think you have to do something, but really you can just step back behind the curtain and leave them to get on with it.'

'Oh dear,' said Simmy. But she found her mood was lightening somewhat, if only because her husband was so wonderfully *engaged* for once. 'But thanks for trying. It's sweet of you.'

'"Sweet",' he muttered. 'I wasn't exactly trying to be *sweet.*'

'Sorry. How about "supportive" or "reassuring"? I'm just happy you're not leaving me to cope with it by myself.'

'As if I would,' he protested. 'I'm hurt that you would even think I might.'

'Sorry,' she said again, pushing away the memory of his reluctance to take his share of baby care when Robin was tiny, and his regular complaints at the way Ben and Bonnie plunged into murder investigations. Apparently, this time was different.

'It's different this time,' he said, echoing her thought. 'You've never been in the spotlight like this before.'

'No,' she said. 'At least, not since we've been together. And never as bad as this.'

'Nearly home,' he soothed. 'I suggest we just sit tight and think about something else for the rest of the day.

Let's not even bother checking out what somebody's put on Facebook. We've done what we can – more than most people would. I could cut the hedge back if it doesn't rain. And we'll need to think about getting a supply of firewood sorted out. Winter's coming.'

'I love that wood burner,' she sighed. 'It's my favourite thing in the whole house.'

'Me too,' he agreed.

But she knew she would be compelled to check the computer the minute they got home. How could anyone not, knowing they'd been publicly named as a suspect in a murder investigation with a picture for good measure?

They were back indoors by half past one, with the dog and baby cheerfully wrestling on the playmat and Simmy searching the Facebook pages for any reference to the Askham business. It took her a while, since it was not something she ever did. Christopher made no attempt to help. At last she found it and read it out loud. '"The word is that the Hartsop resident, florist Persimmon Henderson, has been named as a person of interest in the death of Pauline Parsons. Check out reports of other murders – the lady and Detective Inspector Moxon have known each other for quite a time." Are people allowed to say stuff like that? Where did they get it from? And there's an awful old photo of me from when I first opened the shop.'

Christopher was preparing to go out to his hedge cutting. 'Anonymous, presumably? Has anybody replied to it?'

'Just a few thumbs-up signs. I bet there's more on WhatsApp and other stuff. We'll have to get Ben to find that. I've got no idea how it works.'

'Nor me. Now put it away. I thought you were going to make some coffee. I can take a mug out with me and get cracking on the hedge.'

With an effort, Simmy switched off the laptop and went to boil the kettle. She knew Christopher was aiming for a nice relaxed domestic afternoon doing nothing much. 'Go on, and I'll bring it out to you,' she said.

Five minutes later, she was in the back garden with him. 'I hope they don't have to operate on Ben,' she remarked. 'I wonder what Bonnie makes of it. She might be in a state. I should go down to the shop tomorrow and see that she's all right.'

'I imagine that can be left to Helen,' said Christopher. 'In fact, this might be just the thing to patch up the rift between them. She sounds pretty concerned about him.' Helen Harkness was Ben's mother, an architect suffering increasingly from disabling levels of arthritis. Her early-morning dash to Keswick must have cost her a prodigious effort.

'Let's hope so,' said Simmy. 'But she's not likely to be of much help to Bonnie.'

'She might offer to drive her up to see Ben.'

'It's possible,' Simmy conceded. 'But I'm going to find out for sure when I've got a minute.'

When the doorbell rang at a quarter to three, Simmy knew exactly who it was. She realised she had been expecting him all afternoon. Christopher was outside with the hedge trimmer and Robin was asleep.

'Hello,' she said. 'I thought it would be you.'

DI Moxon wiped his feet and walked in. 'All right?' he asked, peering into her face in search of an honest answer.

'More or less. We went to Askham this morning.'

'So I gather.'

Simmy winced. 'I hate this feeling that everything I do is being watched and reported. It was horrible in the pub there. Everybody knew who we were.'

'And yet you went of your own free will. What did you expect?'

'Not that. We just wanted to see the place where Pauline was found, and then to have a nice relaxed lunch at the Punchbowl. We didn't expect to be treated like pariahs.'

'Did you try to talk to Ms Wilson?'

'Well, yes. Christopher didn't think it would do any harm. I mean – you didn't tell me not to, did you?'

Moxon shook his head. 'I don't have the authority to do that.'

'Really?' She frowned in confusion. 'I thought there must be rules about it. Accuser and accused meeting up must make your job much harder. Doesn't it?'

'That depends. This is a very unusual situation.'

'I know.'

There was a pause, in which she wondered what he had come for. He was a long way from his normal self of earlier times, when he would chat comfortably, ask about the baby, laugh about Ben and Bonnie. They had all come to regard him as a sort of honorary uncle who worried about their welfare while admiring their eagerness to help him solve crimes. Simmy had a suspicion that it all went towards making him rather a figure of fun amongst his colleagues.

'Christopher's off work today, then? I saw his car.'

'He's trimming the hedge. Do you want me to call him in?'

'No, no. What about tomorrow?'

'What about it?'

'Are you going to be here on your own?'

Her eyes widened. 'Why? Do you think I won't be safe?'

'Not at all. I just have a feeling it might be useful to know where I can find you.'

'There's such a thing as phones, you know.'

He smiled patiently. 'Yes, and we all know how unreliable they can be. I only asked because you seem a bit flummoxed, and you might get worse if you haven't got somebody to talk to.'

She looked into his eyes, searching for clues. 'You're not making much sense, you know. This whole situation is utterly illogical. But I can see you're worried. Worse than you were on Sunday, even. And you've never been all tight-lipped like this before.'

He nodded. 'I know. But you must believe it's for your own good. It isn't exactly that information is dangerous, but more that we don't know which bits of information to believe or act on. If it hadn't been for Ms Wilson naming you as she did, we'd have hardly anything at all to go on.'

'You still haven't,' she said hotly. 'Because I had nothing whatsoever to do with it.'

He chewed his lip hesitantly. 'No, but Ms Wilson probably did, in some way.'

'We've been assuming she's got an alibi, and can prove it wasn't her who killed Pauline. That's right, is it?'

'I can't say anything about that. I wish I could. The whole village has clammed up, nobody has a word to say against the victim. She was related to half of them. But word's got out that you've been accused and that makes you vulnerable. Do you see?'

'Sort of. I found it on Facebook just a little while ago.'

'It could make things tricky for you,' he repeated. 'I don't have any firm reason to say that, but it's just common sense, basically. I just feel it would be in your best interest to be amongst other people. Go to your parents, or down to the shop.'

She sighed and gave him a soft look. 'If today at the pub is any indication, then yes, I do see.' Then she shook her head. 'Although I don't really. Do you mean that Pauline's relatives might come armed with pitchforks and take justice into their own hands? A vigilante group or something? I gather she did have relatives.'

He gave a bitter laugh. 'Oh yes. Quite a lot of grandsons, for one thing. Not one of them appears to have inherited her brains, sad to say. They're certainly keeping us all rather busy.'

'Could one of them have killed her?' Simmy asked hopefully.

Moxon sighed. 'That isn't looking very likely.'

'But your "colleagues" don't think it was me, do they? Any of them?'

'I'm not at liberty to say,' he told her, with a reassuring twinkle. 'I ought not to be here without someone to corroborate everything that's said between us, you know. I had to pull rank and make assurances, and even so there's a young sergeant sitting outside, monitoring how long I'm here.'

She savoured the twinkle and smiled her thanks. 'Can he hear what we're saying? Have you got a secret microphone taped to your chest?'

'No. But she – it's a she not a he – might be watching us through the window. Don't look round.'

She almost did, before realising he was teasing. This was more like it. He was telling her she could trust him, that it would all turn out for the best, but that she really ought to follow his suggestions about the coming day. 'Thanks,' she said. 'Am I allowed to tell you that Christopher thinks it might all connect to Humphrey?'

He scratched his neck. 'Craig? The builder who cut himself to bits with a chainsaw?'

'Yes,' she snapped impatiently. 'The man whose funeral we were at on Friday. In Askham. Remember?'

'Of course. And you might be thinking the connection is you. Which I think I've noted a few times before now. In other cases. But I don't think it pertains this time. Nothing to do with flowers, at any rate.'

'So why have I been accused of being the one who did it?'

He had no reply to this. Sometimes, Simmy thought, the police could be extraordinarily frustrating.

'Oh – and Ben's broken his arm. You probably didn't know that. Wrist, to be precise.'

Moxon flinched. He was very fond of Ben. 'Is it bad?'

'He's not sure. His mother took him to Penrith in the small hours of this morning, and he's back there again this afternoon. As far as I know.'

'That's going to slow him down, isn't it. Which arm?'

'Left. He can still operate a phone and computer. He wants to keep working, if Christopher can collect him and take him home every day. It's more or less on his way.'

111

'He could possibly drive an automatic. Maybe that can be organised.'

'Maybe.' She fell silent, sensing that the conversation had run its course. 'Are you going now?'

'Just let me have a quick peep at the baby. Where is he?'

'Upstairs. But it's time he woke up. I'll go and fetch him.'

Which she did, and the childless detective chucked him under his chin and made silly noises and told Simmy she was doing a wonderful job.

Christopher belatedly came in to investigate just as Moxon was getting into the passenger seat of the police car. 'What did he want?' he asked Simmy when they were alone again.

'I think he came to tell me that everything's going to be all right,' said Simmy diplomatically and not quite truthfully. She spent a moment examining Robin's nappy, before adding, 'Pauline had a lot of grandsons, apparently. And they're out for vengeance. He thinks I should get out of here tomorrow.'

'So go and see Bonnie,' said Christopher, with a careless shrug. 'Is he worrying that you'll spend all day wallowing in self-pity otherwise?'

'Not at all. He's worrying that the grandsons might come for me. Aren't you listening?'

'I thought that was a joke. Are you sure he was serious? It doesn't strike me as very likely. What happens after tomorrow?' He was gradually working himself up to a state of unusual annoyance. 'What does he think he's doing, coming up here and scaring you?'

'I expect I'm exaggerating. I don't feel a bit scared of physical attack. Well, maybe a little bit on Robin's behalf,' she conceded. 'But that is what Moxon said. It might not have been the main message, I suppose.'

'You started by saying he came to tell you it would all be all right. Let's hold onto that, shall we?'

'He was subtly reassuring, even though he couldn't actually tell me anything specific.'

'Except the existence of grandsons. How many are there?'

'Quite a lot, to quote his exact words. I guess three or four.'

'If she was ninety, they're probably in their thirties or thereabouts. Are they local?'

'I don't know. Let's not talk about it any more. This boy needs changing. Could you make us some tea, do you think? I'm thirsty.'

'No problem.'

Upstairs, Simmy tried to summarise the day so far, in an unconscious need to have a report ready for Ben next time she spoke to him. Or Bonnie next day, if that was sooner. Much of what she expected to say would be a repeat of Christopher's ideas and theories, since she had very few of her own. The chief suggestion was that Lindsay Wilson was playing some deep game while perfectly well aware that Simmy had not killed Pauline. There had already been a few wild guesses as to what this might imply, and most of them had been dismissed as fanciful. Moxon's uncharacteristic care in choosing his words made the whole thing even murkier. She had been left with an impression that something very serious might be going on below the visible surface. Delicacy, keeping back information, refusal to commit himself – all very different from previous occasions. She wondered whether he was only permitted a role because he knew Simmy and the others. Perhaps he would normally be kept at arm's length by his superiors, for fear he would blunder onto dangerous ground.

Perhaps – the thought smacked her in the face – that had been the accuser's intention all along? Was *that* the reason Lindsay had said what she did – and if so, why would she want the Windermere inspector to be brought in?

Chapter Nine

Ben phoned at six, just as Simmy was cooking and Christopher was trying to entertain Robin at the grumpiest hour of the day. Cornelia was acting the fool, running in and out of the kitchen. 'Hasn't he learnt by now that this is the absolute worst time to phone anybody?' Simmy demanded, not expecting an answer.

She picked up the phone with a greasy hand and almost dropped it. 'Ben? Are you all right?'

'I'm home, with a big green plaster. They let you choose the colour – did you know that?'

'Is your mother still there?'

'No. She went ages ago. She says she'll have to work till midnight to make up for lost time.'

Helen Harkness had five children; she had to be

accustomed to emergency interruptions from one or other of them. Simmy wasted no sympathy on her. 'Does it hurt?'

'Not really. A sort of ache, deep in the bones. What's been happening your end?'

'Moxon came. Christopher has a few theories. We are not popular in Askham. I think that sums it up.'

'Explain.'

'I can't now. I'm cooking. You should never phone people at six o'clock. I've told you that before.'

'Sorry. Shall I try again at eight?'

'You do that.' And she ended the call.

Christopher was determined not to let the subject drop. It turned out that Simmy had been right to suspect that he had deliberately avoided Moxon, staying outside for the duration of his visit. 'I thought it best to let him talk to you on your own,' he said.

'It probably was – although I'm not sure I understand your reasoning.'

'Just human dynamics. We might have started fighting over you, in a very discreet and subtle way, of course. Vying for your affection. It would have muddied the water.'

'The water was already pretty muddy. He didn't tell me anything useful except for the scary grandsons.'

'Maybe *you* told *him* things? Without realising it.'

'I don't think I did.' She tried to recall everything she'd said. 'He already knew we'd been to Askham and seen Lindsay Wilson. At least, he might not have been sure about that until he asked me. And I told him.'

'What did he say?'

'Almost nothing. I thought he might tell me off, but he said he hadn't got the authority to do that.'

'Did he seem worried?'

'Not very. I think he's sad about me being dragged into it, especially as he can't do anything to protect me. He seems to think that's down to you.'

'Back to the scary grandsons, then.'

'I wonder if that's a sort of code? Just a way of telling me to be careful and prepared for anything.'

'Did you get any sense that he knows who the killer is, and has to play complicated games to lure them into giving themselves away? With you as a sort of bait?'

She shook her head. 'Very much not. That's an awful idea. Although . . .' she tailed off thoughtfully. 'It would make a sort of sense, I suppose.'

'It raises an awful lot of questions. Top of the list is what's Ms Wilson playing at? What does she know? Where does she stand?'

Simmy sighed. 'We keep saying that. We need Ben to get us out of this loop. There are all kinds of threads and networks we don't know about. Everybody is probably related to everybody else. There's sure to be history. Pauline Parsons has loads of descendants – who could be married to Lindsay's brother or Sophie's cousin – all sorts of complexities along those lines. Just the sort of good old-fashioned village my father likes so much.'

'And don't I recall us trying to link Sophie with our Bonnie, for good measure, given that they look rather alike?'

She blinked at him. 'So we did. That seems a long time ago now. Don't you dare repeat it to Ben or Bonnie.

Things are complicated enough without that.'

'I wasn't going to,' he said.

'Well, I'm going to Windermere tomorrow to think about flowers all day. If it's not busy Verity can play with Robin while I check the place for cobwebs. Bonnie's brilliant at most things, but cleaning isn't one of them.'

'It's Halloween soon – cobwebs are perfectly acceptable. Almost de rigueur in fact.'

'Gosh – I'd quite forgotten that. We'll have to do a special window for it.'

'Bonnie's done it already,' Christopher told her with a slightly smug expression.

'How do you know?'

'Ben told me, of course. He showed me a photo. How long is it since you were down there?'

'Ten days or so. I've got very slack.'

'You have. Although I suspect you've spent a few hours each day doing the accounts, orders, customer lists, promotion and payments of bills from here.'

'More or less,' she agreed.

'So not slack after all, right?' He laughed at her. 'And I have a feeling that business is actually pretty good.'

'Ben told you that as well, did he?'

'By implication. Tanya reported that they've been rushed off their feet these past few weeks.'

'She'll be wanting a pay rise, then.' Tanya was Ben's younger sister, who had worked at the shop on Saturdays for much of the year.

'I dare say she will.'

Life had to go on – that was the subtext that Simmy perceived in this conversation. Her florist shop in

Windermere had been her pride and joy for years, expanding and experimenting, widening its area of operation and earning a favourable reputation. Bonnie Lawson had drifted into it at the age of seventeen and added a flair and enthusiasm that greatly enhanced the whole operation. The move to Hartsop, an uncomfortable distance away, had threatened to capsize the whole endeavour. The birth of Robin was another blow. But Bonnie was undaunted. A woman called Verity had been engaged full-time, and Tanya filled the weekend gap left by Verity's refusal to work on Saturdays. Simmy anticipated a return to a more active role when Robin was older. How much older was still to be decided.

At Christopher's auction house, entries would start arriving on Wednesday for the next sale at the end of the following week. 'We've got a house clearance in Grasmere,' he told Simmy. 'I'll go with Jack in the van tomorrow and we'll get it all loaded up. Two or three journeys, most likely.'

House clearance was the aspect of his work that Simmy found most engaging. The contents of someone's home, often going back six or seven decades, deemed disposable by uncaring relatives – sent to auction with little hope of substantial proceeds. But since the objects had simply been sitting on mantelpieces and in shadowy corners for so long, the monetary value tended to be underestimated – although most people seemed to believe that grandfather clocks and mahogany davenports were worth a lot more than the reality. Likewise murky old portraits of long-forgotten ancestors. Quite ordinary people still had those tucked away in the attic. But the unsorted boxes of apparent junk that found their way to auctions quite often contained pure treasure somewhere towards the bottom. Collectors of such bizarre obsolescence as Bakelite and rusting tin signs ensured that hammer prices could come as a real surprise. Not to mention penknives, in which Christopher took a particular interest. 'I really love penknives,' he would sigh. 'They always sell brilliantly.'

'It hadn't occurred to Moxon that it could all have something to do with Humphrey,' she said.

Christopher's eyebrows went up. 'I'm not surprised. I mean – I *am* surprised that you suggested it. I hope you didn't say the idea came from me.'

'I think I did, actually. I thought you deserved the credit.'

'Oh, Sim! I was just brainstorming. It wasn't something to be passed to the police. What if they go and upset poor Sophie?'

'Too late now,' said Simmy crossly. 'And it wasn't just brainstorming. It made good sense.'

He shrugged. 'I need to be more careful what I say to you, don't I. You go running off to one of your pals and repeat every word.'

'Do I?' Her immediate instinct to defend herself was quickly overruled by a wish to be fair. Accusations from other people always had to be taken seriously, according to her own peculiar set of values. 'I guess it never occurred to me to keep everything private. And to be scrupulously fair, just for the record, there is a whole lot I never repeat to a soul. Not even my mother,' she added, hoping for a smile.

'I know. I overreacted. Hey – we're good at this, aren't

we! If this was a film, we'd be properly fighting by now instead of being all understanding and patient with each other.'

'Or *The Archers*. They can go a whole episode not listening to each other and getting in a fury about nothing.'

They laughed and Robin laughed with them. 'Time we got you off to bed, young sir,' said Christopher.

'Ben's going to phone again at eight,' Simmy remembered.

The phone call came promptly, but Simmy discovered that there really wasn't very much to say, after all. 'It's all just wild theories and nothing concrete to base them on,' she explained to the impatient Ben. 'I still don't know any real facts. Cause of death, for example. Was she just bashed on the head or strangled, or what?'

'It probably wouldn't take much to kill her,' said Ben. 'I've been thinking what it must have been like to murder somebody as old as that. Would you feel less guilty because her life was almost finished anyway? Or had she done something so awful that her age wasn't relevant? Or could she have actually tricked the killer into doing it because she wanted to die? A sort of alternative version of death-by-cop. Maybe it was a person she really hated and wanted to land in trouble, so she prodded and poked until he – or she – was goaded into bashing her. Or threatened to reveal a secret. That might do it.'

'I think this is what Christopher calls brainstorming,' said Simmy mildly. As always, Ben's imagination filled her with awe. He seemed to overflow with ideas and suggestions that would never occur to anybody else.

'But you're right that we need more hard facts. It's got to be something to do with the people of Askham. They're all so interconnected. And there's Lowther as well.'

'Pardon?'

'You know – I've said it before. That great castle and its estate. It *owns* Askham. It's incredibly feudal. Now they've got into conservation as well, wildflower meadows and all that. Everyone's answerable to Lowther, in one way or another. And that misleading building that looks so majestic looms over everything, like the Old Man of Coniston. It seems to be watching everything that goes on.'

'Why is it misleading?'

'You'll have to go there and see for yourself,' he teased.

Simmy felt herself in danger of being diverted into irrelevance. 'You know all about the place, then? When were you last in Askham?'

'Probably three or four months ago. I was just biking aimlessly around one weekend. I was going to go over again today, but I couldn't because I fell over.'

'I see,' said Simmy. 'And what else do you remember about it, apart from how feudal it is?'

'Nothing in particular. I've been trying to think myself into different people's minds. That can be quite useful you know.'

'Don't patronise, Ben. I've told you about that before.' *About a thousand times*, she added silently.

'No, but it *is*. The Wilson woman, the victim, the average Askham resident, if there is such a person. What are they all thinking? What do they *want*?'

122

'Have you started one of your dossiers?'

'No, because I fell over and broke my wrist and I've only been back from hospital for about three hours, and I want to go to bed.'

'You sound bright enough.' Which was not strictly true. Over the past few minutes, he had sounded more and more weary.

'I'm making a special effort for you.'

'That's very nice of you. But let's leave it for now. I'm going down to Windermere tomorrow. Do you want to speak to Christopher? He's assuming he'll be driving you in and out of work for a while.'

'Okay, then.'

She handed the phone over and sank into the sofa. Everything suddenly seemed exhausting. Perhaps she was catching Ben's sudden drop in energy. They had all had a demanding day, after all.

'He's having tomorrow off,' Christopher reported. 'On doctor's orders.'

'Good,' said Simmy.

But Christopher was manifesting enough energy for all three of them, even as the evening wound down past ten o'clock, when they would normally be in bed. 'I don't know what's come over me,' he said. 'I've got a head full of wild ideas worthy of Ben and then some. I think it's because you've been so personally accused – it feels like an attack on something really crucial to who we are. Do you know what I mean?'

'Hmm?' was all Simmy could manage. She was on the sofa, too weary even to get up and go to bed.

'Simmy!' he said sharply. 'Wake up and talk to me. It's not late. Why are you so droopy?'

She made an effort. 'Sorry. It must be the shock of it all. I feel limp and helpless. Maybe it's hormones,' she added shamelessly.

'Don't give me that,' he warned. 'Or I'll tell your mother of you.' Angie Straw would have no truck with women who used that sort of excuse for feebleness. Simmy pretended to shudder and Christopher went on remorselessly, 'I think we need to focus on Pauline. Who would want her dead? Who benefits, as I think Ben was trying to say on Sunday. There are all these scattered bits and pieces and nothing fits together.'

'We don't know enough. We hardly know any people over there, and I'm definitely not going back to that pub while they're all so unfriendly.'

'No, but don't you think there must have been some deeper reason for that? That maybe all the locals have a pretty good idea of what really happened, and are scared to even think about it? They don't want us marching in and asking dangerous questions.'

Simmy stirred herself. 'You make it sound like one of those films by that Shyamalan chap. Ben says the whole place is feudal.'

Christopher grinned. 'Hey – you're coming along nicely as a film buff. You mean *The Village*, I suppose. It does fit, in a sort of way.'

'Except that would mean that there are alien creatures up on the fells who killed Pauline – and that's a bit too neat. She'd have to have bite marks or disappear leaving only a severed foot.'

'Yeah,' he sighed. 'And if that was the case, the media would have ferreted it out by now.'

'We haven't checked the media, have we? We leave all that to Ben. Except Facebook, of course, and I'm already wishing I hadn't seen what they're saying on that.'

'I had another quick look just now, while you were half asleep. It hasn't caught on as much of a story in the news. Just a flurry of local interest and bland statements from the police.'

'Not surprising, I suppose. And I have no helpful suggestions as to what we could possibly do to move it along – assuming that's what we want to do. My instinct tends to favour doing nothing, if I'm honest. If Ben's out of action, we're sunk anyway. It's all down to Moxon now. I suppose he'll get to the bottom of it eventually. We might as well leave it all to him.'

'No, no.' Christopher shook his head emphatically. 'We're not gonna do that. It's too intriguing. Besides, you have to defend your name and reputation. If you just cower on the sofa for the duration, it'll look as if you're guilty.'

'It won't.' She scowled at him. 'I'm sure Moxon was trying to assure me that nobody at all believes the accusation. That it's part of some deeper plot, if it's not just an innocent mistake. I think he might have been implying that things will happen tomorrow, which is why he thinks I should go to Windermere or somewhere.'

Christopher took this quite differently from what she had hoped. '*Yes!*' he cried. 'So the onus is on us to work out what that's all about. We've been brought into it deliberately, for some reason. We've got a *duty*.'

She lapsed back into exhaustion. 'Okay. You're probably right. But can we leave it for tonight? All I want to do is go to bed.'

'Spoilsport,' he said. But he went to make her a hot milky drink, and by eleven they were both asleep.

Chapter Ten

Windermere at 10 a.m. on an October Wednesday was far from busy. Simmy found a parking space barely a quarter of a mile from her shop, and wheeled Robin along an almost empty pavement. Cornelia had been left at home, which made life a lot easier in the short term. Time enough to worry about torn cushions and incontinent puddles later in the day.

Bonnie and Verity were both there, along with a queue of three customers. They all assumed that the woman with the baby buggy was a fourth, before a closer inspection elicited a wide welcoming grin from Bonnie. 'Hello!' she mouthed, over the shoulder of a small woman standing at the counter.

Verity was bustling about carrying a large colourful

bouquet wrapped in cellophane. 'Oh – Mrs Henderson!' she said, finally recognising her employer. 'Just off to deliver these, all the way up to Staveley. And there's a wedding . . .' She tipped her head towards Bonnie and the computer. 'She'll tell you all about it. Oh – and I want to tell you about my cousin Daphne in Askham. I gather you have reason to be interested.'

Simmy smiled vaguely, repressing her annoyance that Verity had learnt of the Askham connection. *Who told you?* she wanted to demand, but a shop full of customers made that impossible. Verity bent over Robin, the bouquet tilting into his face. When she moved it aside it grazed the sheer nylon legs of a young woman in a short skirt standing too close. Who wore nylons these days? Simmy wondered idly. 'That looks like one of our biggest bouquets,' she said. 'Did you do it?'

Verity had learnt very slowly how to assemble flowers for best effect, putting too much effort into the mechanics of holding them together and not enough into the design and structure of the overall piece. Bonnie had long ago despaired of her. 'Oh no,' Verity simpered. 'Bonnie's so much better at it than I am.'

'Well, better get on,' Simmy encouraged. 'I'm here most of the day, so you can talk to me when you get back.'

'With the little one? Won't he get bored?'

'Let's hope not,' said Simmy.

Bonnie was working steadily through the queue, keeping her focus entirely on the customers. Simmy couldn't imagine how she did it. The woman with the nylons was now being served, pausing every few seconds to peer down at her leg and muttering about a hole coming. She had to be under thirty, but Simmy was reminded of her own grandmother, who was obsessive about laddered stockings and had stories about the war and how precious such objects became. Apparently, they were staging a comeback along with skirts, which seemed very retrograde to Simmy, who only possessed two skirts.

Last in line was an elderly man who regularly came for flowers. Simmy was hurt that he showed no sign of knowing who she was, even though she had served him a hundred times in the past. She expressed her feelings to Bonnie when he had gone.

'He's losing his wits, poor old chap,' Bonnie explained. 'He never remembers what he came in for, so I just give him the usual. I hope he puts them in water when he gets home.'

'So what's this about a cousin Daphne?'

'Who?'

'Verity says she's got a cousin in Askham.'

'Oh – right. Sorry. I was thinking about you bringing Robin here for a whole day. Are we sure that'll work?'

'If he's a pest, I'll take him home. I really only came in because I've got nothing else to do. I know you don't really need me. Let's see how it goes.' She refrained from mentioning that the suggestion had come from Moxon.

Bonnie shrugged. 'We could make him a little play area with boxes or something. Will he go to sleep?'

'Probably.' There seemed to be a lot to say, all at once. Ben's wrist; Verity's cousin; Moxon's visit; Christopher's sudden eagerness to play detective; the cashflow situation in the shop. Customers were likely to interrupt repeatedly, and Bonnie seemed slightly unfocused. Robin was going to need attention as well. Despite all that, Simmy was glad she'd made the trip. She loved Persimmon Petals like an older and more independent child. It was a change of scene and a diversion. She was sorry for Bonnie, left to deal with Verity and separated from Ben. 'I'll probably have to get back for the dog soon after lunch.'

'Pity your parents have moved,' Bonnie sighed. 'I feel completely abandoned now. Everybody's so far away.'

'I know. I must admit I never saw that coming. It's got some advantages, of course – but it hasn't helped me get back into harness down here.'

Bonnie looked nervous, as she often did when the future of the shop was under discussion. It was plain to everyone that Simmy's most sensible move would be to relocate her business to Keswick or Penrith. Driving across the Lake District in summer was nobody's idea of fun. Traffic occupied every available inch of road and parking space, causing immense frustration for both residents and tourists alike. Nobody could think of a solution. 'It'll solve itself because people are going to stop coming,' Russell Straw predicted. 'They'll find somewhere else to go, like Yorkshire or Snowdonia. They're both just as lovely, actually,' he added mischievously. 'With less rain.'

'Ben's off work today,' said Simmy superfluously. 'I expect he'll do some helpful googling about Askham.'

'Bound to,' Bonnie agreed. 'So you've seen Moxo again, have you?'

Simmy nodded. 'He came to see us yesterday. Christopher kept out of the way, but he's really got thoroughly drawn in this time. He keeps brainstorming – you wouldn't believe some of his ideas. He's nearly as bad as Ben. Moxon was nothing like his usual self. He seems quite worried. I didn't know what to make of him, actually.'

'You thought that on Sunday as well,' Bonnie reminded her. 'But it's good that Chris is taking an interest. It's about time.' Bonnie and Christopher had always been wary of each other, using Simmy as their point of contact, but seldom interacting directly.

'I know,' said Simmy peaceably. 'It's nice to have the support, I must admit.'

'So what happened yesterday?'

'The people of Askham have found out that I've been accused. It was horrible in the pub.' She gave a brief report of the previous day's explorations, followed by the uncomfortable lunch. 'They all knew who we were. Even Verity's got wind of it, apparently.'

Bonnie groaned. 'That's the cousin's doing. She wouldn't tell me anything much, but it's obvious she's bursting to talk to you about it. And it's not just her – everyone in Askham must be gossiping about you. Don't forget Christopher's famous in his own right. And they'll have known about Humphrey doing your conversion.'

'That's still a leap to hearing about me being suspected of killing Pauline. Somebody splurged it on Facebook.'

'Must be the Wilson woman.'

'Mm.' Simmy was unconvinced. 'I wonder. Christopher's thinking there's some sort of network, maybe. So many people in Askham seem to be related. Pauline had a big family herself, and Humphrey was local all his life. There are countless connections we'll never get to grips with.'

'Ben might. But it's got to have come from that woman

in the first place. Who else would know that she's accusing you?'

'I suppose that's right. We saw her at her house. She wasn't nasty, but she didn't want to talk to us.'

'That's not surprising. She must have thought you would start shouting at her. You've got a lot to be angry about, after all.'

'Christopher thought she might be trying to tell us something, just by the tone of her voice. He says I interrupted at a crucial moment and ruined it.' Simmy found that she was still feeling sore about that. 'He's probably right,' she admitted. 'I can be very clumsy.'

'She might be following orders from some Mr Big,' said Bonnie, with wide eyes. 'And wanted to make you understand.'

Simmy sighed. 'That's pretty much what Christopher thinks as well. Oh – and a man came to see me on Monday. A Mr Isaacs who's from somewhere near Carlisle, apparently. He said he was a builder like Humphrey and was going to take over his business. He made it sound like a charitable move for the benefit of Mrs Craig and the girls.'

'Oh! That might be important, don't you think? What's his first name?'

'Howard. He doesn't look like a builder. More a banker or jeweller. Very clean hands.'

Bonnie laughed. 'Didn't Humphrey have clean hands?'

'No, not very. Not the way I mean.'

Bonnie had slipped instantly into detective mode at the mention of this new character. 'So the Isaacs man is too senior to do the actual work. He just orders other people about and handles the money.'

'Do you think Verity might know him? Or maybe this Daphne person does. We never got back to that, did we?'

'I'm not sure it's relevant. Verity just likes to muscle in – and she does know an awful lot of people. Same as Melanie, in a way.'

Simmy took a moment to regret the disappearance of her first assistant, who had indeed known a significant proportion of the population of Cumbria. 'Go on,' she said.

'Well, the minute Askham came up, Verity started on about these people who live there. Daphne is a proper cousin, a bit older than her and has always lived in Askham. It doesn't sound at all helpful. I think she was just desperate to feel involved somehow. You know what she's like.'

'It didn't take her long to catch on to the way you and Ben like to do detective work.'

'It started when the woman at the auction house was killed in the summer. Even then she was really quite slow on the uptake. She's very dim, you know.' Bonnie heaved a martyred sigh.

'But she has useful talents and you're stuck with her. All part of life's rich tapestry.'

'That's what I keep telling myself.'

Two customers came and went, and then Verity came back from the Staveley delivery. Bonnie had found three new orders on the computer, and Simmy went to the back room to revive her floristry arts that had languished badly for most of the year.

Robin was on his stomach in a sort of makeshift nest beside his mother in the back room. He was slowly mastering the rudiments of crawling, to the extent of getting his knees under himself and raising his bottom in the air. His front end was still failing to cooperate, but he did manage a small amount of forward progress. Verity ran noisily in, eager for some playtime. 'Isn't he cold down there on the floor?' she accused. 'Look how he's almost crawling! Doesn't he look like his daddy?'

She always said this, and Simmy always wanted to argue that the child was actually far more like his grandfather, Kit Henderson. Verity had only seen Christopher once or twice, so her comparison carried little credibility. 'He seems rather top-heavy,' Simmy said. 'Crawling isn't coming easily. Not that I mind. I like to know he'll stay where I put him.'

Verity laughed scornfully. 'He'll be all over the shop before you know it.'

Simmy was tempted to raise the question of the residents of Askham, and specifically Howard Isaacs, while at the same time reluctant to give the woman any encouragement when it came to investigating a murder. Verity's self-censorship mechanism was rudimentary, and whatever information she might elicit would quickly be spread all over Cumbria. Given that the Askham case appeared to be even more sensitive and secretive than usual, this was clearly undesirable. Simmy only had to mention an individual's name and Verity would most likely soon be telling the world that he was the killer. Over the past months the woman had tried to convince herself and others that Simmy was 'carrying on' with Detective Inspector Moxon, that Ben and Bonnie were splitting up, and that Russell and Angie Straw had made a quarter of a million pounds profit on the sale of their Windermere B&B and purchase of a modest bungalow in Threlkeld.

'She's a menace,' moaned Bonnie at regular intervals.

The main worry was that Verity would soon discover that Simmy had been accused of committing murder. Since word had evidently got out in Askham itself, there was no guarantee at all that it would not fly all around the world – go viral, as Ben would say. In fact, was it not already highly likely that this had happened? Perhaps nobody beyond the village concerned was actually very interested? Or was the story so vague and unpersuasive that people just dismissed it? Had there been suggestions that the accuser was as suspicious as the accused? Or what?

Bonnie appeared in the doorway, looking harassed. 'Sorry, but there are two more orders for delivery to Newby Bridge and Crook. Both by the end of today. And there's another big funeral next Monday. Somebody in Bowness died and wants everyone to send flowers. I've just had the undertaker on about it.'

Simmy felt an inappropriate thrill of pleasure. She had always enjoyed a big flowery funeral much more than a wedding. There was something so much more genuine and sincere about funeral flowers. It seemed to matter so much more that she should get it right. 'Great!' she said.

'Oooh!' gasped Verity, still not accustomed to the particular values of the floristry business. The others both ignored her.

'Better get busy, then,' said Simmy cheerfully. 'Feel free to take Robin for a stroll if you've got time,' she invited Verity. Suddenly she was congratulating herself for finding solutions to three or four different difficulties all at once. Amuse the child, divert the woman, give Bonnie a break and leave Simmy to get on with her job.

Verity was not quite as dim as the others believed. She

knew she was being sent off deliberately, but she could not resist the offer. Her expression amply conveyed her feelings. 'Just for ten minutes or so, then,' she agreed. 'If you're sure he'll be all right with me.'

'He's going to be hungry before long, but I'm sure he'll be happy to see all the new things in town. He doesn't get out as much as he should.'

'Hey – thanks!' said Bonnie as soon as Verity was safely outside. 'We'd never have been able to talk with her hanging about. If she's not doing deliveries she just sort of *hovers*, waiting for something to happen.'

'I know. Anyway, how are you, really? You must be worried about Ben and his wrist. He might not be able to drive for a while.'

'I was going to ask you about that. Do you think I could have Saturday off, so I can go up there for the weekend? Corinne says she'll take me.'

'That'll mean I've got to come and take over from you here.'

'Yes, but there's no sale this weekend, so Christopher can have Robin. Or your mother. I am due some time off, you know.' The words were meek, but the tone had a sliver of steel behind it. Simmy was forced to accept that the request was reasonable.

'Rather short notice,' she muttered, before agreeing that she could manage. 'It'll be nice to see Tanya again.'

'Anything else new from Askham?' Bonnie finally enquired. 'It doesn't feel as if you've told me everything.'

'I can't think of any more. I know it feels very scrappy, but the problem is I wasn't paying proper attention on Saturday. You heard the important stuff on Sunday, I think. There's bound to be loads more, obviously, but my head's so scrambled, I don't think I'm the person to ask. I'm hoping Ben's spending all day on his computer, tracking down connections and backgrounds and so forth. Pauline Parsons sounds as if she was quite a character. Just because a person's old doesn't make them boring – I suppose.'

'Corinne says most people are boring at any age, but it gets more difficult to be taken seriously as you get older. She rants about care homes and the way they play music that was a hit when the residents were young, just assuming they all liked the same things, and went to the same dances and stuff. It must be awful for the ones who love Stravinsky or Philip Glass, or even Louis Armstrong.'

Simmy could hear the quotation marks, as the girl repeated her foster mother's views. 'Philip Glass?' she echoed.

'Yeah. I don't get it myself, but Corinne says he's a genius, and she would never have got where she is without his influence.' Corinne did gigs at country fairs and festivals, making her own unique sounds that did at least attract notice. Simmy had to admit that she had never heard of Philip Glass.

'We're wandering off the subject,' she said. 'The point seems to be that Pauline was some sort of threat to somebody, or had done something that made them want revenge. When we went up onto Askham Fell yesterday and tried to work out if she could have walked to the Cockpit from her house, it did look rather a stretch.'

'You think she was taken up there somehow?'

'Inconclusive. When I saw her on Saturday she was walking quite well, but fairly slowly. A better question is probably – why? Why would she struggle up there by herself on a windy day?'

'She wouldn't. Somebody must have gone with her.'

'Which Lindsay Wilson must have told the police was me. What else can she have said? But Moxon won't give me any details at all. It's all guesswork.'

Bonnie stared at a corner of the shop and nibbled a fingernail. 'None of this is new,' she said. 'We said it all on Sunday.'

'Not quite. There might not be any new facts, but Christopher's being brilliant at working out all kinds of theories. He's made everything look a lot clearer.'

'So what does he think you should do?'

Simmy gave a frustrated laugh. 'It's quite a list. When I said I'd prefer to do nothing and just wait for Moxon to figure it all out, Chris would have none of it. He has no intention of letting me off the hook. That's if I'm really *on* a hook. Nobody seems to be watching my movements or tapping my phone. I think Christopher's right that Lindsay Wilson gave them my name as a way of making them take it more seriously. It sounds mad, but it does fit with how she was yesterday.'

'Oh?'

'When we went to knock on her door, she just leant out of a window upstairs and told us to go away.'

'Right,' said Bonnie dubiously. 'You already told me that – and Chris thought she was trying to get some kind of message across. People could hear her, probably, so she had to avoid saying anything directly. And yet . . .' She shrugged. 'It could all be imagination.'

'I know.'

'Have you said all this to Ben?'

'Not really. He was too taken up with his broken bone.'

'Bones,' Bonnie corrected her. 'He says he broke *two*.'

'Well, we need him. I think Moxon is hoping he'll make some headway, too.'

'Lazy old so-and-so. Haven't the police got computers? I can't really see that Ben has much to go on this time. He doesn't know anybody in Askham.'

'No, but he has at least been there a few times, which is more than I had before last Friday. I think we can assume he'll have worked up a few ideas by now.'

'He usually does,' laughed Bonnie proudly.

Speculation ran dry just as Verity came back. She reversed through the shop door, pulling Robin's buggy behind her. She was talking to a person not yet visible. When the threesome had finally got themselves inside the shop, Simmy and Bonnie could only stare in blank incomprehension.

Chapter Eleven

'But you're Sophie!' Simmy finally managed to squeak. 'How . . .? Why . . .?'

'She was at school with my young sister,' said Verity as if that was obvious. 'Lost touch, as you do. It was Daphne who reminded me, a little while back. I've been meaning to say for a while now that I knew her, with her husband doing your conversion and all that, but there was never a chance.' She gave Simmy a reproachful stare, reminding her that opportunities for a proper gossip had been extremely rare ever since Verity had come to work at the shop. 'It was thanks to you, though, that we got back together, in a sort of way. My sister's moved over to Hawes in Yorkshire now, but she's going to be thrilled. Of course, I knew Sophie was called Craig now, married to a builder.' She turned to the newcomer. 'I was gutted that I couldn't make it to the funeral. Now you two can properly get to know each other at last.'

Sophie, with the same pale frizzy hair as Bonnie's, smiled weakly and shook her head. Robin was dozing in his buggy, his cheeks red from the October air. Verity was almost bursting with gratification at having finally gained some meaningful notice, despite the fact that most of the attention was on Mrs Humphrey Craig. With her and Bonnie in the same space, the likeness between them was unmistakable. Simmy kept looking from one to the other. Sophie was more than twenty years older. She had a lot more flesh on her bones, and was two inches taller. But the faces were the same. Bonnie was completely oblivious to Simmy's thoughts. Instead, she stepped back until she was standing by the till, as if claiming her rightful role in the shop. Any mildly tentative customer might well be deterred by the crowd of women, plus baby and a very peculiar atmosphere.

'I've always wanted to meet you now you're grown up,' Sophie said to the girl, speaking fast and not very coherently. 'I'm ashamed at the way I've just left it all these years. Ever since your mother gave up on you, I've been saying I should get in touch. She never was a person to rely on, poor old Samantha. I wished I could have taken you on, but I'd just had Berta at the time and was rather snowed under. She was an awful baby – never slept. It wouldn't have been fair to any of you. Humphrey would have done it, of course, but I never gave him the chance. Seems as if you turned out all right in the end, anyway.'

'My mother?' whispered Bonnie. Simmy shivered and

wondered whether she should try to prevent any further disclosures. This was definitely not the time or the place. Sophie evidently assumed that Bonnie knew what she was talking about – quite wrongly.

'I'm sorry, pet. Didn't you know about me? It just burst out of me – blame Verity here. She's been encouraging me to come and see you for a while now. The thing is, I'm your aunt. Your dad's sister.'

'My dad?' Bonnie repeated blankly. This was a person who had never once featured in any conversation that Simmy had had with Bonnie or Ben. For all she knew his identity was an insoluble mystery.

'Harrison,' Sophie nodded. 'Last seen headed for the South Atlantic on a container ship. Never been heard of since. Before you were even born, Lord help us.'

'She didn't give up on me,' Bonnie corrected. 'The social took me away because they said she wasn't coping. She put up quite a fight – I remember it all.'

'Which she wasn't – coping, I mean. She'd leave you on your own at night, barely remember to feed you, bring all those men home with her. But we all kept giving her another chance. It wasn't really her fault.'

Bonnie's face registered distress, but she made a swift brushing-aside gesture, and took a deep breath. 'You're my aunt?'

'Course she is,' came Verity's loud insensitive voice. 'Just look at the two of you. Peas in a pod. That hair!'

'Where do you live?'

'Askham. Just by the car park on the Sockbridge road. We've been there all along. You were born there – surely you knew that?'

Bonnie shook her head. Her place of birth had never been an issue. Corinne had handled the paperwork, such as it was. Very little bureaucratic formality intruded into Corinne's life, if she could help it.

'Well, you were – in my back bedroom, as it happens. The house was my mother's before Humphrey and I took it on. Samantha turned up one night in labour, and before anyone could think what to do, there you were. Nobody ever doubted you were Harrison's. My dad was thrilled, silly old coot. He paid the rent on the flat you lived in until he died.' Sophie's eyes grew misty and her voice faltered. 'What is it with men – the way they go and die so young?'

The ghost of Humphrey hung over them all and even Verity deflated slightly.

The sudden determined approach of a customer sent everything into a flurry. Simmy pushed Bonnie, Robin and Sophie into the back room, and gave Verity an uncompromising look. She took an order for a birthday bouquet with a shaking hand. The word *coincidence* kept repeating in her head. She wanted time and space to consider the implications and to persuade herself that it was not so much coincidental as inevitable. The surprise was that it had taken eighteen years for Bonnie to learn the identity of her father and to rekindle a connection with his sister. Who happened to be married to Simmy and Christopher's builder. She smiled vaguely at the irritated customer and wondered what she should do next.

The door of the back room was open, with Robin's buggy halfway through it. She ought not to have brought him, she knew. It wasn't going to happen again. His presence meant she could not give her full attention to anything. Nor could she rush off to remote Cumbrian villages and confront mendacious witnesses. If only her parents had stayed in Windermere a bit longer, she could have deposited him with them at a moment's notice.

But was that what she wanted to do – go off to Askham again and find Lindsay Wilson? If so, why? Where had that leap come from? Whatever the chain of reasoning had been, she now lost it – and when she found it again she knew it would be full of gaps. But perhaps at least one of those gaps could be filled by Sophie Craig. She put her head into the little room and said, 'Do you know Lindsay Wilson?'

She had interrupted an obviously agitated conversation, with Bonnie looking pale and unsettled. The girl should not be overwhelmed with too much information in one go, Simmy decided.

'What?' said Sophie.

Simmy waved the question away and changed the subject. 'Look, Sophie, this needs to be done somewhere else. Corinne should probably be there as well. Or somebody.' *Me*, she suspected. 'You can see we're already in a bit of a muddle here, with the baby and everything.'

'Yes, I know Lindsay Wilson,' Sophie answered the first question. 'She came to Humphrey's funeral, didn't she? I saw you talking to her. What about her?' She was composed, but her eyes were bright with a worryingly manic expression.

'I can't explain it now. But it's important.' Simmy glanced back into the shop, where Verity was fiddling with bits of paper on the counter. She was obviously very upset at being excluded, and might therefore prove troublesome. Simmy went out to her. 'Well, that was a surprise,' she said heartily. 'All thanks to you. And you've got Robin nice and sleepy after his walk.'

'Huh!' sniffed Verity. Simmy was reminded again of Melanie Todd, who often found herself left out of exciting adventures that included Ben and Bonnie, Moxon and Simmy. Somebody had to mind the shop, Simmy kept repeating to them all, with little effect. She could remember seeing Melanie thinking it should be the proprietor a bit more often.

'I'll go, then,' said Sophie. 'Give me your phone and I'll put my number in,' she told Bonnie. 'We've got a lot of catching up to do. I can meet any time, anywhere you like. Is there a boyfriend or anything? You could come up to us for a meal one evening. Have you got transport?'

Simmy marvelled at the depths of ignorance displayed by this new-found aunt. How could anybody not know about Ben Harkness? But Askham was a long way from Windermere. Almost another world, with meres and fells and becks and roads in between.

Bonnie handed over her phone but said nothing. She glanced from one face to another with very little expression, looking about ten years old. Simmy felt the revival of a concern that had gone into abeyance over the past year. Bonnie was fragile, recovering from considerable damage wrought largely by her mother's awful boyfriends. Ben had saved her, showing her a shining future where her talents and interests could be fully engaged. He avoided discussion or analysis of her past with a firm conviction that it could serve no useful purpose. Simmy, Corinne and Ben's mother all applauded this approach.

'She's with a boy called Ben. He's got a car, but at the

moment he can't drive. He broke his wrist. He works with my husband in Keswick.'

Bonnie smiled gratefully at her. 'That's right,' she murmured.

'Okay. Well, there's no hurry. But you might want to meet my girls, Chloe and Berta. After all, they're your cousins.'

'Oh!' said Bonnie as if this was the final straw. 'Cousins . . . How old are they?'

'Fifteen and twelve. Berta looks quite like you. Chloe's at an awkward stage – you never know where you are with her. And now with Humphrey . . . well, you can imagine, I expect.'

'Oh,' said Bonnie again, helplessly.

The phone rang, two customers came in at once, and Robin stirred himself with a wail. Sophie had the sense to make a rapid departure, and Simmy answered the phone. Verity stepped up to welcome the customers and Bonnie faded invisibly into the back room. Nobody took any notice of Robin until the second customer leant over him with a big face and frightened him into silence.

By midday Simmy was exhausted, and coming to the conclusion that she had been wildly optimistic to think that she and Robin could spend even half a day at the shop. It wasn't fair to anyone, including Bonnie and Verity. She had considered sending the girl home, after the shocking revelation from Sophie Craig, but Bonnie insisted she was better staying on and focusing on the work. 'Nothing's really changed,' she said three times. 'I guess it had to happen eventually. I just can't quite work out how to process it all.'

'She shouldn't have dropped it on you like that with no warning,' said Simmy. She found herself feeling mainly annoyed with Verity for instigating the whole thing. 'Anyone would feel shaken after something like that.'

'It's like those telly programmes – long lost families,' said Verity, who clearly found the whole business romantic and stimulating.

'I've never watched them,' said Bonnie, with a little frown.

'You're too young,' Simmy realised. 'At your age, your ancestry doesn't seem relevant. It hardly does to me, to be honest. I think it only starts to feel important when you hit sixty or thereabouts.'

'Ben does family history,' Bonnie reminded her. 'He found all those weird relations in the Cotswolds.'

'Ben's different,' said Simmy, making Bonnie smile.

Mother and child were back in Hartsop by half past one, having paused to do some shopping on the way. Cornelia was overjoyed to see them, and Simmy endured an excessively lavish welcome before pushing the dog out into the garden. The house appeared to be undamaged, with not so much as a puddle to reproach Cornelia with.

But the afternoon stretched emptily before her, unless she pulled herself together and formulated a plan of action. There was now a major new layer of information to think about. Bonnie's link to Askham made everything that had happened feel much more relevant. How, she kept asking herself, had the connection with Humphrey been missed over all those months when he had been working on the conversion? Had he and Bonnie not once coincided in the house? Actually not, Simmy concluded. Bonnie had only ever visited on Sundays or in an evening, when the builder was at home. Ben might have glimpsed Humphrey a few times, but that would be of no consequence at all. Even if Humphrey had encountered Bonnie, he might have missed the close resemblance to his wife. Men could be very unobservant, even though it had been Christopher who first noticed the coincidence of the fluffy hair.

She gave Robin an hour of quality attention, and then put him down for a nap. A growing list of people to call was dominating her thoughts. Ben, Christopher, Moxon, Corinne, her parents . . . and there was a nagging sense that she should somehow try to make contact with Lindsay Wilson. Everything had to link to her – she probably knew who killed Pauline Parsons, as well as how and why. If she could be persuaded to talk, wouldn't the whole silly business be quickly resolved?

Perhaps it was the association with getting people to talk that prompted her to phone her father. Russell Straw was an excellent conversationalist, his skill honed by years spent running a Bed and Breakfast establishment. He would gently interrogate his customers, eliciting their life stories, reasons for being in the Lakes, knowledge of history and general outlook on life. For years he remembered what they had told him. In some dimly nebulous way, Simmy thought he might be persuaded to go and speak to Lindsay. She was also vaguely conscious that Moxon had hinted at possible danger, and who would a girl go to if not her father at such a time? Russell was not big or strong but he had infinite good sense.

He answered the phone quickly, and Simmy imagined

him sitting with it beside him, just waiting for some diversion. He would be worrying about her and the Askham accusation and wanting to hear the latest developments. The fact that he had attended Humphrey's funeral meant he would consider himself closely involved.

Simmy updated him on events of the previous day, emphasising how engaged Christopher was for a change, and how cleverly he was producing theories to explain the mystery of Pauline Parsons' death. She described Moxon's restrained visit, and then diverted into a brief summary of the morning's revelations about Bonnie.

'I don't think it occurred to any of us to wonder about her father,' she concluded.

'What I think is odd is that Humphrey never said anything. Surely he knew she was working in your shop? Why didn't he ever mention it? I mean – that would be the natural thing. "I hear you're employing my poor little niece." Something like that.'

'I guess he thought it was none of his business. Maybe he'd forgotten about her. They never once tried to see her. Maybe the authorities told them not to. Bonnie's mother was *persona non grata* for most of the time, and more or less ignored once they'd taken her child into care. They probably insisted she sever all connections while Bonnie settled in with Corinne.'

'I don't think they do that,' Russell corrected her. 'They're all for maintaining links with blood relatives.'

'Are they?' Simmy realised she did not know much about the ways of the social services.

'Never mind that now. What about your accuser? Is she still sticking to her story?'

'Apparently so. I keep wanting to speak to her, but she told us to go away in no uncertain terms when we knocked on her door yesterday. Christopher thinks she's under some sort of pressure from person or persons unknown, and daren't be seen talking to us. At least, I think he thinks that. He keeps coming up with new theories.'

'And Ben?'

'Oh, I forgot to say. He's broken his wrist. But he does know Askham a bit. He seems to think there's something sinister about that Lowther place. But he won't waste much time before getting online and trying to figure out how everything connects. He'll want to forget about his broken bones.'

'But now he'll be needed to make sure Bonnie's all right.'

'That's true. He's off work today. I should try and catch him and find out what he's doing. He might want me to drive him down to Windermere.' She quailed somewhat at this realisation.

Russell was silent for a moment. Then he said slowly, 'You know, this accusation business is very strange. Nobody seems to be watching you, do they? Have they asked to see your phone or laptop or anything? I don't think so,' he went on without letting her reply. 'So they obviously don't believe what that woman said about you. They've wheeled your pal Moxon in, as a result of your name being bandied about, which could well be the intention all along. Do you see?'

'I do. Christopher says the same thing. But *why*? Moxon doesn't know anyone in Askham, and isn't famously brilliant as a detective, let's face it. If that idea is right, it would mean that Lindsay Wilson knew beforehand that

I had links with Moxon, so that by accusing me he'd probably be consulted, at the very least. It makes me feel all jangled to think that's how it was. Makes my skin crawl. And when Moxon came to see me last night he made some scary hints about being in danger.'

Russell was clearly fired up. 'It wouldn't take much googling to figure out that you and the good detective inspector go back a long way. Your names must have been linked in quite a number of news stories. Think of that murder at Storrs, and then Coniston. And the awful business in Hawkshead. Thousands of people across the whole area will take it for granted that you and Ben are unofficial police assistants. It's not really at all sinister. Just somebody acting clever. And it would not be a bit clever to accost you in your own home in broad daylight, would it? I don't think you need worry too much about that. It's just DI Moxon being overcautious.'

She sighed. 'How is it that you always make me feel better?'

'I'm your father, silly. It's what I'm for.' Then he said, 'And I'm reading *Dombey and Son*. I thought I might find some clues.'

Simmy laughed. 'Of course you are,' she said.

Chapter Twelve

Simmy felt nervous of phoning Ben until she knew whether
Bonnie had spoken to him. While the girl often texted him
and other people from the shop, actual phone calls were
discouraged. A Wednesday afternoon in October was not
likely to be especially busy, but it gave a bad impression
to customers if the only person available was deep in
conversation with an invisible boyfriend. And if Verity was
there, Bonnie would be deterred anyway, knowing she was
being overheard by Windermere's biggest gossip.

Thinking about Bonnie, Simmy feared that she had been
remiss in not sending the girl home, after receiving such
a shock. She had not shown enough concern, it seemed
now. Perhaps it would be a good deed to call Corinne
and warn her about what had happened. The whole

situation felt volatile, with Bonnie a vulnerable victim of circumstance. *Damned Verity*, Simmy thought fiercely. It was all her doing.

But Corinne did not answer her phone, which was not at all unusual. She considered herself free of all obligation now that Bonnie was eighteen, content to let the girl share her home and provide company when it was convenient. Quite how she would respond to the sudden appearance of unsuspected relatives was hard to predict. Corinne had a natural wisdom and a relaxed outlook on life, but she put her own interests first. Bonnie's involvement with Ben and numerous murder investigations left Corinne unmoved. She had mentioned once or twice that she was relieved that no harm had been done during any of the girl's adventures, because picking up the pieces was something the erstwhile foster mother no longer felt constrained to do.

It was approaching four o'clock and Robin was tetchy. The days generally began to feel uncomfortably long by that time, with Simmy often reproaching herself for having given him insufficient attention, fresh air, healthy food or social intercourse. There was never a day when he got everything that she assumed was his due. At the clinic they had been carefully non-judgemental at the way he had not managed to sit up by the age of six months. Everything else, Simmy had wanted to protest, was exactly as it should be. And see what a cheerful little soul he was. The same clinic kept asking her about contraception as well, which was never a welcome question. 'We're hoping for another one fairly soon,' she always said with a smile. *Mind your own business* she shouted silently.

Ben phoned at four fifteen. 'Bonnie told me what

happened this morning,' he said, without preamble. 'She's in a bit of a tizz about it.'

'I've been trying to get hold of Corinne and warn her, but she's not answering.'

'I can't get down there,' he wailed. 'I can't ask my mother to keep taxiing me about. I can't even ride the bike like this.'

'Oh dear,' said Simmy weakly, knowing what was coming. 'Are you sure? I mean, your fingers work, don't they?'

'Not really. The plaster covers half my hand. I might do a mile or two, but not all the way to Windermere.'

'She'll be all right. You can do Facetime or something – it'll be almost the same as being there.' Simmy spoke from considerable ignorance. Phone calls in which you could see the person still felt like a step too far to her. She had done it a few times under duress and hated the way faces were distorted.

'It's not. You know it's not,' he corrected her.

'All right. Well, she's got Saturday off, if that's any consolation. She can get the bus to you, or somebody might drive her. It's not long to wait.'

He groaned his disagreement.

'Meanwhile why don't you get down to some research into the Askham people? There's a whole lot to find out. Mrs Parsons had grandsons who sound a bit scary. And a man called Eldon in the pub was throwing his weight about, as well. Lindsay's related to a whole lot of Askham folk, from what she says. Oh!' She suddenly had a thought. 'What about her connection with Sophie Craig? Do you think that means *Lindsay* might be related to Bonnie as well? Gosh!' The implications began to swirl around her head, raising potential coincidences that would amaze them all. 'Or have I got that all back to front? Every time I think I've got it straight, something new crops up and I'm all confused again.'

'Hold on,' begged Ben. 'For a start, most of these connections are by marriage, with distant cousins the most likely thing. You know that most people have several hundred fourth and fifth cousins, don't you? Especially if they come from one of those huge middle-class families from the nineteenth century. It's futile to try and trace them all.'

'I'm sure it is. But maybe you could just go back one or two generations to start with. You know what fun it'll be.'

He reverted to his main preoccupation. 'Bonnie says Verity thinks the Craig lady looks just like her.'

'Yes, she does. Christopher noticed it on Friday at the funeral. I'm guessing there's Scandinavian ancestry. Her father works on ships. That would fit, wouldn't it?'

'Possibly. We don't know what he's doing now, or where he is. He might even be dead.'

'No,' said Simmy firmly. 'We can't have that. After all, he must know Bonnie exists. He'll come back and find her one day.'

'That's sentimental rubbish,' he shot back at her. 'If anybody finds anybody, Bonnie's going to have to do all the work.' He went quiet for a moment. 'And who says he knows he's got a daughter? Who would have told him? According to Bonnie, he disappeared before she was born.'

'Oh,' said Simmy, aware of treading on delicate ground. 'I suppose I thought there were letters or something.' She was still trying to imagine even one cousin, let alone several hundred. The Straw family was embarrassingly small. All she had were two childless uncles.

'Well, let's leave that for the time being, while I see what I can find about the Parsons family,' Ben suggested. 'I've got plenty of time, after all. I just wish Moxon would be a bit more forthcoming. He must know far more than he's telling you.'

'I get the impression he's being sat on by his superiors. He's sorry about your wrist, by the way.'

'Huh. Our best hope is that he's just biding his time, for some reason. He must know how useful we can be. Why can't he persuade his superiors or whatever they are?'

'I don't know, Ben.'

'I can think of a few reasons. I was wondering if there might be some sort of ongoing investigation in Askham that we don't know about. People they're trying to trap, who'd take flight if they thought they'd been noticed.'

'That would explain why they brought Moxon in, I suppose,' she said slowly. 'What made you think of it?'

'I don't know. I must be channelling Christopher. Didn't you say he keeps coming up with wild ideas like that?'

'Did I? It's true, anyway. His brain's working overtime. Most of it seems much too fantastic for my liking.'

'Anything's possible, I suppose,' said Ben, sounding disgruntled. He was the one with the wild ideas, as a rule, Simmy realised. 'You'll have to go back to Askham, you know,' he went on quietly. 'You probably don't want to, but it's where everything's happening. You really ought to give the pub another try, if you can face it. Pubs are often full of vital information.'

'I'm not sure that's true.' Just at the moment she could not think of one instance where this had been the case. Then she remembered an overheard conversation in the Mortal Man's garden in Troutbeck, and one or two revelations at the Ellory in Windermere. 'Maybe you're right, come to think of it.'

'Take somebody with you tomorrow. Baby, dog and friend. Camouflage.'

'What friend?'

'I don't know,' he said impatiently. 'Isn't there anybody in Hartsop or Patterdale you could take?'

'Can't think of anyone.' All her lukewarm efforts to make the acquaintance of other mothers in the area had come to nothing. Plans to join a mother and toddler group had not yet reached fruition. There had been slightly more success in befriending other dog owners, but that had mainly been Christopher's doing. 'I'm just not a very sociable person.'

'Okay. But listen – you've been dragged into this murder for a reason. You've got an obligation to do something about it. There's a game going on, which feels pretty nasty. We don't know how far it'll spread. I keep thinking about that sinister Lowther place. The way the building seems to be visible for miles. It works both ways. It's as if it's watching everything that goes on.'

Simmy had barely registered Lowther Castle. 'I think that's just you,' she said diffidently. 'Isn't it a big tourist attraction these days?'

'Probably. That doesn't change anything,' he said darkly.

'Next thing you'll be telling me the Ghost of Lowther Castle is haunting Askham and making the people do crazy things.'

'I might have been watching too many horror films,' he admitted with a laugh.

'You and Christopher both. Just get back to some googling,' she told him, and ended the call.

Cornelia was definitely a help when it came to entertaining Robin. She would nudge a ball towards him and then grab it back when he reached for it, causing peals of infant laughter. Simmy had some slight concern for the welfare of his fingers, but the dog was descended from the most soft-mouthed breeds and took impressive care to do no damage. The enjoyment of the game was so palpable in both youngsters that Simmy found herself actively glad of Cornelia's presence. Christopher and Angie had both had been right that every boy should have a dog, even when only seven months old. Cornelia had effortlessly become part of the family, finding her niche and making herself indispensable.

At least I'm not bored, Simmy thought, as she tried to assemble the day's events into a manageable pattern. Revelations, theories, suggestions all filled her head. Christopher would come home with new ideas and propositions that would occupy the evening very nicely. If this was how it turned out when a person was accused of murder, she told herself foolishly, then there were worse things that could happen. The accusation itself had receded through the day into something much less alarming. The fluttery feelings from Sunday had gone completely. It was still a huge mystery, but small threads were beginning to appear, which when followed might well provide answers. Pauline Parsons had been dead for three days, and Simmy had not been arrested or even asked any more questions. Much more likely, surely, that Lindsay Wilson was the object of greatest police interest. They should be grilling her mercilessly until she confessed her reasons for telling such an outrageous untruth.

Over the past day or so Simmy had become increasingly aware of a simmering resentment against Moxon. He had been a coward, going along with opaque orders from above and refusing to give her any proper information. His visit the previous day had shown concern, and perhaps an admission of his own shortcomings, but it had not moved anything along. On the contrary, he had exuded an air of stasis and frustration. His reaction to the news about Ben's wrist suggested that he had been relying on the young man to solve the case for him – as he had done on previous occasions, without openly acknowledging the fact. Moxon's inertia had left a void that was being filled with unlikely hypotheses created in the minds of Christopher and Simmy herself. As for Ben, his fantasies about Lowther did not deserve any consideration at all.

The afternoon was darkening, after a cloudy day. The trees were still in full leaf, but they sensed the oncoming winter, the cycle that dictated the many changes to come. The big tree behind the house blocked the view of Hartsop Dodd for half the year, and then when the leaves came off, the fell was suddenly visible, its detail quite vivid on bright frosty days. The Hendersons had not yet seen a full year round in this home, with the autumn colours, holly berries and hungry birds still to be enjoyed. The end of British Summer Time would mark the change of season more palpably than any calendar.

There were domestic tasks to perform, which warranted little conscious thought. Feed the dog, peel potatoes, chop some onions, go and find another jumper to put on as the chilly evening advanced.

Christopher appeared ten minutes earlier than usual. He greeted his wife, son and dog in the prescribed sequence, and then went outside for an armful of logs. 'Cold enough for a fire,' he said.

'We need to get more wood. They say prices are up again this year.'

At precisely six o'clock Simmy's phone tinkled. 'If that's Ben I don't know what I'll do,' fumed Simmy. 'He knows not to phone at this time.'

But it was Moxon. 'Bad time, I know,' he said before she could reproach him. 'But it's important. Miss Wilson's gone missing. We can't find her anywhere.'

Initially, Simmy could not understand why this would matter to her. Granted, there were interesting implications and pressing questions, but nothing that couldn't have waited a while. 'Oh dear,' she said.

'Never mind *oh dear*,' he snapped. 'This changes everything. We're concerned for her safety, obviously. And yours,' he added ominously.

'What? Why? How do you work that out?'

'We still don't know why she made the accusation against you. It could be a perfectly innocent mistake, but if it was meant maliciously, then you're the object of something unpleasant, to put it mildly. If she did it under duress, and is now being kept against her will, then that could affect your situation.'

'Stop talking like that. Say it in normal English, why don't you?'

He cleared his throat. 'Sorry. The trouble is, we have to take care not to defame anyone, or convey restricted information. We have no actual grounds for suspecting that you're in direct danger, but nonetheless, there's a possibility . . .'

'Oh, for goodness' sake!' she shouted. 'You're just covering your own backs. You know perfectly well nothing's going to happen to me.' She stopped and took a long breath. 'Sorry. I imagine there are people listening to what you're saying. I've got the point – you're not a free agent in this investigation, right?'

'That's right.'

'This isn't on some sort of speakerphone, is it? Can they hear what I'm saying?'

'No, no. But there'll be a record.'

'Honestly, this gets more like Soviet Russia every day.'

He let that pass and said, 'I don't have to tell you that we would very much appreciate it if you'd tell us if by any chance you encounter Miss Wilson. It's unlikely, I know, but we're still a long way from understanding her motives. There's a chance she'll be wanting your help.'

'How hard have you looked for her? Is she supposed to tell you everywhere she goes? Maybe she's just tired of the whole thing.'

'It's possible. But until things get a bit clearer, we should err on the safe side.'

'All right,' said Simmy with a sigh. 'Thanks for calling.'

Christopher was staring at her, trying to follow the gist from what he could hear. 'Soviet Russia?' he queried.

'It's infuriating. He sounds as if he's under observation – I don't know how to describe it. He isn't his usual self at all. He seems scared of putting a foot wrong.'

'I heard you say he's not a free agent. Did he agree?'

She nodded. 'Poor man. It must be awful for him. But it's also very irritating for me.'

'I bet he's done something he shouldn't and is being given another chance. He probably used the wrong word about somebody and was deemed to be offensive.'

'That's ridiculous.'

'It's not, though, is it? It's the same everywhere. I have to watch how we describe things in the auction – I'm never sure that "tribal" is acceptable these days, for a start.'

'But how does that stop Moxon telling me what's really going on in Askham? They've brought him in – and now they won't let him do anything.'

'I'm sure he is doing something. Why did he phone, anyway?'

'Oh – they've lost Lindsay Wilson.' For the moment that seemed entirely unimportant to her. 'And he thinks she's been abducted and the same people might come for me. Or something equally crackpot. She'll have gone off to check something for her thesis. Why should she keep the police informed of where she goes anyway?'

'If they think she's been abducted, there must be some signs to suggest that. A mess in her house, or somebody hearing screams. Or missing an appointment. Did he say anything like that?'

'No. He didn't say anything much. It's been like that all along. Nothing but vague hints and threats, which always make me think there's much more just below the surface that I'm supposed to be able to guess.'

'To me it looks as if there really is some very delicate police investigation going on, possibly going back way before Pauline Parsons was killed, and they're wary of letting it all slip through their fingers.'

'But that's so unlikely in nice little Askham, of all places.'

He gave her a look from under his brows, which made her laugh. 'All right. I should know better by now. There are bad people everywhere. Why should Askham be exempt? Ben thinks the Lowther place is sinister as well. There's got to be a whole lot of history that people round there care about.'

'Your dad's the man for that angle.'

'He's reading *Dombey and Son*, which is a start, I suppose.'

'If you ask me, I think Moxon should give it a look as well. It could yet turn out to be the key to everything.'

'I seem to remember it's terribly long. If Lindsay is living and breathing it, there's bound to be scope for every sort of bad behaviour for her to get obsessed with. Her thesis is about cruelty.' She frowned. 'Do you think she's got so into it that she's acting out the story? Does anybody make false accusations in it?'

'Don't ask me. We'll have to wait for your father to finish it, and then ask him.'

'Lucky he's a fast reader.' She sighed. 'We should probably be a *bit* worried about Lindsay. We already thought she might be in some trouble – this could prove it. Even if she's just hiding from someone she's scared of, that's not good, is it?'

'None of this whole thing is good,' he said glumly. 'An old lady got murdered, don't forget.'

Through the evening Simmy had a sense of a network of people all working away at the puzzle of what was happening in Askham. Ben, her father, Moxon – and alongside that there was Bonnie's bolt from the blue to be factored in. Sophie Craig must have plenty of other stuff to think about but without Humphrey she might well find herself focusing on her long-lost niece as some sort of replacement. At the very least it was somebody else to include in her life and distract her from her awful loss. Bonnie herself must be in a state of bewilderment, and perhaps excitement at finding relatives she had never been told about. And where was Samantha now – the woman who had failed so badly as a mother?

Christopher was as actively engaged as ever, still coming up with suggestions and theories. 'Just wait till Saturday,' he said. 'When I've got a bit of time, I'm really going to stir things up.'

Simmy inwardly cringed. *Let it all be settled before Saturday*, she prayed. The prospect of a rampaging Christopher Henderson, well-known and more-or-less-respectable auctioneer, was not enticing. She didn't dare ask him exactly what he intended, but she was reasonably sure it would involve another visit to the unfriendly Askham pub. 'Gosh,' she said faintly.

'Yes. And you know where I'll go first?' He paused for dramatic effect. 'Mrs Sophie Craig! She's right there in the middle of it all. She connects to everything, when you think about it. The Wilson woman's related to her, for a start. She's waited all these years to get in touch with Bonnie – which is weird, you have to admit. You know how Ben says you should ask "Why now?" Well, what if it's Humphrey dying that sparked everything off? Everybody getting together at the funeral, meeting old enemies for the first time in years, stirring up old battles. Doesn't that make sense to you?'

She met his eyes with unfettered admiration. 'You know what – it absolutely does,' she said.

Chapter Thirteen

'I love you, Christopher Henderson,' said Simmy, somewhere towards midnight. They had slept for an hour or so and then woken to a cry from Robin in the next room. Both parents lay still, waiting to see what would happen next. When nothing more was heard, they turned to each other in the dark and enjoyed a spell of marital relations that went very well indeed.

'What brought that on?' he asked with a chuckle.

'I just wanted to say it. It came over me in a great big wave. You don't have to say anything back.'

'Okay.' He was quiet and she thought he'd fallen asleep, but then he said, 'You're the best thing that's ever happened to me, you know. But I have a hunch that great big wave might have been hormones. And you know what hormones do, don't you?'

'Oh hush,' she said.

Thursday dawned slowly, the dark morning feeling a lot more like winter than the middle of autumn. 'It'll be better next week,' Christopher assured her. 'The clocks going back mean we get lighter mornings.'

'Good,' said Simmy, who knew that already. 'Is Ben going to work today?' she asked, changing the subject.

'No idea. I thought he'd have told you yesterday.'

'He said he thought he'd be fit, but couldn't be sure. Presumably he'll be asking you for a lift if he is going to be in.'

'Right.' Christopher's expression was severe. 'It would be helpful to know. Why are young people so sloppy about this sort of thing these days?'

'I expect we were the same at his age. I think we should assume he's having another day off. He didn't sound very robust yesterday. It might take a little while to get over the shock.'

'Did he actually have a proper operation on it?'

'I'm not sure. Possibly not, since they sent him home so quickly. We talked about other things and I never got around to asking him.'

They were still in bed, their phones downstairs. 'There's probably a text from him, anyway,' Simmy added.

She was proved right when Christopher inspected his phone, but was prevented from commenting when she found a message of her own, from Corinne, sent late the previous evening. 'Bonnie not doing so well. Think you might have to come and help.'

Suddenly the day felt complicated and stressful. Was Bonnie going to be off work, and if so, what should Simmy do? Close the shop, she supposed. Verity could manage the basics for a day or so, perhaps, but only by some intelligent juggling, which might be beyond her. Tanya might do a couple of hours after school, allowing Verity to make deliveries. Simmy could possibly put in an hour or so as well, with Robin in tow. Already she was figuring out logistics and wondering who to speak to first.

'Ben says he'd appreciate another day off, but is sure he can get back to work tomorrow,' Christopher announced, before noticing the look on her face. 'What's the matter?'

'Bonnie's having a crisis. Corinne thinks I should go down there.'

He made a tutting sound, and said, 'Why does everything have to happen at once?'

'This is probably only the start. We've got Moxon and Sophie and Lindsay to worry about as well. Not necessarily in that order.'

'Pity we can't just leave them all to worry about each other.'

'Good point. But you don't really mean it. You know we've gone too far now. In fact we – or I – were too far into it right back on Sunday. It's unthinkable to stop caring now. I couldn't do it if I tried. In fact, I *have* tried and it doesn't work.'

'I know,' he said. 'I'm the same.'

Which left them precisely nowhere, as far as action went. Christopher would have to go to work, and make sure Ben's absence was covered. Despite being new to the business, the young man had quickly made himself useful, suggesting improvements to the computer system and researching some lesser-known historical backgrounds to Chinese porcelain, Pacific Island artefacts and the dubious realms of ivory and tortoiseshell. The last was the most contentious, with the auction house always inclined to turn a blind eye on items that fell into the grey area of legally permissible dates of origin. The arbitrary cut-off of 1947 was impossible to adhere to precisely, and scarcely credible stories of great-aunts definitely buying the item in 1936 were treated as proof positive. Ben Harkness was an awkward voice at such times, casting doubt on unconvincing tales. 'He's right, of course,' Christopher would sigh. 'And yet . . .'

'You'll be thanking him if you get the customs people turning up for an inspection,' said Simmy.

On this particular Thursday, the saleroom was anticipating a delivery of china that was rumoured to contain at least three pieces of Martin Brothers. It would be the first time that Ben had laid eyes or hands on anything from that workshop and he had been excited. Now Christopher would have to identify and catalogue the objects in Ben's absence. He relayed all this to Simmy over breakfast. 'He can see them tomorrow, of course, but it won't be the same.'

'I've never heard of Martin Brothers,' said Simmy. 'Have I?'

'They made those grotesque birds with big beaks and sinister eyes. You can't miss them. But they did a lot of other stuff. The things coming in today won't be anything like as exciting, but it would have been a first for Ben.'

'He'll see them tomorrow,' she said, unable to feel much concern for such a detail. 'I'm more worried about Bonnie. I'll have to call Corinne and see how things are today.'

'She'd have told you by now if she wasn't going into the shop. There's nothing actually *wrong* with her, is there? She's got no reason to take to her bed. When you think about it, it's really good news for her.'

Simmy suddenly felt a strong desire to speak to her mother. Something about families and blood ties and the way people behaved made Angie the go-to person. She had her own special understanding of how strange life could be, and how easy it was to do the wrong thing. Twenty years of running a Bed and Breakfast had taught her a great deal. That meant a decision would have to be made between Windermere and Threlkeld – although both would just be feasible with Angie's co-operation. Simmy's gut reaction, however, was to avoid Windermere, if at all possible. Christopher was very likely right in his assumption that Corinne was overreacting and there was little need for Simmy to rush down there. The apparent fact of Lindsay Wilson's disappearance never quite went away, with its implication that the really important events were going on in the Askham area, and Simmy would be wise to remain within reach. And yet she could not just abandon Bonnie if she really was in distress.

'Time you were off,' she told Christopher, aware of wanting him out of her way. 'Have a nice day and see you later.'

'I've got five more minutes,' he said. 'I haven't finished my coffee.'

'I really ought to ask Mum if she'll have Robin this

169

morning so I can go down to Windermere and see what needs doing.'

He gave her a long look. 'She won't like the short notice. You'd better be sure you're wanted first, don't you think?'

'Probably. But Corinne wouldn't have sent that text unless she meant it.' She had another thought. 'And I could take Ben with me. I'm surprised he hasn't asked already.'

Christopher made a gesture that came close to throwing up his hands, relinquishing all attempts to argue or make suggestions. 'Well, good luck,' was all he said.

Progress on making arrangements for the day was greatly impeded by the dog and the baby. Robin was crochety and Cornelia forgot the toilet rules and deposited a large and unpleasantly loose turd on the hearthrug. Simmy came within an inch of rubbing the animal's nose in it, understanding the temptation to do so for the first time. Instead, she made the message perfectly clear with a hard smack on the dog's rump and a shove out into the garden. '*Outside!*' she ordered.

Robin's left cheek was red and he kept rubbing it. 'Can that be a tooth?' Simmy wondered aloud. So far he only had one tiny incisor on his bottom jaw. She had been assured there was no prospect of any molars for years yet. 'Almost certainly not,' she told herself in answer to her own question. She put him on his playmat, having thrown the damaged hearthrug outside for future attention. Then she tried to think.

There had been nothing from Bonnie to say she was unable to work, which made it seem less urgent to dash down to Windermere on Corinne's command. The best thing would be to phone the woman first and take it from there. On calmer reflection, there was nothing so terribly traumatic in what Sophie had revealed the day before, anyway. A shock, yes. Emotions such as regret and anger might well come to the surface, along with a sense of having been kept in the dark for much too long. But nothing had really changed. Information had been added, but the few essential facts that Bonnie knew already were still true. The new-found cousins must be exciting. On the whole, Simmy concluded that within a short while Bonnie would be feeling quite positive about the whole thing. She found herself once again wanting to talk everything through with her own mother, who was well versed in Bonnie's history and would have views to express.

She was also aware of an increasing wish to contact Ben, out of a mixture of motives. Simmy had not read the wording of the boy's text to Christopher, merely understanding that he was taking another day off work. She felt mildly concerned for him, alone with his laptop and his broken wrist, on a cool day in Keswick, missing his girlfriend and probably feeling frustrated. But Ben did have a mother of his own, who was the rightful person to minister to him if ministrations were required. Simmy's own priorities, regarding being accused of murder and experiencing bewilderment at the strange attitude of her friendly detective, might be shelved for another day or so, but that didn't mean she was perfectly free to spend all day roaming the byways of Cumbria. Ben would very probably have to wait for her to get things sorted out.

So the first call she made was to her parents. There were three choices of phone number – two mobiles and a landline. The most likely way of reaching her mother was to use the last of these, which she did.

'Hello?' came a somewhat groggy response after several seconds.

'Mum? Are you all right? It's me.'

'What time is it? I was in bed.'

'It's nearly nine. Where's Dad?'

'Downstairs, I think. I nearly didn't answer it. We're *retired*, remember? We don't have to get up if we don't want to. It's still dark out there.'

'It's not a bit dark, just cloudy.'

'You want me to have your child,' Angie accused. 'Again.'

'Only if you don't mind. He is a bit tetchy today. He's got a red cheek.'

'Teething.'

'Maybe. Why does that make their cheeks red? He's rubbing it in a place where no teeth are meant to happen for ages yet.'

'I don't know,' said Angie. 'It just does. Except I never really believed what they told me about teeth. It's just a sort of code for various uncomfortable things that babies are heir to. Like growing pains. Meaningless, but oddly comforting.'

Simmy was still trying to process *heir to*, which she heard as something quite different. Eventually it clicked. 'Oh,' she said. 'So . . .?'

'Of course we'll have him if it's important. He's quite good with us usually. It won't be all day, will it?'

'No, just the morning,' Simmy rashly promised. 'I'll bring him some lunch if you like. He can have it any time

172

from half past eleven, if it helps to amuse him.'

'And there's always the CBeebies,' said Angie, who was rapidly warming to the blandishments of children's television. 'He likes that black rabbit thing.'

'I think he really likes the way *you* like it so much,' teased Simmy, having watched her mother enjoying Bing. 'It's much too old for him, actually.'

'You like it as well.'

'I do,' Simmy confessed. 'It's very philosophical.'

'So where are you going that won't allow babies?'

'I'm not entirely sure yet. But I might need to be free to drive Ben down to Windermere or possibly to Askham. It's all rather unpredictable. I'll update you when I bring Robin. I do want to talk to you, actually. Can we come about ten or just before?'

'What about the dog? Is that coming as well?'

'Only if you want her.'

'Not in this weather,' said Angie decisively. 'I think it looks like rain.'

It was all amicably arranged, with Angie audibly calculating the number of hours she would be required to mind the baby. Assuming Russell would take charge for at least half of the time, with the chance of a walk or a prolonged play session, Angie was left with little to complain about.

Simmy was galvanised into action, phoning Ben briefly, filling a bag with Robin's necessities, calling the dog back in. The last was an afterthought, accompanied by a moment of panic at the possibility that Cornelia had escaped through the very insubstantial hedge and gone over the fells by herself. Instead, she was shivering pathetically a few feet from the back door. 'I forgot all about you,' said Simmy. 'They don't want you in Threlkeld, so you can just stay at home and behave yourself.'

Ben had wanted to talk, but Simmy told him she would be in Keswick in under an hour and he should save it all until then. 'Too much to say on the phone,' she said.

The day was indeed cloudy, and getting worse by the minute. No wonder poor Cornelia had been shivering outside. Thoughts of log fires and woolly jumpers were getting closer by the hour. Traffic was thin all the way to Threlkeld. Russell met her at the door with the news that he would not be taking Robin for a walk up Blencathra. 'I don't blame you,' said Simmy. 'I'll stay for a bit and bring you up to date on what's been happening.'

But this turned out to be impossible. Robin wanted all the attention, and Angie still wasn't dressed. 'It's about Bonnie,' Simmy began, twice. But she got no further than that. Realising it was hopeless, and might well occupy an uncomfortable amount of time once she did get her parents' attention, she prepared to leave. 'I'll be back by about one,' she assured them.

She was away again by ten fifteen, and with Ben five minutes later.

He had a green plaster cast halfway up his arm, with his fingers protruding from it, looking rather swollen. 'Does it hurt?' she asked.

'Aches,' he said. 'I can't do much with it. And I feel giddy when I stand up. It's horrible. They say driving is out of the question for about a month.' He sighed. 'That's the most annoying part.'

'Have you spoken to Bonnie?'

'Course I have. Actually, she's more bothered about Corinne than the new relatives. She seems to be in a real tizzy about it. Bonnie's okay.'

'That's not how it sounds to me.' Simmy showed him the text from Corinne. 'I was thinking I should dash down there now, as she obviously wants me to, but I'm assuming Bonnie's gone to work as usual, so it might not be as urgent as I first thought.'

'It's not urgent at all. We'd be better off going to Askham.'

Oh?'

'Don't you think?' He looked at her in surprise. 'Surely that's where the most important stuff's happening? We need to try and talk to people there, find out more about the Pauline lady, and how she was killed. We should have done it *days* ago. My wrist has slowed everything down horribly.'

Simmy made a calming gesture with both hands. 'Slowing down is no bad thing. We need to think, and talk, before we do anything rash. No way am I going back there asking rude questions of total strangers. Except they're not strangers, because most of them seem to know who I am, and that I've been named as a suspect. I might get lynched if I go there again.'

'Who knows you? Just one or two men in a pub.'

'Somebody put a *picture* of me on Facebook,' she reminded him.

'It doesn't look much like you,' he assured her. 'There was only one tweet that said "Windermere florist named as a person of interest in Askham murder" or something like that. It was barely even retweeted two or three times, and nobody's put a name to you. It's pretty much the same on Facebook and the other sites. Less, if anything. You're old news – it was days ago now. You're overreacting.'

'I don't think I am. Christopher says there's got to be some explanation of why I was accused, and now Lindsay Wilson's gone missing he's got even wilder theories about what's going on. He really believes there's a major conspiracy behind it all.'

'Lindsay Wilson's gone missing? When did that happen?' Ben was tapping his keyboard in bewilderment. 'There's nothing about that anywhere.'

'Moxon phoned last night and told me. I forgot you didn't know.'

'Has she been murdered?'

'I hope not.'

'What does Moxo think?'

'He didn't really say. He was being all stilted and weird, so I asked if people were listening and he said they were. Christopher thinks he's there under sufferance, or under a cloud, and hasn't got a free rein at all.'

Ben's eyes sparkled and he tapped his front teeth. 'That would fit perfectly!' he triumphed. 'Didn't we say from the start that you were only accused as a way of involving us – me and Bonnie rather than Moxon – in the investigation? Through you, I mean. The question is – who wants us involved? And why? And is Moxo just collateral damage or something?'

'I don't know what that means.' Simmy was starting to feel weak.

'He might just be an afterthought, with no real part in the investigating team. Just a link to you that nobody thinks is important. If the Lindsay person is playing some sort of game of her own, she'll be manipulating the police until they have no idea which end is up. I can see that fitting the facts as we know them, can't you? There are plenty of perfectly credible explanations for her disappearing,' he assured her.

'Are there? Everything you or Christopher say just sounds like something out of a fairy tale to me. Or a film.'

He shook his head at her. 'No – listen. She might be scared to point a finger at the real killer, because they'd come for her if she did. But she knows who they are, and decided it would be very helpful to conscript outside help from people known to have been useful in the past. She met you on Friday, and then again on Saturday and did some quick thinking, and decided to rope you in by concocting a story about seeing you on the verge of bashing the old lady.'

Simmy shuddered. 'Nobody would be so cold-blooded as that. And it leaves about a hundred glaring gaps that we can't hope to explain.'

'We can try.' He tapped his teeth as he often did when thinking. 'Wasn't there something about some grandsons? Do we know their names?'

'I don't. I thought you might have found them by now.'

'I should have done,' he nodded. 'I thought I had plenty of time yesterday, but then Bonnie called and I didn't get back to it. She talked for nearly an hour.' He shook his head. 'That never happens. But she was better at the end of it.'

'Good.'

'Now, then. I wonder where we should start . . .' He tapped his keyboard again using the protruding tips of his left-hand fingers more deftly than Simmy would have believed, chewing his lip and shaking his head. 'Pity she hasn't been dead long enough to warrant an obituary.' He looked up. 'I'm sorry to say it, but I really think this is one of those times when we'd be much better off going to the village and talking to real people. We could start in the shop, if you don't like the pub.'

'Oh dear – are you sure?' She wondered what time it was. 'How long is that going to take? There are still some things I haven't told you. It's been terribly scrappy up to now. I can't remember who said what to who. I keep thinking there must be more that Lindsay said on Saturday that I can't remember. Clues.'

Ben said nothing for about four minutes during which he went on rattling the keyboard and made notes on a pad beside him. He then sat back with a grin. 'Pauline Parsons had five children, three sons and two daughters. Husband died twenty-five years ago. One son was killed in a farm accident at the age of twenty or thereabouts. A granddaughter called Scarlett currently has some kind of heart trouble and there's talk of a transplant. And there's a fund collecting money for her. Three adult grandsons, two brothers, Luke and Kieran, and their cousin Eldon Franklin. I might have missed a few.'

'Eldon! Did you say Eldon?'

He nodded.

'There was a man in the pub called Eldon. He was the one most hostile to me and Christopher. He never said he was related to Pauline.'

'He's the son of Pauline's daughter Adela. That's a nice name.' He repeated it slowly. 'It's always interesting to know what makes people choose certain names, don't you think?'

Simmy waved this away as irrelevant. 'And a man called Franklin,' she reminded him. 'That's Eldon's father.'

'Obviously. Eldon Franklin works at Askham Hall, by the way. He's some kind of groundsman, apparently.'

'I don't know how you do it all so quickly,' she marvelled. 'It's like magic.'

'Facebook goes a long way,' he told her. 'The electoral register, of course. And one or two local newspaper reports. Instagram often comes up with pictures of the people concerned. It's all there for the taking. Everybody uploads their entire personal history for the world to see.'

'I suppose that's rather sweet, in a way. Innocent. Trusting. And it must be good for raising money for the kid with a bad heart, poor little thing.'

'She's not so little. Sixteen, I think. Something like that.' He consulted his notes. 'I didn't write that down.' Then he shivered. 'Imagine having a heart transplant! Yuk!' He put a protective hand over his own heart.

'Better than dying,' said Simmy.

'I guess so. And she's old enough to decide for herself, anyway.'

'I'm not so sure about that.' Simmy reminded herself that to someone of nineteen, sixteen was relatively grown up. 'It's really awfully young, for something as massive as that.' Then she said, 'We have to follow up on Eldon. If we go to Askham, we should see if we can find him. You might have to defend me, though.'

Ben gave her an amused smile. 'Why? Because he looked like a murderer?'

'He did, actually. But he wouldn't kill his granny, would he? If he lives in the same village, he must have grown up knowing her well. And if he was some sort of criminal already, wouldn't he be a prime suspect?'

'Too many unknowns,' said Ben with a wise look. 'Eldon doesn't do Facebook or WhatsApp, but he's listed by some of the others. Looks as if he's single and has some sort of small business – maybe he hires himself out to other places, not just the Hall.'

Simmy had a sudden thought. 'Can you check a man called Howard Isaacs as well? He's a builder, who knew Humphrey. I can't help feeling he's connected somehow. He turned up out of the blue on Monday and gave me some spiel about keeping Humphrey's business going and wanting photos of what he'd done to our conversion.'

Ben renewed his tapping, which did not look to be very productive. 'All I can see is an entry on a list of local businesses that says "Isaacs Enterprises", which could mean anything. Doesn't appear to be very active.'

'Some people rely on word of mouth, I suppose. But he struck me as fairly upmarket. Something rather slick about him. I told him he didn't look like a builder, and I don't think he liked that very much. But it was true. I told Bonnie about him,' she added.

'Could be they advertise under someone else's name. If he's the big cheese behind it all, he might well have various smaller outfits under his umbrella, so to speak. They might all have their own listings, which wouldn't be obviously his. I mean, they'd use their own names and look as if they were independent.'

'Oh.' She was even more impressed than before. 'How do you know all that sort of stuff?'

'Actually, I got quite a lot from Christopher. I do this sort of thing for him sometimes. Don't tell him I told you. It's not always entirely legit. Industrial espionage, you might say.'

Simmy laughed. 'I definitely don't want to know, if that's the case.'

'It's great, you know – working for him. No two days are the same.'

'He says it's a shame you're missing the . . . something Brothers. He says you'll be sorry about that.'

'Martin Brothers. I am a bit sad about it, but I can see the things tomorrow. I'm definitely going to be fine by then – if he can drive me. I'll try and make it easy for him. It's going to be a real nuisance if it goes on for a month.'

'He'll cope,' said Simmy.

'So – are we going to Askham, then? It's eleven o'clock already. We could see if the pub's open. Isn't there another one besides the Punchbowl? We could try there if you're worried about being recognised again.'

'We should have a proper plan. I don't want to just stroll aimlessly round the village hoping something jumps out at us. That's silly. So is going to either of the pubs, really. Why do we have to be there? You've got loads of information off the Internet. Isn't there a better use we can make of the time?'

'How much time do we have?'

'Two hours or so. Three at a pinch. I told my mother I'd be back after lunch, which they'll probably have early, so that means one o'clock or thereabouts. She's not going to be happy if it goes past two. Robin's not in a very good mood. They'll probably be totally frazzled already.' She sighed, feeling as if she'd behaved unfairly. Other mothers left their offspring with people pretty much all the time, but it still felt wrong to her.

'It might be useful to speak to Moxon,' Ben mused. 'Do we know where he is?'

'No idea. There's something going on with him, and he's obviously not happy about it. I think he'd love to talk to us, if he thought it was off the record. I feel sure he's got all sorts of things he wants to say and isn't allowed to.'

'That's very peculiar.'

'Actually, I think you might be right that we're all being used like pawns in some horrible big game that we don't understand, including him. Isn't that what you meant just now? I can't decide whether I think Lindsay Wilson is in the same boat and somebody's forcing her to do what she's doing, or if she's one of the prime movers. And what about Sophie?' She moaned helplessly.

'Why would you be worrying about her?'

'Christopher thinks she could be at the centre of everything.'

'Well, I don't agree. I can't see that she has anything whatever to do with it.'

Simmy hesitated, not knowing which to believe. 'I keep seeing her face, and how like Bonnie she is. She must be so *sad*.'

'Hm,' was all Ben said to that.

Simmy kept on with her list of worries. 'And you mustn't forget that Bonnie's going to want you to be there for her.'

He waved this away. 'Don't fret about Bonnie. She says

she's got Saturday off. Does that mean you'll be down at the shop?'

'I guess so. Me and Tanya.'

'Which means Christopher will have Robin. And *that* means nobody will be around to drive me anywhere.'

'If you can be ready early enough, I could take you with me,' she offered. Saturday still felt quite a distance away. 'I could collect you from here at about half past eight.'

'Great!' he said, alerting Simmy to the strength of emotion he had been concealing when it came to the needs of his girlfriend. 'So now we just have to decide what we do next.'

Chapter Fourteen

Ben lived in one room in a house occupied by a couple in their sixties. 'It's called "digs",' he announced in wonder. 'Like something from the nineteen-thirties.'

The couple had invited him to share their breakfast but not their other meals. 'We go out a lot,' said Mrs Lewis. 'We like to be spontaneous. There's two takeaways and a Tesco Express within easy reach. But please don't eat food in your room. Even the most careful person spills things now and then. You can use our dining area any time you like.' Ben had declined the offer of breakfast and survived mainly on the lunches he ate at work, since using the designated area was awkward and embarrassing. The lunches came from a mobile catering van, which did hot dogs, sandwiches, sausage rolls and soup. It toured the industrial estate which was home to the auction house. For an evening meal, he mostly cycled to a small supermarket and ate his purchases in the very pleasant park in the centre of Keswick when weather permitted. When it was raining, he hurriedly consumed the food as Mrs Lewis had instructed. Nobody believed that he was eating a healthy diet, but nor could anyone suggest viable methods of improving it, other than including quantities of apples and oranges.

The Lewises did not in fact go out much, but sat in their living room with the television on, or played interminable games of Scrabble, which explained why sitting at their dining table was not to Ben's liking. It was all part of the same room and he felt like an intruder. Another reason for seldom joining them was the discovery of their taste for soap operas and rom-com films. It was no hardship for someone of his age to spend evenings in his room with his laptop and phone, augmenting his unsatisfactory diet with illicit Mars bars and packets of crisps.

Visitors were expected to call ahead, so that Ben could meet them at the street door. So when someone knocked at five past eleven on a Thursday morning, he assumed it was a parcel delivery for his landlady, and of no significance to him.

'They're out, aren't they?' said Simmy. 'Shouldn't you go and answer it?'

He made no move to do as she suggested, sitting resolutely at the little table that functioned as his desk. 'They can leave it next door or something.'

'Ben! That's awful. Listen – they're knocking again. I'm going to see who it is.'

'Suit yourself,' said Ben.

It was Corinne, looking breathless and bad-tempered.

'Thank Christ,' she said. 'I thought I'd come all this way for nothing.'

'You're lucky,' said Simmy. 'We were just going out. What's the matter? Have you brought Bonnie with you?' She peered round the woman for a look.

'No, of course not. She's working in your shop, obviously. I *told* you. Didn't you get my text? Bonnie's in a real state, and needs somebody more than just me. All I can do is make soothing noises, which isn't helping. When I got no response from you, I thought I should try Ben.'

'Come in and let's do this properly. Bonnie can't be as bad as all that if she can work. Ben thinks she's perfectly all right.'

Corinne gave her a withering stare. 'I don't believe you said that. Don't you understand *anything*?'

Simmy flushed and led the way upstairs to Ben's room. She'd known Corinne could be outspoken, with considerable experience of life's darker corners, but up to that point the two of them had always amicably agreed about almost everything. Bonnie could not have wished for a better foster mother, and it seemed odd that she was apparently panicking now.

'It's Corinne,' she said, pushing Ben's door open.

'Hey!' he said, still not getting up from the table. 'What brings you here?'

'What do you think?' She sat down on the bed.

'You think Bonnie's not okay, right?' He sighed. 'She said you were overreacting. Listen – she's not blaming you, if that's what you think. Not much, anyway. We assume you did know about the Craigs and Bonnie's dad and everything, but chose not to say anything. Maybe the social people told you not to. I can see it would be hard to find the right moment. And you never had any reason to go to Askham or think about the people there. It's all right, anyway. She's basically quite happy about it – so far. The worst bit is wondering about her dad. Is he even still alive? Does anybody know? She wants me to try and find him, but that needs a bit of thought. You hear stories of people rejecting their children all over again – especially men. It doesn't mean much to some of them whether they've got any kids or not. Besides, he might have a dozen others scattered around. I'm inclined to think it might be best just to leave him out. That's what Bonnie's wrestling with now. She's got to do it by herself. She can do that.' He gave her a kind smile. 'No need to panic.'

Corinne sniffed. 'I'm not *panicking*, as you call it. I just want to explain that I didn't know it was the Craig man doing Simmy's conversion. If I'd known that I would have said something. He was always the best person in the whole miserable business. He used to take Bonnie out for the day when she was very small. She remembers him a bit. She called him Uncle Humpie. You think you know better than me how she's doing, but I can tell you she's really upset that he's dead and she never got a chance to know him again. It's tragic.'

'Yes, it is,' Simmy interposed. 'His death is tragic for everyone. We all feel it.'

'Bonnie wishes she'd gone to the funeral. She had every right to be there, after all.'

'That's true. But it wouldn't have been a very suitable moment to get to know her cousins, would it? You have to rewrite a lot of history, with any number of "what ifs" and "might have beens" and "if onlys" to make any of it work out. It's futile. What's done is done, and you've got to take it from here.' She stopped talking, realising she was parroting her own painful discoveries, following the death of her baby daughter. 'You know that as well as I do,' she finished.

Corinne's head drooped. 'It was such a shock,' she muttered. 'After I'd seen her through a dozen years and more, keeping her going through all that eating business, and never knowing if her bloody mother would show up out of the blue, and getting her to relax with dogs and other kids – the whole package – and now this. She was the hardest of them all, you know. I thought at one point she'd go and die on me. This has brought it all back. I dare say I'm making too much of it.'

'She's eighteen now,' Simmy reminded Corinne. 'And she's got Ben. And me. And a job. And you're still watching out for her. What would she think if she knew you were here, saying all this?'

Corinne gave a weak smile. 'Good question.'

'She'd think you weren't keeping up,' said Ben. 'You're scared she's going to slide back into how she was at twelve. But she won't. She's a different person now.'

'There's always going to be setbacks. Tragedies and disappointments, and horrible feelings,' said Simmy. 'That's pretty much the same for everybody, after all.'

'Yeah,' sighed Corinne. 'And there was me thinking my life was going to be all song and dance and smelling the roses from here on.'

Ben and Simmy both laughed. It was only slightly forced.

* * *

Corinne stayed almost an hour, making any sort of trip with Ben impossible unless Angie and Russell could be persuaded to keep Robin all afternoon. Simmy made some fairly disgusting instant coffee with powdered milk, thanks to the electric kettle Ben kept in his room. It seemed he was at least allowed to make drinks for himself. 'Can you do this with your arm in plaster?' Corinne wondered. 'How do you get dressed? Or use the computer?'

He waggled the fingers of the affected arm, saying, 'They work quite well, luckily. I can just manage to oppose finger and thumb, look.' He demonstrated. 'As long as I don't do anything strenuous, it's okay. The keyboard's not much of a problem.' Again he demonstrated. 'But they're still quite swollen, so it is a bit awkward.'

'It just shows,' said Corinne vaguely. 'You never know what's round the corner.'

'Careful! You sound like Verity,' said Simmy. 'Anyway, listen – Bonnie's having Saturday off. I might take Ben down to yours when I go to the shop. He can stay in Windermere all weekend – his parents might be glad to see him. Then by Monday he'll probably be able to do a lot more, and we can take it from there.'

'What about the murder?' asked Ben. 'I still want to go to Askham. I want to talk to Moxon and see what the matter with him is.' He looked at Simmy. 'Did we say it all – about him, I mean? Have we missed anything?'

'I don't know.' She was having difficulty getting her thoughts away from Bonnie. 'He won't talk to me properly. He's gone all different. I don't know where I am with him. I expect he'll explain it all eventually.'

'Do you get the impression he wants us to stay out of

it? That it's something too nasty and dangerous for us this time?'

'Possibly.' She thought about it. 'I don't know, really. He doesn't seem to be a free agent, but I get the feeling he doesn't dare argue with whoever's ordering him about.'

Corinne was looking more and more alarmed. 'You two!' she scolded. 'You'll get yourselves into terrible trouble if you go on like this.'

'What – worse than having a broken pelvis and being kidnapped?' said Simmy, referring to two previous occasions where trouble had resulted from getting too close to violent criminals. 'We know how horrible people can be, believe me.' She smiled. 'But you know what? I think the worst moment was when that woman threw the flowers I'd just delivered right across a farmyard. It had nothing to do with anything I'd done, and she lives in Patterdale now. I see her once in a while and she's nice. But it was a real shock at the time.'

Corinne departed a few moments later, leaving Ben and Simmy at a loss as to what to do next. 'We're wasting the day,' he said urgently. 'We haven't got anywhere all week, and I said I'd go into work again tomorrow. That only leaves this afternoon.' He lapsed into some serious thought. 'You could take me to Askham now and leave me there. Fetch the baby and do whatever you have to do, and then come back for me at two o'clock or thereabouts. Bit later, maybe. I can keep in touch on the phone.'

'What's the point of that? I've already told you I don't want to go there again, especially as I can't see how it would get us anywhere.' She looked at him, aware of a niggle that had been irritating her all morning. 'Shouldn't you be wearing a sling? That arm looks heavy and stiff, as if it needs to be held up. Don't people with broken arms always have a sling?'

He grimaced. 'I can't type in a sling. Or anything else.'

'I think that's rather the point of it. To remind you not to try to use it.'

'I'll put it on when I go out. There'll be people to help me then.'

'I feel sorry for Corinne,' Simmy said. 'She's obviously feeling guilty.'

Ben nodded. 'She'll get over it. There was never going to be a right moment, was there? If anything, this is probably it – Bonnie can handle the shock now when she might not have done before. Besides, it's nothing very awful, is it? She always knew she had a father somewhere – she just forgot because nobody ever talked about him. There were plenty of other kids around in the same boat when she was at school. Decent fathers are a bit of a luxury these days.'

Simmy thought of her own father and how unimaginable life would be without him. But David Harkness had never been very present to his offspring, appearing for meals and nagging about homework, but not much good at outings or games or listening to their worries. Tanya had once described him as 'a typical teacher, more interested in other people's kids than his own'. At the time, Simmy had thought that rather unfair to teachers. More likely he was just a man who could only focus on one thing at a time, and the demands of his job took precedence.

'At least you all had each other,' she said to Ben now, reading his mind as he considered his own parent's shortcomings.

'He was okay, really. Stabilising, you might say. You always know where you are with him, which is not nothing. Mum's going to be more and more dependent on him, the way her arthritis is going.'

In a sudden leap, Simmy remembered Chloe and Berta Craig and how their very decent father was lost to them for ever. It made her tearful, which she hid from Ben. 'So what are we going to do?' she asked, taking a deep breath.

'Make a plan,' he said.

They went back to basics, as they had learnt to do over the past few years. 'You forget things otherwise,' Ben said. 'So – where did it all start?'

'Humphrey's funeral,' said Simmy promptly. 'That's where we met Lindsay and Sophie. Although I don't think the Isaacs man was there.' She frowned. 'Actually, he said he was, but I didn't see him. There was quite a crowd, so that's perfectly possible.'

Ben dutifully made a note on his pad. It always gave Simmy a twitch of relief to see that he could still use a pen and paper and not be entirely dependent on the keyboard. 'What about old Mrs Parsons?' he said next.

'Good question. Let me think. No – she can't have been there on Friday, because when I saw her next day she was asking Lindsay about it. She doesn't hold with churches, either. Lindsay told me a bit about that. She's a Jehovah's Witness – which I have heard of, but have no idea what it involves. But she obviously cared enough about Humphrey to go and look at the grave next day.'

'Same as you did. I'm not sure I get why you needed to do that.' He gave her a careful look. 'Am I being insensitive?'

'Not really. The thing is, we all hung back when they were doing the interment. That's meant to be family only. I wanted to see the flowers, and just . . . well, spend a few minutes thinking about Humphrey, by myself.'

'Except you weren't, because old Mrs P and Lindsay Wilson were there.'

'Right.'

Ben made another note. 'So you spoke to Lindsay both days, right? She clocked you and Christopher on Friday, probably knew exactly who you were and how you connected to Humphrey. Got her ducks all in a row right there and then at the funeral. When you were back again on Saturday she must have been thrilled. More than she could have wished for. Handed her the whole thing on a plate.'

'Slow down!' she ordered. 'You're making way too many assumptions. And too many metaphors about ducks and plates.'

'Hypotheses, not assumptions,' he corrected her. 'Now – did Lindsay seem especially friendly with the old lady? Had they known each other for years? Did they *touch* each other?' His eyes sparkled at his own cleverness. 'That would be a real giveaway.'

'I don't know,' wailed Simmy. 'I don't notice things like that.' Then she forced herself to think back, waiting for the memories to come into focus. 'I'm running through it again, and no – they didn't touch. Mrs Parsons was slow, especially when we were out in the road, but she didn't need any physical help. I had the buggy and the dog, so I was pretty encumbered. We just crawled along the road for a little way, after we'd left the grave. and then Mrs P went off without us and Lindsay and I chatted for a bit and then I got back in the car.' She slumped against the back of the only comfortable chair in the room. 'And then she died the same day, poor old thing. Nobody kills a ninety-year-old woman for no reason, do they? Why would anybody do that?'

'Just because she was old doesn't mean she wasn't a threat to someone. Or had something they wanted. Or made somebody really angry. Age doesn't have to come into it.'

'She was quite sharp in her wits. She asked me a few personal questions. And to answer your question, I don't think she did know Lindsay very well. She kept giving her curious looks, as if wondering about her.'

'She's an anomaly – Lindsay, I mean. Doing that thesis all by herself in a quiet little village. It's almost Dickensian in itself.'

'My dad's reading *Dombey and Son*,' Simmy remembered. 'He thinks there might be some clues in it.'

'He could be right. Does anybody falsely accuse anybody of murder in it?'

'I don't know. She said it was full of cruelty and she wanted to put it in context, so she was researching cruel aspects of Victorian society. Something like that.'

'Is your dad a fast reader?'

'Fairly. But he's got Robin today, so he won't have much of a chance to get on with it.'

'Let's take a shortcut, then.' He turned back to his laptop and woke it up. Simmy watched him use the fingers of his left hand, the plastered wrist resting on the front edge and the fingers hardly moving as they limited themselves to the first five or six keys on the left. The right hand compensated effortlessly.

'You make it look so easy,' she said admiringly.

'What? Ah – here it is. Students' notes. Synopsis. Character list. Themes. Lovely.' He scanned rapidly. 'Hey – there's someone called Cornelia in it. Did Lindsay tell you that?'

'No! There can't be. That's crazy.'

'There is. Cornelia Blimber, daughter of the owner of the school Paul Dombey goes to. There's a cast of thousands, as usual. It says that child cruelty is one of the main themes. Do you think Mrs Parsons was cruel to her children?'

Simmy gave no reply to this, but she thought about Eldon, the grandson. He looked as if he might have had a difficult childhood. That took her directly to Bonnie, which was an uncomfortable association.

'Is there someone called Good Mrs Brown?' she asked.

'Oh yes. She's not good at all, as far as I can see. But she's important near the end.' His eyes were flying down the screen. 'I need to take this slowly. It looks horribly complicated. Why did you ask about Good Mrs Brown?'

'Lindsay said Pauline Parsons was like her.'

'Did she! Mind you, she probably fits everybody she meets into the story in one way or another. You might even be Florence. Or maybe Susan Nipper. Or Mrs Toodles. She's called Richards as well, for some reason. These are all in the first few lines. Sophie Craig could be Mrs Chick – she's Mr Dombey's sister. Her husband sounds a bit like Humphrey.'

'Stop it. You're getting silly. You can't base a murder investigation on a book.'

'Except when one of the main people involved is completely consumed by that book. Have you any idea of the intensity and focus needed for a PhD thesis?'

'Not really,' she admitted.

'Well, it's no joke.'

'But she won't expect anyone else to have read it or know the story. Not the police, anyway. It can't really be relevant. Maybe it would be if we thought she did the murder, but Moxon says she's got a good alibi.'

'Did he say what it was?'

She shook her head. 'And actually, it was mostly just implied. He didn't say it directly. We assumed he was sure she didn't do it, or what would be the point of questioning me?'

'He'd have to if she made a direct accusation, regardless of what she said about her own movements. She might have been trying to say you and she did it together.'

Simmy moaned. 'There's not much defence against outright lies, is there? It's like fake news. People can say anything they like about other people, and somebody will believe it.'

'Nobody believes you murdered the old lady,' he assured her. 'We got past that ages ago.'

'I must admit I've stopped worrying about it now. It doesn't feel exactly personal to me. It's more of a puzzle than anything else. I don't even feel especially victimised – just used for some weird purpose.'

'All will become clear,' he predicted. 'We just need a few more clues.' He gave her a look. 'And my hunch is they're sitting right there in Askham, staring us in the face.'

'Well, it'll have to wait. What time is it?'

He glanced at his screen. 'Twelve forty-nine.'

'It's not, is it? I'll have to go. I should take Robin home and let the dog out. I won't surface again until about two, if then. You can keep doing your googling or whatever it is. Phone me if you find anything important.'

Ben sighed. Looking at him, Simmy could see he was pale and tired. 'Did you sleep last night?' she asked.

'Sort of. It aches, even when I take a pill.'

'Have a nap, then. I might see you later. And tell Christopher if you're not up to working tomorrow. He won't mind.'

'Go,' he told her with a boyish scowl.

Chapter Fifteen

Thinking back over everything she and Ben had talked about, Simmy became aware of some glaring omissions. First among them was the fact that Lindsay Wilson was missing. That had scarcely been mentioned. It was all very well going back to basics, but they had barely moved forward from there. She also reproached herself for not ensuring that Ben had something for lunch. There had been no sign of anything in his room. She was hungry herself, come to that, and hoped there'd be something available in Threlkeld even if lunch was technically over.

It was a very short drive from Keswick to Threlkeld, along the A66. The consequences and implications of the relocation of the whole Straw family from the softer southern Lakes to the more mountainous north were still not completely understood by everyone concerned. Bonnie would never again be a daily part of the little group, even if she eventually acquired a car and a driving licence; the distance was too daunting. Simmy and Christopher were out on a limb in Hartsop, near the tourist-clogged banks of Ullswater. Nothing could be done quickly, especially in the summer.

And what about Moxon? When Simmy had lived in Troutbeck and worked in Windermere, he was on her doorstep, knowing the same people and local businesses. Now he, like Bonnie, had been left behind. Had that made it easier for him to be so withholding and strange over the Askham business? She hoped not – and after events in Threlkeld on the day she married Christopher, she could not seriously believe that the detective would ever willingly let her down.

She arrived at her parents' bungalow well after one o'clock, fearing her mother's wrath at her lateness. Instead she walked in to find a scene of joyful frolicking that she could never have imagined. She stood watching in amazement for a good two minutes before anyone noticed her. Robin was half-lying on a big rubber ball, spreadeagled across it and clinging on tightly. His grandparents were rolling it from one to the other, the child squealing with excitement at every move. At times it was on top of him, which he appeared to find even more thrilling. Russell had to push it into its former position, punching it unnecessarily to joggle its passenger. 'It's like being on a waterbed,' Angie laughed.

Eventually Simmy's presence was acknowledged and the game subsided. 'Doesn't he bump his head?' was all the astonished mother could say.

'That's all part of the fun,' Russell assured her. 'We were spinning him round and round at first, and then he started rolling it. It's the perfect size for him.'

'Remember that spacehopper thing you had?' said Angie. 'This is the same sort of idea, although there's nothing to hold onto. He absolutely loves the sensations it gives him.'

'So I see,' said Simmy, watching her little son using his legs to steer the ball as he draped himself over the top of it. He rolled forward onto his head without showing any sign of distress. Then he shifted from side to side. 'It does look like fun,' she conceded.

'He'll crash out in a minute,' Russell predicted. 'He hasn't slept at all so far.'

Fifteen minutes later the prediction came true, and Simmy settled down with a large coffee and a cheese sandwich. 'How's Ben?' asked Russell.

'A bit pale and droopy. I've never seen him like that. But his brain seems to be working much as usual. We spent ages going over what happened in Askham on Friday and Saturday. I need to go back, really, because we didn't cover everything. It's got to be important that Lindsay Wilson is missing, for a start. We barely even mentioned that. And then there's the whole business about Bonnie and Sophie Craig.' She was thinking aloud, forgetting that her parents needed some detailed updating. Russell reminded her with a strong dash of reproach.

'Oh, sorry.' Simmy closed her eyes for a moment, wondering how much summarising she could get away with. 'Quite a lot happened yesterday. And then Corinne came up to Keswick this morning while I was there, and had to be pacified. That took up some of the time.'

'Does this have anything to do with the resemblance

between Bonnie and Mrs Craig? I heard Christopher remarking on it at the funeral.'

'She's her aunt. Sister of Bonnie's absent father. She always knew about Bonnie, and meant to establish a connection, but somehow never did. Bonnie was born in her house.'

Angie Straw was pottering about, collecting the toys strewn around the room. Now she stopped and stood up straight. 'What?' she said. 'What on earth are you saying? Isn't that a completely impossible coincidence?'

'I thought the same at first. But I suppose it's not really. You could say the big surprise is that Bonnie hasn't known anything about it until now. Humphrey used to play with her. There was even talk of them taking her on when her mother was so useless. But it was all just swept aside when Corinne took her on. She told us a little bit about what that was like, just now. It sounded awful – much worse than I realised.'

'Did Corinne know about the Craigs?'

'Sort of, I think. She's feeling very guilty and upset about it. She wanted me to go and see if Bonnie was okay, but Ben insists she's fine. It just needs time and everybody keeping calm, according to him. I'll take him down on Saturday and they can have the whole day together.'

'Talk about a red herring,' said Russell. 'A major distraction from the case in hand. Did you say the Wilson woman is missing?'

'According to Moxon, yes. At least they can't find her, and he thinks that means there is foul play afoot and we're all in danger. He told me I shouldn't be at the house on my own. Cornelia isn't much use as a guard dog, I admit.'

Russell rubbed his forehead. 'I must be getting dim in my old age. I can't follow that logic.'

'Don't worry about it. It's all guesswork anyway. Ben's our best hope, as usual. He's found out a whole lot of stuff about Mrs Parsons, trying to work out why anyone would want to kill her.'

'Most people want to kill someone,' said Angie. 'And it must cut both ways. I mean, most people must be in the sights of someone who wishes they were dead.'

'However much awful behaviour I get involved in, I still don't entirely believe that,' said Simmy. 'Who do you want to kill? And who wants to kill you?'

Angie smiled and shook her head. 'The list got shorter once we moved up here and I dropped off that dreadful committee. I might have strangled the appalling Molly Mitchell otherwise.'

'We're getting off the point,' said Russell. 'Without the Wilson lady the whole thing's stuck, surely?'

'We don't know for sure. The whole thing's going on without us this time. Moxon doesn't want to tell me anything, as far as I can see.'

'Those girls are Bonnie's cousins, then,' Angie suddenly realised. 'That'll make quite a change in her life. Are you saying she's never once met them?'

Simmy had to think. 'She might have done when they were very tiny. When she was still with her mother, she played there, apparently. I'm not certain how old she was when Corinne took her on. Five or six, maybe. All that part of her life is still rather a jumble.'

'In and out of care, presumably,' Angie nodded. 'The older girl must be – what?'

'About three years younger than Bonnie,' said Simmy. 'Maybe a bit more.'

Russell was still focused on Lindsay Wilson, ignoring the talk about Bonnie. 'Can we stick to the point?' he asked, rather more irritably than was usual. 'Don't you think it's more important to clear our daughter's name than to go over old history that has nothing to do with the matter in hand?'

His wife and daughter gave him identical looks of surprise. Angie made an exaggerated gesture of apology, putting her hands together and bowing her head. 'Yes, master,' she said. Simmy laughed.

'So – does Moxon think they'll find Ms Wilson's body up on the fells next?' Russell went on. 'Or what?'

Simmy felt justly chastised. 'I should have made Ben concentrate more on her. We somehow just set her to one side. But listen – she works at Lancaster University on Fridays. I'm sure that's what she told me. I remember thinking it wasn't a very convenient day to have to drive down there and back, and I don't imagine students are at their best by the end of the week. Anyway, I should probably tell Moxon that, and he can go and check whether she shows up for work tomorrow. I bet she will.'

'He doesn't need to go in person, does he? A simple phone call would serve the purpose.'

Simmy laughed again at her father's impressively clear thinking. 'Hey Dad, this is new. With you and Christopher and Ben all putting your minds to it, we'll have it all settled in no time.'

Russell smirked. 'Let's hope so,' he said.

Angie made a sound suggesting scepticism. 'Look at

that rain,' she said. Nobody had noticed the thickening cloud over Blencathra, and the slow onset of a fairly heavy downpour. 'You'd better stay the afternoon. Not much sleuthing scope in this, especially with a baby to consider.'

'No,' said Simmy with some reluctance. 'I've got to get back for the dog. I'll go as soon as Robin wakes up.'

It's you. You're the connection. This remark had been made by Moxon two or three times over recent years. Persimmon Petals had delivered flowers to people in crisis, setting events in motion, heightening dramatic feelings and revealing hidden histories. There in the middle of it all was Simmy, innocently carrying out orders as part of work that had initially seemed altogether blameless. But now she was even more centrally involved, perhaps the only person who had spoken to Lindsay Wilson, Pauline Parsons, Eldon Franklin, Howard Isaacs, Sophie Craig and DI Moxon in the space of a few days. If the revelations about Bonnie's origins were added in, that made Simmy even more pivotal. All of which made her feel responsible, and obliged to do everything she could to set things right. At the same time, she was thwarted by Moxon's unusual reluctance to share any of the investigation with her. Even if it wasn't his fault, there was a sense of irritation with him. His air of caution made her uneasy, not so much for her own sake as for his. He gave an impression of expecting something terrible to happen that was unnerving, while at the same time discouraging her from contacting him. Everything he had said and done since Sunday exuded an atmosphere of apprehension and helplessness. He was not his own master and that was awful. He had clearly not wanted to interview her on Sunday, with the outrageous information that she had been accused of murder. He knew it was idiotic; that it made him look ridiculous in his own eyes, if not hers.

All this meant she did not dare try to approach him, after his warnings of the day before. Not only was he apparently not free to speak frankly to her, but he had implied that any clumsy step might jeopardise the investigation and get him into trouble. There was a sense of a delicate balance in Askham, with suspects, witnesses, potential future victims and wary villagers all suspended on a flimsy structure that the police were almost afraid to touch.

Fanciful, Simmy told herself, as this stream of consciousness flowed through her on the drive back to Hartsop. It was half past three, and Robin was wide awake again. His red cheek had subsided and he was in high spirits. If this was the new normal, she allowed herself to entertain plans of leaving him with her parents more often. Perhaps a regular day a week, rising to two when he was a year old. She would go down to the shop and get back into harness, chasing up new business, freshening up her knowledge of more obscure plants, and finding a wider range of work for Bonnie.

Cornelia was impatient for attention, not surprisingly. The rain had not stopped, so any notion of a walk or even a romp in the garden was out of the question. A quick toilet trip outside was all that was on offer. 'Play with Robin,' Simmy told the dog, but somehow neither child nor animal could fix on any satisfactory game. Simmy had to sit on the floor between them, with a ball and a much-chewed rag toy and give herself up to entertaining both her young charges.

Inevitably the phone interrupted after twenty minutes

or so. It was Bonnie, who almost never phoned. She would send a text now and then, but generally waited for Simmy to make the approach.

'Corinne saw you this morning, didn't she?' she began.

'Yes, she did. At Ben's. She's worried about you.'

'I know. She can't let it go. I've just had her here in the shop. She's convinced I'm going to hate her because she never told me about my father and his relations.'

'I thought Ben had persuaded her you don't blame her. You don't, do you?'

'Not at all. But she's driving me mad. Look – I think I need to go and see Sophie again, right away. I do want to meet her girls. My cousins.' She paused. 'That sounds so weird.'

'What does "right away" mean?'

'This evening. As soon as I shut the shop. There's a bus I can get as far as Keswick. And another one that goes to Penrith, which I can get off not too far from Askham. But it's a real hassle and I don't know how I'd get home again.'

'You mean you'd get off at the Rheged place? That must be at least three miles from Askham. Are you intending to walk? In the rain and the dark?'

'I could phone Sophie and ask her to come and get me.'

'It's a crackpot idea,' said Simmy firmly. 'You can't just turn up like that. Wait until the weekend and do it properly.'

'No. It won't wait. Everything's too volatile. You can't understand what it's like, being landed with this stuff out of the blue and then left to deal with it on your own. I can't do it. There's no point in waiting.'

'Corinne will take you there, surely, if it's that important?'

'She's just *been* up there. The car's overheating and one of the brakes is making a nasty noise. Typical, let's face it. She's never any good for a lift – never has been.' Bonnie laughed indulgently. 'She's getting worse, if anything.'

Simmy was trying to convince herself that none of this was actually her problem. Bonnie had not asked her to go with her to see Sophie; nor had she requested a lift. Not directly, anyway. 'Why did you call me about it?' she asked.

'Ben said I should. He thought you might have an idea.'

'Since when have I been the ideas person? That's his job. All I can think is that you'll just have to wait another day or two. If all this is just to get Corinne to calm down, it might not work anyway.'

Bonnie made an exasperated sound and then said, 'There must be some way we can make it work. All these cars and people – you, Chris, your mum and dad, Ben's people – and nobody can figure out a way to get me to Askham. So I'll do it on the bus if I have to, and sleep in the church or pub or somewhere. That means I won't be at the shop tomorrow, though.'

Simmy remembered that she was speaking to a teenager who seldom felt any fear and who lived by the uncompromising tenets she had learnt from Ben Harkness. They had demonstrated that nothing was impossible if you considered all the options and took a few risks. 'You could use your bike,' she said. 'It wouldn't be the first time.'

'I was hoping you wouldn't say that,' came the quick reply.

'Why?'

'It's mean. It would only take you half an hour to get

down here and fetch me, and then the same later on, taking me home.'

'That's two hours driving,' Simmy pointed out.

'So?'

'God, Bonnie – why didn't you just ask me at the start instead of all this nonsense about buses?'

'Is that a yes?'

'Not until you've spoken to Sophie and asked if it's all right with her. She's got plenty to worry about without you foisting yourself on her at a moment's notice.'

'She owes me,' said Bonnie flatly.

Which Simmy could not deny. 'Even so, you've got to phone her. If she agrees, then go and stand where I can see you, in the lay-by at the top of Windermere,' she said. 'At five past five. If Sophie says it's impossible, let me know right away. I'm leaving here at half past four.'

Bonnie would know where she meant. They had used the rendezvous before, avoiding the one-way system through Windermere and saving time. 'Thanks,' she said. 'You won't regret it.'

Robin was not pleased at being bundled into the car again having been hurriedly renappied, and fed with a few swift spoonsful of tepid vegetable mash, made of peas and tomatoes. 'Just enough to keep you going,' his mother told him. She gave Cornelia a similar small meal, an hour before the usual time. 'I might be gone some time,' she warned the dog.

There was just time to text Christopher with minimal information. 'On a rescue mission for Bonnie. Dog had half its supper. Will be back with Robin at some point. Could be late.' It broke a number of rules concerning good mothering, but she felt little guilt on that score. Even less at her failure to make any mention of her husband's supper.

Bonnie was waiting in the drizzle as instructed when Simmy drove into the lay-by five minutes late. 'Sophie's okay with this, then?' Simmy said.

Bonnie flashed a sickly grin and said nothing. She turned round to look at Robin on the back seat, avoiding Simmy's eye.

'Bonnie? You can just get out again if she said not to come.'

'She didn't say that. And you can't waste all this time and fuel for nothing. You're here now. Just drive, okay? It'll be fine.'

The car was still stationary. 'Tell me properly or I promise you, I'll throw you out.'

'She said it was awkward, but she didn't tell me not to come. Not exactly. I think if you're there as well she'll be okay about it.'

Simmy tried to visualise the encounter to come. 'Don't forget Robin. I'll probably just sit outside in the car with him and let you get on with it. If the rain stops I can take him for a little walk or something.'

'The rain won't stop,' Bonnie said. 'Look at it.'

The afternoon had slumped into a thick grey wasteland, with poor visibility and everything dripping wet. The fells had disappeared and a million sheep drooped into depression. 'Isn't this how it should be in November, not October?' said Simmy.

'Huh,' said Bonnie.

'Cheer up. Isn't this what you wanted?' Simmy knew

she was being unfair and impatient, but it had been a long day and she was feeling exploited. Christopher would not take a benign view of this escapade, and Robin shared his father's attitude. 'Talk to Robin, will you? I should have put you in the back to entertain him.'

'I can climb over,' offered the girl, and did so before Simmy could stop her. The agility was prodigious and Simmy wondered if she had ever been so light and flexible at Bonnie's age. 'Hey, Robin – it's me,' the girl chirruped. The child seemed willing to listen to anything she might have to tell him.

The road wound up to Kirkstone, full of traffic as workers made their way home to scattered dwellings between Windermere and Ullswater and tourists searched for somewhere to eat. 'It'll be six before we get there at this rate,' Simmy complained. 'Christopher is not going to like this at all.'

'I hope we can find the house,' said Bonnie. 'Askham's only small, isn't it?'

'You've got the address, I assume?'

'Sort of. It's just the name. They don't have numbers. She said something about a car park. I think I can remember all right.'

'You'd better,' said Simmy darkly.

Chapter Sixteen

Thursday had been very disheartening for Detective Inspector Nolan Moxon. His role was anomalous, to say the least. He was not officially part of the small team investigating the death of Mrs Pauline Parsons, and yet he had been asked to remain at the Penrith station where he could be quickly put to work if necessary. That meant a tortuous drive backwards and forwards from his home in Windermere every day, for no clear purpose. The Senior Investigating Officer was a man called Mark, who was affable and patronising and apparently in possession of confidential information that belonged more appropriately to MI5 than the Cumbrian constabulary. 'This could prove very delicate,' he kept saying. 'It's come right in the middle of another operation, and we have to assume it's connected.' Then he scratched his head, and added that he couldn't actually see any conceivable way in which a woman in her nineties could be linked to the case – which he was not permitted to describe in any detail. Moxon was left to imagine a whole range of criminal activities involving trafficking anything from small boys to forbidden tiger skins. He had initially attempted to force more information out of his superior. 'If it's a genuine police investigation, surely the whole force ought to be informed of it?' he persisted. 'How can it operate otherwise?'

'It's not for me to say. It goes a lot higher up the chain than our little section. All I can tell you is that we've been asked to keep a watchful eye on certain activities not a million miles from here. Now we've got an unlawful killing, we've drawn attention from the Top Brass, and we have to tread very *very* carefully.'

Eventually Moxon understood that Mark himself had not been apprised of the exact nature of the case, which made him feel slightly better. The more he dwelt on Lindsay Wilson and her disgustingly mendacious testimony about Simmy Henderson, the more he concluded that the murder had nothing to do with Mark's secret investigations. It was something about women, resentments and feuds most likely aroused from dormancy by the funeral of Humphrey Craig. Until Simmy herself mentioned that event, no police person had made the slightest connection between it and the death of an old woman. Now it seemed to Moxon that the link was obvious. With Lindsay's disappearance, his conviction merely strengthened. And yet he could give no rational account of it to himself. On the face of it, the facts might well look to support the opposite theory: that old Pauline

Parsons had been involved with something very serious at some point in her life, and needed to be eradicated in case senility kicked in and she inadvertently spilt the beans. It was conceivable that the funeral had alerted her killer to the fact that she was still alive and presented some sort of threat.

But had she actually been at the funeral? On Moxon's repeated advice, the attendance list held by the undertaker had eventually been examined, and no P. Parsons appeared on it. 'Of course, not everybody bothers to give their name,' warned the undertaker. 'And the crowd at the gate were not considered to be actual mourners in any case.'

So much for that, sighed Moxon to himself. More urgently, he was determined to locate Lindsay Wilson. He had no serious concern that she had come to harm – rather she was hiding away because of what she had told the police at the weekend. As a competent adult, she was not even deemed to be officially missing anyway, without any sign of violence or distress. She was free to go where she liked, and had not been requested to keep the police informed of her movements. That, actually, struck him as an oversight. Given that she claimed to have practically witnessed the attack on the old woman, she ought to have been kept in sight much more effectively. He had made notes based on what the Penrith police had told him, but had not actually interviewed her himself. 'She says that florist woman from Windermere did it,' they told him on the phone on Sunday. 'The one you've been involved with a few times. Can you come up and talk to her for us?'

He had taken it all as a joke for far too many minutes. The conversation with Simmy had been agonisingly constrained, due to the limits that had been placed on him. 'Don't tell her any details. Just ask where she was, whether she knows the Parsons lady, what she was doing in Askham in the first place.' Simmy had drawn most of the correct conclusions, of course. She knew almost instantly that she was being accused. She also knew, before ever arriving at the police station, that a woman had been killed, and it was highly likely to be Pauline Parsons.

Subsequently, Moxon had come to see that there were subtle advantages to being an anomaly. It was almost liberating to realise that the investigation into the murder was being left more and more to him and his unorthodox friendships with amateur sleuths. He had been given a set of instructions at the start, and supervised for a few days, but the demands of the mysterious Lowther case, or whatever it was, took virtually every working moment of almost the entire Penrith force – even if very few of them knew exactly what it was they were looking for. Moxon had overheard mutterings about *intercepts* and *surveillance*, which worried him enough to deter him from asking any questions.

He took it upon himself to discover as much as he could about Mrs Parsons. He had interviewed three of her relatives at some length, and spent two hours in the middle of Wednesday conspicuously sitting in the Punchbowl, waiting for nervous individuals to approach him. It had worked reasonably well. He was going to do it again today. He had a foolish superstition that the whole case should be solved by the end of the week. Local interest was already waning, Simmy was under a disgraceful cloud, and Moxon was fed up with the drive every day. He could feel himself losing heart with every passing hour. *One last push*, he told himself sternly, while having very little idea what that might mean in practice.

Lindsay Wilson was crucial, of course. Everything kept coming back to her. And yet none of the people he had spoken to admitted to knowing her other than vaguely by sight. 'That little university woman,' as one man finally identified her. 'She keeps herself to herself mostly,' said another. 'Not healthy, the way she spends all day crouched over that computer,' said a middle-aged neighbour who had once been admitted to Lindsay's home. And yet she was related to the Craigs. Moxon had eventually got round to speaking to Sophie, just that morning, thanks to Simmy's input. Nobody at the Penrith station had alerted him to the death of the builder and his all-consuming funeral last Friday. If there was a connection – and Moxon was now convinced there was – not one police officer had spotted it. It made him despair of the IQ of his colleagues. Having got to know Ben Harkness and his wide-ranging practices when forming theories about a murder, the narrow-focused, rule-following habits of professional detectives was dispiriting. They delved into DNA and forensics, surveillance and known criminals, but seldom really listened to the jumbled testimonies of real people with real knowledge.

Nobody could really think that a known criminal, under the eye of extremely senior investigators, could have whacked a ninety-year-old woman on the head, on a fellside on a Saturday evening. Nobody *did* think that, but they were at a loss as to what to think instead.

Sophie Craig had been pale but lucid. She explained how her husband had done the Hendersons' barn conversion. She accounted for the family link to Lindsay Wilson. 'I

215

don't know her at all, really. She's never been to visit me after the first time when she came here, even though it's about a minute's walk from that house she's renting. We had coffee and established the way we were related, and that was about it. Just a wave if we passed in the street.' Sophie knew Pauline Parsons as a colourful local character, with a story about everybody and a sense of humour that many people found disconcerting. 'She used to make awful jokes about people not being the children of who they think they are – if you see what I mean. Not always from the very distant past, either. Humphrey didn't like her at all.' When asked if she had any notions as to who might want her dead, she said, 'Nearly everybody, I should think.' Which was not helpful.

'What about you?' Moxon asked.

She huffed a mirthless laugh at him. 'Me? I've got other things to worry about than her, haven't I? But if you must know, I'm rather glad she won't be sticking her nose in when we get to know Bonnie Lawson again. She'd be sure to make a real meal about that.'

Moxon's heart thumped. 'Pardon? Did you say Bonnie Lawson?'

'That's right. She lives in Windermere. Works at the flower shop. Oh!' She put a hand to her mouth. 'You know her, of course. I never thought. Well, she's my niece. Her father was – is – my brother. Harrison Lawson. Samantha gave Bonnie his surname, which I thought was crazy, when he never even met her. He scarpered before the baby was born. As they do,' she added crossly. Moxon raised his eyebrows. Her Humphrey had been a famously good husband, as far as he could gather.

'You surprise me,' he said weakly. His brain had frozen; he knew there had to be implications, but he could not grasp any of them. 'Does Bonnie know about this?'

'She does now. I spoke to her yesterday. All thanks to that Verity woman who works there as well. She made the connection not long ago and has been itching to bring us together ever since, apparently. She bumped into me in Windermere and dragged me into the shop. If she goes on like that she'll turn into another Pauline Parsons before long.' She smiled ruefully. 'I suppose they're quite a common type, really.'

'What were you doing in Windermere?' said Moxon, thinking this was about the least relevant question he could have asked. His brain was still seized up.

Sophie narrowed her eyes. 'What does that have to do with anything?'

'Not much,' he admitted. 'You don't have to tell me.'

She leant towards him. 'The police go too far, these days. They stop you in your car and ask where you've been, as if it's any of their business. Humphrey used to fume about it. We can't call our lives our own any more. I've got no problem helping you with finding Pauline's killer, obviously. But I know my rights. I don't have to share the details of my personal life with you. Do I?'

He shook his head, but she hadn't finished.

'But now you're wondering if I was up to something shady. What do I have to hide? Why don't I simply tell you everything I've said and done and seen and thought for the past week? After all, most people put that stuff on the Internet. It's normal these days to live like that. Except that I don't like it, and neither did my husband.'

'You're right,' he said forcefully. 'I actually agree with you completely. I never meant to ask you that and I'm sorry. I'm still stunned by what you've told me about Bonnie.'

She gave him a watery smile. 'You know something? I think you're a very unusual policeman, and I like you.'

I like you too, he wanted to say.

'And I'll tell you why I was in Windermere, even though it has nothing to do with anything. Humphrey's accountant lives there, working from home. I had to go and see her about his finances – as you would expect. Simple as that.'

Moxon shifted on his chair and could think of nothing to say. The woman had lost her husband barely three weeks ago and here he was interrogating her. For a moment he hated himself. If there was more to ask her about the death of Pauline Parsons, it had escaped his mind, so he got to his feet.

'It was nice to meet you,' she said. 'Humphrey would have liked you, too.'

He left, stumbling over uneven ground in the car park on his way to his vehicle. The Craig house was accessed through the somewhat impromptu parking area, the Askham and District Community Centre standing opposite. It had the air of something unfinished, perhaps abandoned. A letter was missing on the Centre's large white sign over the door. He stood looking at it for a minute. An odd shape, painted black with minimal windows, the place struck him as slightly sinister. Then he shook himself – he had been paying too much attention to the mysteries hinted at in Penrith. Any wild notions of secret meetings in this out-of-the-way building should be banished instantly. They might sit well with young Ben Harkness, but Moxon was made of more realistic stuff. Besides – unless it concerned Mrs Pauline Parsons, he actually wasn't even interested.

It was time to take up his post at the pub again. He was not especially hungry, but ordered a ploughman's and a pint of draught ale, which he would make last as long as he could. The girl working at the bar nodded in recognition and smiled. On the previous day he had asked her a few questions about Mrs Parsons; enough to alert her to his role. 'I won't make any waves,' he had assured her. 'Just sit here quietly and see who shows up.' In the event, three people had sidled up to him and said they'd heard he was looking into the old lady's death. One had asked why there was no incident room in the village. 'Just assume this is it,' Moxon had grinned. 'We're a bit short-staffed at the moment.'

The would-be informants had little to add to what he already knew. Pauline Parsons was a matriarch with numerous grandchildren and great-grandchildren. She was of the fourth or fifth generation of Askham locals, and had connections to just about everybody. Had anything happened recently that might explain what had befallen her? Not that anyone could think of. A woman mentioned that there was a superstitious expectation of a third death. 'These things always go in threes,' she insisted. 'Everybody knows that.' Moxon made no promises, thinking there could well be a road accident or a natural death in the neighbourhood, but merely said, 'Let's hope not, then.'

The name of Eldon Franklin occurred twice. 'He was close to his gran,' Moxon was told. 'He's been all over the place since Sunday, drinking too much and shouting his mouth off. When someone told him that florist had been seen behaving suspiciously, he was all for accosting her. She was here yesterday, with her husband and baby, and he gave her the edge of his tongue.'

It came as an unpleasant shock to hear that Simmy was widely known in Askham as a possible suspect. 'Not that it would make a lot of sense,' said the person speaking. 'Most likely it was all a mistake. There was a thick old mist up here on Saturday, don't forget. Funny weather, that day. Started with a chilly wind, and then the mist just rolled in, all in a couple of minutes. Must have caught a few walkers by surprise, I shouldn't wonder.' This was yet another detail that the police had failed to register. Every fell had its own micro-climate, or so it often seemed. It could be impossibly foggy in one place and perfectly clear five miles away. Penrith, home to most of its police force, had not seen any mist that day. It therefore stood to reason that visibility had been perfectly good everywhere.

It was perhaps a blessing that Ben Harkness was out of action, if violent grandsons were on the loose. And yet Moxon missed him. The boy was a genius at assembling small details, constructing flowcharts and compiling eccentric 'dossiers' describing every individual who might qualify as a suspect, however remotely. He would send Simmy and Bonnie out for informal chats with relevant persons and snatch at their findings, putting them into his composite picture. At least, that was what Moxon believed Ben was doing. The actual process was never completely revealed to him. The first he knew was often a presentation of a miraculously logical analysis of what had happened and why, and who did it. When the boy went off to study forensic anthropology at Newcastle, Moxon had felt a powerful personal satisfaction. He had not yet quite recovered from his disappointment when it all went wrong.

Now, on his second session at representing the entire police investigation, he again waited for volunteers to step forward and tell him things he could never hope to glean in any other way. He doodled in his notebook, trying to establish a comprehensive list of individuals connected to his quest. The undertaker's list of mourners at Humphrey Craig's funeral had worried him. There had been sixty names, which had to be a hefty proportion of permanent Askham residents, with some from further-flung villages and towns. There were no addresses. And the undertaker had pointed out that another dozen or two had lingered out in the road, a kind of second division who knew who the Craigs were, but had no direct claim to be actual friends. 'Anomalies like me,' Moxon muttered to himself.

It was twenty past one before anything happened. Then a man with a beard approached, one eyebrow raised under dark curly hair. He held out a hand and said, 'Howard Isaacs. You'll be the detective bloke.'

Moxon took the hand and introduced himself. The name was familiar from his repeated scrutiny of the mourners list. He waved the man to the chair waiting for just such a person. 'Drink?' he offered.

'I've got one coming, thanks. The young lady said she'd bring it over.'

Moxon indulged in a spot of old-fashioned detecting. The man did not know the barmaid's name, therefore he did not frequent this pub. The conclusion did not feel very significant.

'You might know that I paid a visit to your friend Mrs

Henderson on Monday,' Isaacs began. 'Given that she's got herself tangled up in this business with old Mrs P, I thought I ought to come and clarify that if I can.'

'Er . . .' said Moxon, feeling painfully unprofessional. 'No, I didn't know that. I have barely spoken to her, as it happens. Just a quick visit the other night.'

Isaacs nodded. 'She didn't do it, obviously.'

'Why do you say that?'

'Well – look at her! Why would she? New house, new baby, happy marriage, thriving business. She must score ten out of ten for a contented life and not a worry in the world.'

It was a new view on a woman for whom Moxon felt a profound affection. In his direct experience she had had quite a lot of worries in recent years, and a catastrophic tragedy before that. 'I suppose there's always something,' he said vaguely.

'I admit she did seem somewhat *tense* when I called on her. Upset about poor Humphrey, of course.'

'Why *did* you call on her?'

'Oh – I had some idea of using the conversion in a publicity exercise, keeping the building business running, for the sake of the lads who worked with Humphrey. I still think we can do it – if I lend them some cash to keep it afloat and maybe wheel in someone who can carry a bit of heft. There's always work for builders, after all. And Sophie can't just be left to sink or swim, can she?'

Moxon sighed. 'How does this fit with the death of Mrs Parsons?'

'I doubt if it does – but you never know, do you? Look at the timing. The way the whole place has been shaken up by what happened to Humphrey. All sorts of stuff's going to fall out of the woodwork because of that. I'm a builder myself, in case you hadn't realised. We're a bit like florists, if you think about it. We stumble across people's secrets, hear their phone calls, see what's in their houses. And Humphrey was a friendly chap, always going the extra mile, blurring the boundaries, as they say.'

'Yes, but . . .' Moxon was out of his depth. Was this person a quiet philanthropist or a determined mischief-maker? 'You don't look like a builder,' he said idiotically.

'That's exactly what Simmy Henderson said. She thought my hands were too clean, I think.' He spread his flawless fingers, with short perfect nails, and waggled them. 'I've been more at the admin end these past ten years or so,' he admitted with a laugh.

The man's defence of Simmy had been endearing but not especially meaningful. Nothing that would hold up in court. But it would never come to that. Not one single person thought it would. Even Lindsay Wilson must know that she'd committed a major mistake in naming such an unlikely killer. A mistake or a wicked calumny.

'Do you know a Ms Lindsay Wilson?' he asked Isaacs, almost at random.

'Who?'

'She lives here in the village. Related in some way to the Craigs. Very much in the middle of things.'

'Oh! The name doesn't ring any bells. I don't live here, you know.'

Moxon toyed with his notebook. 'If you're here to give me some relevant testimony, I should have your contact details,' he said.

'I'm not, though, am I? I just wanted to show my face,

223

so you won't have any doubts about me. It crossed my mind that nice Mrs Henderson could have got me wrong, and said something damaging about me. Looks as if I was worrying for nothing.' He cocked his head, trying to appear disingenuous. 'Reputation is everything in my line of work. You see that, don't you?'

'I do,' said Moxon, who thought he probably did. Here was a self-made man, an entrepreneur who had grasped the financial opportunities in the building trade and perhaps set up a number of apparently independent businesses under his nebulous umbrella. None of that need imply dishonesty or dodgy manipulations. But what mattered most was his reputation – hence the philanthropy. 'Well, thank you for taking the trouble to talk to me.'

'Looks as if I'm your only catch today. The whole thing's already fading into the background, isn't it? Disconcerting the way that happens.' He drained the drink that had been gently placed at his elbow five minutes earlier. 'Well, best get on, then. I don't envy you, I have to say. Not that I think there's much mileage in the death of the old lady, but the ghastly business with Humphrey has made a mess that we'll not see the end of for a time. His family life wasn't always straightforward, you know. Well – whose is? Teenage girls are never easy, are they? Sophie's a clever woman, though. She'll land on her feet, with a bit of help from the likes of me.' He winked and Moxon's heart thumped. Men were not supposed to behave like this any more.

'I can't say,' Moxon evaded.

'No. Well. No suggestion of foul play with that one. And this won't be your usual patch, as I understand it?'

Moxon squared his shoulders and tried to recapture the

high ground. He should insist on having the man's address, for a start. But it was too late to do that easily. His emphasis on the wrong death made the encounter feel more like a social chat than a police interview. 'Well, thanks,' he said. His own lunch had been consumed long ago. 'I can't see much point in hanging on here. Let me know if you think of anything else that might be helpful.' He handed the man a card. 'My mobile number's on there.'

'Course it is,' said Howard Isaacs.

The next hour or so proceeded unprofitably, with Moxon spending much of it in his stationary car, making idle notes and trying to think logically. At three o'clock he gave in to an impulse that had been growing stronger every day since Sunday. He phoned Ben Harkness and asked if he could come and see him.

Chapter Seventeen

'Ben knows we're doing this, I assume?' said Simmy, as they followed a slow procession of vehicles across the more northern realms of Cumbria. 'We should have stuck to the main roads,' she realised belatedly, as they crawled through the Kirkstone Pass. 'It's much further, but would have been quicker.'

'Yes, Ben knows everything. I'm not sure about this being slower, actually. Grasmere to Keswick can take ages, even though it's a better road.' Bonnie spoke from several months' experience, since Ben acquired his car and the route became increasingly familiar to the young pair.

'It's the worst possible time to turn up at a person's house, you know. I can't even cope with a phone call at this point in the day.'

'You've got a baby,' Bonnie pointed out. 'It's not the same.'

'Even so. Does she expect us to want food?' Simmy was feeling more and more nervous as Askham came closer. Askham had acquired a menacing aura for her since Tuesday. If she and Robin were required to amuse themselves while Bonnie got to know her new-found relatives, where would they go?

'She'll want you to come in,' said Bonnie decisively. 'Anybody would. The girls can play with Robin and you can mop me up if I get weepy.'

'Is that going to happen?'

'It might. It's a very emotional situation. For a start, I'm really sad I didn't get to know Humphrey. And they'll be all over the place because he's only been dead a few weeks.'

'Right. This is all Verity's fault,' Simmy said crossly. 'She's forced the whole issue.'

'She didn't mean to, I suppose. She's just a busybody who likes to think she knows everything about everyone. Her own life's pretty dull. She thinks she's got dozens of friends, but I doubt if any of them really likes her much.'

'Oh dear,' sighed Simmy, reproaching herself for the hundredth time for foisting the woman onto poor Bonnie.

'Can't be helped,' said the girl, as she generally did. 'And you must admit there's a chance I never would have met Sophie at all if Verity hadn't taken charge. I might have moved away and married Ben and never thought about my father at all.'

'You would have needed his name for your marriage certificate,' said Simmy. 'Come to think of it, I'm surprised Ben hasn't tracked him down long before now. He must have been curious. Where did you think your surname came from?'

'It never occurred to me to wonder. I have a hunch Corinne warned Ben not to go there, when we first got together. He would have thought there'd come a time when we could just ask her. She might be sloppy with paperwork, but there's got to be some official stuff tucked away somewhere. And if I really try, I can remember quite a lot. I was six before Corinne had me permanently. That's quite old, really.'

Robin chirped, as if in confirmation of this assertion, and both women laughed.

They found the house with little bother. The name was on the gate and there were lights on in the two front windows. Sophie evidently assumed that Simmy and Robin were part of the package and ushered them all in with a good grace. 'I hope this is okay?' said Bonnie, in a small voice. 'It must seem like a bit of a panic to you, dashing up here so soon.'

'Making up for lost time,' Sophie smiled. 'No sense in leaving it, is there? Although you might have to give my girls a bit of time. They're still trying to get to grips with losing their dad.'

There was no sign of Chloe or Berta in the open plan ground floor rooms. A living area connected to a space that was clearly used for eating, homework, crafts and general mess. There was a schoolbag on the big table, as well as a piece of needlework and a lot of papers. Sophie indicated the sofa in the sitting area and the two sat down, with Robin on Simmy's lap. 'They break up for half-term tomorrow,' sighed Sophie. 'I'll have to amuse them for a week.'

Conversation was slow to get started. Without Bonnie's cousins, there seemed to be less purpose to the visit. Sophie offered hot drinks, biscuits – even cheese and fruit – but was plainly not planning to embark on a full-scale meal. Outside it was almost dark. 'So where *are* the girls?' Bonnie finally asked.

'Actually, they're both upstairs. I told them they had to be sociable and come down to talk to you, but I can't promise they will. It's really Chloe that's the problem. Berta just tags along and does whatever her sister does.'

'I saw them at the funeral,' Simmy offered. 'It must have been dreadful for them.'

'And you,' said Bonnie.

'That whole weekend was a nightmare. Do you know – people still bring food at times like this? I thought it was mainly an American thing, but evidently they do it here as well. Even Lindsay Wilson turned up with a box of flapjack she'd made. I ask you – flapjack!'

Simmy was careful to maintain a bland expression. 'Could be worse, I suppose.'

'She probably thinks it's comfort food. One woman I barely even know almost threw a massive lamb casserole at me on the doorstep. You have to wonder what people like that are thinking. She said she had a lot to thank Humphrey for and didn't know what else to do. Sweet, in a way. But both the girls are vegetarian. I split it into about six portions and froze them. I mean – you can't just throw good food away, can you? And she wanted the dish back.'

'So you'll eat it yourself, will you?' said Bonnie.

'Probably. It was meant kindly, and I do admit it's nice not to have to worry about shopping and cooking for a bit.

It was just such a surprise. Like the way so many people were at the funeral. As far as I knew, Humph was just a normal builder, getting on with it. I never saw anything special about him – that sounds bad, doesn't it? He was a decent husband, doing his best as a father, lending a hand around the village. Nothing special,' she repeated, with a faraway expression. 'That policeman reminded me of him, funnily enough. The one from Windermere who looks as if he's running the whole investigation into who killed Pauline Parsons. He could have been Humph's brother, the way he walks and listens as if he's really interested.'

'That sounds quite special to me,' said Simmy, recognising the description of Moxon and feeling embarrassingly moved by it. She hugged Robin to her, like a shield.

'When did you see him?' asked Bonnie with a frown.

'Oh – he came here this morning. I can't really remember what he said, but I thought he was nice. I assumed he was just going round the whole place asking if we could shed any light on what happened to Pauline. He sounded as if he was running out of ideas.' She looked at Simmy. 'You've helped him a few times with nasty murders, haven't you? Humphrey found all that stuff fascinating. But he said you never really talked to him about it.'

'That's right,' Simmy agreed. 'I don't think the subject ever arose. He was ever so good with Robin, though.'

'Oh, well,' said Sophie, with an ominous sniff. The emotion that Bonnie had predicted was gathering strength. Simmy could feel a familiar sensation at the back of her nose, as she remembered the friendly builder. Bonnie herself had all kinds of reasons for becoming weepy. Didn't long-lost relatives always cry on each other?

'I really do want to see the girls,' said Bonnie. 'That's mostly why I came.'

Sophie went pink and glanced at Simmy. 'I know you do. Obviously you do. The thing is – you might not know there's a local Facebook group for Askham and there's been all sorts of silly talk about who might have killed Pauline. And . . . well . . .'

Simmy interrupted her. 'I know. I get it. My name's on there. It's me that's keeping the girls away. Although . . .'

'It's not that simple, but you've got the idea. They know their dad was at your house a lot, and somehow it's got all mixed up in their heads.'

Bonnie was first to draw a very unpleasant conclusion. 'You don't mean they think she really did kill Pauline?'

Sophie heaved a deep sigh. 'Who knows what they think? As far as I can see, Chloe's trying to protect her sister somehow. There's an added complication, to do with Chloe's friend Scarlett. She's ill and everybody's in a state about that.'

'Scarlett?' Simmy repeated. 'Isn't she Pauline Parsons' granddaughter?'

The atmosphere changed in a second. Sophie's eyes flashed a range of reactions: suspicion, shock and something that looked like *I-knew-it-all-along*. 'Great-granddaughter, as it happens. Seems you don't know everything, after all.'

'I should go,' said Simmy, before things could get more acrimonious. 'I'm very much in the way. It's just that somebody had to bring Bonnie . . .' She gripped her child even harder and prepared to get off the sofa.

Bonnie stood up first. 'This is completely my fault. I don't know what made me so desperate to come and see you. I should have waited. Ben should be with me. It was mainly Corinne, I suppose . . .' She tailed off, unequal to the task of explaining herself.

Sophie's focus remained on Simmy. 'I really don't know what to make of you. Humphrey thought you were the bee's knees. Always talking about you. So kind and sweet, such a good mother, too good for your husband, he said that as well. But a clever businesswoman, keeping up with the shop on the computer, with the baby only a month old. And always in the papers, solving murders for that detective, with your young friends.' Finally, she turned to Bonnie. 'The truth is, we were a bit scared to approach you, with everything you've been doing the past year or two and the people you mixed with. I'm nobody special, no great asset in anybody's family. Stay-at-home mother, and couldn't even make a decent job of that. Your Corinne made it look so easy.'

She paused for breath, but it was clear she hadn't finished. 'I'm still scared of you now. *Both* of you. I'm not clever like you. All I know is my husband chopped himself in pieces with a chainsaw – probably because he saw a long-tailed tit or heard a chiff-chaff and forgot what he was doing. And now I'm left with these bloody girls, to manage the best I can.'

Robin stared round at the three female faces, all of them creased and wet. Not to be outdone, he emitted a hearty wail, twisting and pushing in his mother's arms.

Like magic, the two invisible girls upstairs suddenly materialised. 'It's a baby,' said the smaller one wonderingly. 'It's crying.'

'So is Mum,' said her sister. 'What's going on?'

232

'What do you think?'

Bonnie moved towards them. 'Chloe. Berta,' she said. 'Hello. I'm your cousin.'

'Yes, we know,' said Berta. She was a solid twelve-year-old with a defiant expression and impressive self-confidence. She stood just in front of her tall older sister, as if defending her. 'You look like Mum. We don't. That's quite funny, isn't it?'

'And this is Dad's favourite customer,' said Chloe, looking at Simmy with something close to a sneer.

Simmy jiggled Robin and tried to persuade herself that there was nothing to panic about. Sophie's angry words about Humphrey had been nothing more than the dumping of bad feelings arising from her bereavement. She had every reason to envy the woman her husband had admired, after all. Simmy's sudden tears had sprung from her own sense of tragedy at Humphrey's death. Whatever accusations might be thrown at her, they paled into insignificance when the reality of the accident was brought into focus. And yet, they had hurt. They were unfair, untrue, unfriendly. And now here was a teenage girl with the same disagreeable emotions on her face.

'I'll go,' she said again. 'Don't worry about me. The baby's not going to settle unless I walk him around outside. Come and find me when you're done, Bonnie – okay? I'll phone Christopher and tell him where I am.'

They let her go with very little sign of concern. She had been an intruder from the start and even Bonnie would benefit from her departure. Nobody pointed out that it was dark and damp outside, which was not conducive to walking a baby around. Robin was hungry and worried.

Nothing was as usual, and he did like his routines. Where was his supper? And when was he going to have his lovely snuggly bedtime feed from his mother, who could not quite bring herself to wean him completely?

'Hey,' she whispered to him. 'Let's pretend it's bedtime now.' She got into the back seat of her car and hoped nobody could see them. Not quite able to believe his luck, Robin eagerly grabbed the reassuringly familiar food source, and slumped into a blissful state of near-catatonia within seconds.

Simmy herself was half-asleep when a gentle tapping brought her back to wakefulness. A man's face was peering through the window, comically revealing embarrassment, reassurance and hesitancy.

Chapter Eighteen

It was Moxon, materialising rather as Chloe and Berta had done a few minutes earlier. Simmy pulled her jacket over the baby's head, and tried to open the car window. Since the ignition was off, nothing happened. 'Open the door,' she mouthed at him. He obeyed tentatively, the hesitancy dominating his other feelings.

'Sorry,' he said. 'I never thought you'd have the baby with you.'

'You knew I was here?' She was still not quite awake. 'How?'

'Ben told me. Are you waiting for Bonnie?'

'Why are you here? It's nothing to do with the police. Is something happening?' She fumbled with her clothes, detaching Robin and putting him on the seat beside her.

'We're completely disorganised, as you can see.'

'Looks pretty normal to me,' he said, keeping his eyes firmly on her face as she reassembled herself.

'But why are you here?' she asked again more loudly.

'No special reason. Ben told me about Bonnie and the Craigs, and how he wished he could be with her, but that you would make sure it would all be all right. But when I saw you were in the car, I thought there might be a problem.'

She wondered whether it was her hearing or logical processes that were at fault, since Moxon's reply had made no sense at all. 'That doesn't explain anything,' she protested. 'Why were you speaking to Ben? What did he tell you? Haven't you already been here once today, talking to Sophie? Isn't it time you went home? And what does Bonnie's personal life have to do with anything anyway?'

'I am going home. I just came round this way on a whim. I'm not really being a policeman for the moment.' He was still standing beside the car, in shadow, so his features were unclear. As he spoke, he seemed to take another step or two away and turn his gaze on the Craigs' house. 'I had a funny sort of hunch, which I can't explain logically. It has to be stressful for Bonnie – so why are you in the car?'

'They don't trust me,' said Simmy flatly. 'Thanks to bloody Facebook.'

'You're not telling me they think you really did kill the old lady?'

'You can't blame them. More than that, it sounds as if Sophie's been feeling jealous of me ever since Humphrey

236

started work on the house. He must have sung my praises to her and been horribly tactless doing it.'

Moxon's eyebrows went up, but he found nothing to say.

'Now Bonnie's got caught up with it all, and it's obviously not going to be smooth sailing for her. I was just making everything worse, so I came out here.'

'Would you like me to go and get Bonnie for you? It's not right for you to be sitting in the cold. Have you got to take her all the way back to Windermere?'

Enlightenment dawned. 'Oh! *That's* why you're here. You and Ben hatched it up between you. How sweet!'

'I don't know what you mean,' he said with a chuckle. The light from one of the houses caught his eyes, just as he made an elaborate wink.

'I suppose it is on your way. She can walk from your house, so you wouldn't have to drive one extra yard.'

'Right then,' he said. 'So you can go now, if you like. That'll give her no options.'

'She could stay the night. But then she wouldn't be able to get to work tomorrow, so she won't do that.' Simmy was feeling drowsy again, exhausted by the never-ending logistical considerations that rural life made necessary. 'Can I really go? What time is it?'

'Five to seven. You'll be hungry.'

'I am. Thanks.' She wanted to say his name, but had never once done so. What would she call him? Nolan? Detective? Neither was remotely possible. 'I expect I'll see you again soon.'

'You will.'

* * *

237

She drove back through the little lanes, Robin strapped into his seat, trying to stay awake so as to express his opinion of this disgracefully aberrant evening. Simmy turned the radio on loud, drowning the baby's protests with Radio Two. As she got closer to Hartsop, it was her husband's complaints she began to worry about, much more than her little son's.

The brightest and warmest element of the day had been Moxon's gallantry. Thinking of her convenience while trying to conceal the extent of his benevolence, he came over as almost incredibly kind. She brushed aside questions concerning his reasons for speaking to Ben that afternoon, his progress on the murder investigation and his impressions of Sophie Craig. All that would become clear soon enough. The revelations involving Bonnie would have to be dealt with in the coming days, as well. If Sophie and her daughters continued to be hostile towards Simmy, that would be awkward.

And far behind all this, in a small corner of her mind, was the figure of Lindsay Wilson, who created a new mystery every day, or so it seemed.

Christopher was resigned and not in the least reproachful. When she tried to give a clear account of herself, he simply said, 'You didn't have much choice, then, did you? No harm done. We should be grateful to Moxon for coming to the rescue. Robin seems to have survived it all, even if his routine is in shreds.'

'I won't do it again,' she said, making the promise more to herself than to him. 'It was pretty silly all along. It could easily have waited for the weekend. I have a hunch that

Corinne was behind it. She's the most worked up of them all. Did I tell you she came to Ben's this morning in a right old state?'

Christopher waved this away. 'No more. We've got ourselves into a whole shoal of red herrings, when we really need to focus on the murder. And even that can wait a day or two. I made us one of my risottos. It's got prawns, mushrooms and spam in it.'

'Pardon?'

'Joking. It's a thing that's going round at work. Everybody says "spam" all the time. Simple pleasures. It's driving me mad, but I seem to have caught the bug.'

'Is Ben going to work tomorrow?'

'He says he is. We'll take it slowly and see how much he can manage to do. I can find him plenty of admin, I expect. Making lists, answering the phone, and so forth. There's always more to be done with the website, as well.'

Simmy felt a pang of envy at the busy variety that went on every day at the auction house. She was starting to miss the social side of her own work, with unpredictable customers appearing at unpredictable moments with unpredictable requests. The man who wanted to buy a wreath made entirely of holly; the young girl who wanted a black tulip in October for a Halloween event. The weddings and the funerals and the mystery trips to remote farms for a delivery. She sighed.

'What?' said Christopher.

'Oh, nothing. I just remembered how much I enjoy the world of work.'

He rolled his eyes. 'You women – never satisfied.'

239

'Robin would agree with you. Although – did I tell you what fun he was having in Threlkeld today? My mother didn't want to give him back.'

'I guess there's a lot you haven't told me about today. Eat your risotto and then I'll debrief you. Will Robin have some?'

'I'm sure he'd find spam perfectly delicious,' she said.

By half past eight, they were snuggled on the sofa and Robin was peacefully asleep upstairs. Cornelia was on her master's lap, having made it clear to him that she had not enjoyed a good day. 'I forgot all about her,' Simmy confessed. 'But I really can't be taking her everywhere with me, can I?'

'She can come to work with me when she's a bit more grown up. She'll be an asset.'

Simmy was unsure as to whether to believe that this would actually happen. The animal would get under people's feet as they carried valuable antiques, and perhaps cause friction if anyone in the team was antagonistic towards dogs. 'That'll be good,' she said. 'Because she can't come with me to the shop.'

At ten to nine, Simmy's phone jingled. 'Don't answer it,' said Christopher, before she could read the caller's name.

'It's Dad. I'll have to.'

'Are you still up?' asked Russell.

'Just about.'

'So listen. I finished *Dombey and Son*. And I think there has to be some sort of clue about the Wilson woman and the game she's playing.'

'All right. Try me.'

'I can't work out any details, but the whole plot

240

involves families and old resentments and an awful person called Carker. I could easily see someone getting much too deeply into it and trying to make real life somehow resemble it. You told me yourself that she said Mrs Parsons was like Good Mrs Brown. That just shows how obsessed she is.'

'It's terribly speculative. You can't run a murder investigation according to the plot of a Victorian novel.'

'I know. But I'm *sure* there are clues in it somewhere. The whole thing is so rich and dense and *passionate*. Do you think Lindsay Wilson might have a child that nobody knows about, and she's stricken with guilt at how she treats it, and Mrs Parsons made it all worse? Maybe the father is part of her family—'

'Dad – we could go on like this all night and it wouldn't get us anywhere. You're right that Lindsay might well be playing some sort of game, and it's perfectly possible that she's got fact and fiction all confused – but we must have evidence. Ben's the person we need for that. He's got all sorts of information about the Parsons family, which I suppose the police have found as well. I haven't told you any of it. There are probably in-laws and cousins all over the village who know Lindsay and might well have upset her. But she's gone off somewhere, so nobody can ask her anything.'

'And what about you? Are you still under suspicion?'

'Around Askham I am, yes. And I suppose technically the police have to take notice of what Lindsay said – which I still don't know exactly. But I don't feel very worried about it. I saw Moxon this evening. He's being very sweet and reassuring, but he's still not telling me anything specific.'

241

'Did he come to the house?'

'No. It was in Askham.' She gave him a brief summary, aware that she was leaving out far too much. Her father was never going to be an active participant in any unofficial investigations, despite his wishes. He had been there on Sunday when everything had taken off, and that made him want to participate in the ensuing detective work. He had seized on the Dickens novel as one way of getting involved. He was doing his best to understand the story, and learn all relevant names and facts. Simmy was not playing fair with him by failing to convey every detail. 'Sorry, Dad,' she concluded. 'I'm too tired to remember everything now. Let's sleep on it, and start again tomorrow.'

'If you say so,' he accepted meekly.

'Poor old Dad,' she sighed to Christopher. 'He's so keen to clear my name. He must have been sitting with that book ever since I left. It's seven hundred pages.'

'I expect he skimmed some of it.'

'He wouldn't do that. He says it has to have some clues to the murder in it. I very much doubt if he's right.'

'Of course he's not right,' said Christopher.

Simmy awoke on Friday morning when it was still dark, and the name *Eldon* was echoing inside her head, the last remnants of a dream. As she muzzily surfaced, she acknowledged her own insight – that man was by far the most like a murderer of any she had met in the past few days. Followed, perhaps, by Howard Isaacs, the soft-handed builder. But then she snagged an awkward thread of logic that made her think again. Eldon had been hostile and accusing in the pub on Tuesday and unless that was all a deliberate act to impress the other drinkers, it had to mean that he did not kill his granny. Perhaps the murky dream which had flown away completely had been trying to tell her that Eldon Franklin might well be the ideal person to talk to. Which would mean that Ben had been right in wanting to go to Askham the day before. Having Ben's company would have made the prospect of confronting the man very much less fearsome. Now it was too late because Ben was going to work. The only person who would be more than willing to go with her was her father.

'I think I'll see if Dad will come with me to Askham today,' she said to Christopher, who was even less awake than she was.

'Oh?'

'Sorry. I didn't mean to say that out loud. Now I've woken Robin up.' The baby's acute hearing had registered parental voices and was calling out his wish to join in. 'Coming, kiddo!' Simmy sang out.

Half an hour later Christopher said, 'You're not really going to Askham again, are you? What for?'

'I've been thinking about that Eldon man – the one in the pub. He seems to be quite important, on reflection. Ben wanted us to go there yesterday afternoon, but I thought I should go and get Robin, and then it was all too late. And I didn't want to go anyway. Ironically, Bonnie made me take her after all. So now I've had second thoughts, but I don't think I can face him on my own, so I could ask Dad to come as moral support. He'll be thrilled. Mum can have Robin.'

'And Cornelia?'

'Probably not. She's too young still. She'll just be a pest.'

'Poor doggy,' he said daftly. 'Let's go for a quick sprint up to the car park and back, then,' he consoled his pet. 'Tomorrow we'll go for a proper long walk – and again the next day.'

Cornelia lavishly expressed her gratitude and Christopher forgot all about his wife's intentions for the day.

When Simmy phoned her father with her idea, he raised a number of objections. 'How are we going to find him? Surely he doesn't spend his entire life in the pub? What are we going to say to him? What time do you want to leave? Your mother has something on this afternoon. I think she's out for lunch as well.'

Simmy held her ground, and they agreed to aim to be in Askham for half past ten. Simmy would drop Robin off and be certain to collect him again by midday. 'Eldon works at Askham Hall,' she remembered. 'And that's just across the road from the pub where I saw him on Tuesday. We're sure to be able to find him.'

'I believe you,' said Russell, reminding her that he was taking a great deal on trust. 'But you're going to have to talk fast in the car, because there's an awful lot I don't understand.'

'Don't worry, I will. It'll help me to go over it all again, anyway.'

She was out of the house soon after nine, with Robin in a blessedly co-operative mood. Rather than having been deterred by the strange events of the previous evening, he seemed to associate the car with variety, society and even perhaps an unscheduled feed from his mother's breast, which he suspected might be shortly to cease entirely. Officially they were down to one bedtime session, which was getting briefer by the day.

Being left with his grandmother was not what he had expected, especially the hurried way he was deposited and then ignored in favour of his grandpa. *Hang on a minute!* he wanted to shout. *Can we do this properly?* Angie was equally disconcerted. 'What's the rush?' she wanted to know.

'We need to be back, so you can go out for your lunch party,' Simmy said. 'It's all going to be a bit tight. We don't know how long it'll take to find Eldon.'

'Don't try to explain. And it's not a lunch *party*. It's a lunchtime meeting of the Conservation people I foolishly said I would support. I'm only going so they don't put me down for bramble clearance.'

'Or squirrel slaughtering,' added Russell with a wry smile. He had taken a perverse position on the squirrel situation in the Lake District. Grey squirrels were exterminated ruthlessly, in an attempt to clear the way for a return of the reds. Russell called it 'genocide' and made all the noise he could about it.

'I keep trying to tell them that the most effective way to give nature a chance is to just step back and do nothing, but nobody will listen,' sighed Angie. 'And I do agree that bracken is an abomination. I don't mind spending a morning attacking some of that.'

'So we've got to go,' Simmy insisted. Her sense of urgency was hard to explain, but it was growing stronger all the time. 'It's a week since Humphrey's funeral now. If this goes on much longer, I don't think they'll ever find whoever killed Pauline Parsons.'

'If it was this Eldon man, we might regret confronting him,' said Russell.

'We might anyway, but I don't think it can have been him. I know it's probably crazy, but I just think he might be able to fill in a few gaps. He might even know what Lindsay told the police about me.'

'Didn't you say she'd gone missing?'

'That's what Moxon told me, yes.'

'So maybe this man knows where she is, as well.'

'Maybe he does,' smiled Simmy.

Chapter Nineteen

They left the car in the road that ran down to the church and the river, and walked up the driveway into the grounds of Askham Hall. 'It's a hotel,' said Simmy. 'We can pretend to be enquiring about an event, if anybody stops us.'

'These gardens used to be open for anyone to walk in,' said Russell. 'But look at this.' He pointed to a board on which was written the news that the gardens were only open for hotel residents. 'That's a shame.'

'It is,' she agreed. 'I could also see if they'd be interested in some regular flower displays, although it would be a long way to bring them. I did it in Hawkshead for ages, before it all got too difficult with Robin.'

'We've got all the cover story we need. Let's just have a look for your man. That's not him, is it?' He pointed to a figure spreading mulch over a rose bed, close to the Hall itself.

'I'm afraid not. We can ask that one where he is, though.'

The young gardener showed no surprise at their request and pointed to a stone wall beyond the building. 'He might be over there,' he said. 'Part of the wall needs patching up.'

Eldon Franklin was readily located at the far end of the wall in question. Stones of various shapes were scattered on the ground, along with a quantity of dry sandy soil and tufts of moss. Russell stared at it. 'What happened?' he asked.

'Dirty great charabanc bashed into it last week. Trying to turn round, the idiot. Look at this mess!' The wall itself was noticeably injured at the point where it ended and an upright wooden gatepost took over. The post was askew and the gate had been unhung.

Russell tutted in sympathy and Simmy began to relax. Eldon wasn't as bad as she'd feared, after all. But then he looked at her properly and realised who she was. 'You!' he spat. 'What do you want?'

She took a deep breath and delivered a little speech she had prepared in the car. 'Listen – can we start on the assumption that neither of us killed your grandmother? It looks as if there are people around who suspect us both, so we're kind of in the same boat. This is my father. He was at Humphrey's funeral last week. Will you get into trouble if you talk to us for a bit?'

Eldon shrugged. 'Doubt it. As long as I get the job done, nobody's watching the clock.'

'Skilled work,' said Russell admiringly.

'Not so much. Common sense. So long as you keep

it straight, it's easy enough.' He looked at Simmy again, shifting from one foot to the other, as if making a difficult decision. 'What's there to talk about?'

What do you think? she wanted to shout, but instead she kept a calm voice as she replied. 'I want you to help clear my name. You live here in Askham. You know all the people – Pauline's family and neighbours. You probably know the person who killed her, even if you haven't got any suspicions . . .'

'Oh, I've got suspicions right enough.' He scowled at her.

'You mean me? Because of what Lindsay Wilson said? But the police don't believe her, you know. What earthly reason could I have had to do such a thing? I only met the woman once.'

'Lindsay doesn't tell lies.'

'Then she made a mistake. Someone told me it was foggy up here on Saturday evening. Whatever she thought she saw must have been very indistinct. I absolutely promise you, on my baby's life, that I did not kill Pauline Parsons. Do you believe me?'

He made no direct response, but said, 'Is someone saying I did it, then?'

'Well . . .' She looked at Russell. 'Your name has been mentioned now and then.' This was stretching the truth considerably. The only person she knew who had even registered Eldon as of any relevance was Ben Harkness.

Her father chipped in. 'You know what people are like. They'll slander anybody at a time like this. But the idea can stick, especially if the rightful villain isn't caught. You'll be getting funny looks for years to come.'

Eldon's chest swelled in indignation. 'All because I had a few drinks too many,' he protested. 'I was right fond of my nanna, let me tell you. Spent all my summers at hers when I was small. We're a tight family, watching each other's backs. If you're thinking one of us did her in, then you're barmy.'

'So what does the family think happened? How did she get all the way up to the Cockpit? How exactly was she killed?'

'Steady!' he warned her. They were still standing by the broken wall, a conspicuous trio obviously in very earnest conversation. Eldon and Simmy simultaneously realised this. 'Come over here a way, where we're not so obvious.'

They moved further from the Hall, to the lee of a large barn or stable. 'Now listen,' Eldon went on. 'The way I heard it, Lindsay was coming back from a walk down by the church, just as it was getting dark and she saw two people going the other way – up towards the Cockpit, not far past her house. It was a bit foggy, yeah. She admits that. And she only had a back view. But she knew it was Nanna right away. The other person was a woman, youngish . . .' He looked Simmy up and down and briefly grinned. 'Long dark coat, short hair. She said she was something like fifty yards away, and nobody said anything. Thinks the others never even noticed her. When she thought about it, she realised it was you. There was nobody else it could be. She said the coat was the giveaway.'

Simmy looked down at herself, and her dark blue coat, which was indeed distinctive. It had a big collar and reached down to her knees. She had had it for at least ten years, and had taken to wearing it when pregnant with Robin. She had worn it to the funeral, but not on Saturday. 'Oh,' she said. 'Lindsay told you all that, did she?'

'She told Luke and he told the rest of us.'

'Your cousin,' said Simmy without thinking. Too late she chastised herself. *You've done it again!* she silently shouted. The reaction was much as Sophie Craig's had been the previous evening.

'Oh, right. Been snooping on us, have you? Got the names of the cousins and all the dirt on us. I know who you are, Miss Amateur Detective Florist. I knew back in the week when you came into the pub. Always interfering where you're not wanted, getting things wrong.'

'I had to do what I could to clear my name,' she said, her voice shaking.

'It does look bad, I know,' said Russell, with a placatory smile. 'I wouldn't like it either. But then, you know, it's all right there on Google or whatever it is. And you can't blame us for being interested.'

'So why not finger Luke for the killer instead of me?'

'Nobody's fingering you,' said Simmy impatiently. 'All I know is you've got two cousins called Luke and Kieran and another one called Scarlett – is she a cousin as well?'

'She's not anything for much longer,' said Eldon in a pained voice.

'Pardon?'

'Scarlett's at the end of the line. My mother keeps on about deaths coming in threes, and the poor girl's aiming to be the third, any time now.'

'That's terrible,' said Simmy. 'Can't they do anything?'

Eldon suddenly stood taller and looked towards the Hall. 'Best get back to work,' he said softly. 'If you're not residents, you're not meant to be here. It's not open to the public any more.'

'So we saw. Seems a bit mean. Is somebody watching us?' Russell was very carefully not turning round to check.

'One of the admin women, always bossing us about. So – before you go, I should say I didn't mind talking to you. You should go and find Luke. He's in Tirril. A good mate of Humphrey's, as it happens. You'll have seen him on Friday. And he's got a thing with Lindsay. We've all told him she's well out of his league, but we're wasting our breath.'

'Does he know she's gone missing?'

'What? Don't be daft. She's there with him now. Has been since Wednesday. Didn't like the way people kept banging on her door and distracting her so she moved in with him for a bit. He's in clover, of course. Makes all the other worries disappear, having her there – even if she spends all day on her computer.'

'She works in Lancaster on Fridays,' said Simmy.

'Which you would know, of course. Watch out – the dragon's heading this way.'

'Is Lindsay at work today, then?'

'Presumably.' Eldon gave an exaggeratedly deferential gesture to the woman bearing down on them.

'Good morning, Mr Franklin,' she said stiffly. 'Friends of yours?'

'You might say that. They're from away, and didn't know the gardens had been closed to non-residents. They'll be going now.'

'That's all right,' was the vague reply, and she marched back towards the big house.

'Thank you for that,' said Simmy warmly. 'I'm really

glad we've cleared the air. You've given us a lot to think about. And I'm so sorry about your niece.'

'Niece? Oh – you mean Scarlett. She's my great-niece, actually. My dead uncle's granddaughter.'

Simmy buttoned her lip successfully this time, refraining from blurting – *Oh yes, the one who was killed when he was twenty.* Instead, she pulled a sympathetic face, and merely nodded. Her brain was calculating relationships and implications, wishing she had Ben beside her to help. 'Can I give you my phone number, just in case?' she asked Eldon. He put out a hand for her phone without saying anything and tapped competently for a few moments. Then he handed it back.

'I've put mine in as well,' he said.

'Your family's had more than its share of trouble, then,' said Russell, without knowing any of the facts.

'Not so bad, really,' said Eldon, already walking back to his wall, plainly wanting them to go. 'Others have it worse.'

In the car, Simmy listed on her fingers everything they'd gleaned. 'Lindsay isn't missing. She gave a good description of the person she thought was me. The Luke cousin is having a relationship with her. Scarlett's dying. Eldon is much nicer than I thought. What have I missed?'

'We don't know how the old lady died, exactly. We don't know whether Lindsay Wilson was telling deliberate outright lies. We don't know how *Dombey and Son* fits it all.'

'It probably doesn't, Dad. That would be too fantastic.'

'You'll see,' he said stubbornly.

253

'It's only eleven o'clock. We've got nearly an hour. What are we going to do now?'

'Do we know where Cousin Luke lives?'

'Just Tirril. That's not much use. The person I most urgently want to talk to is Lindsay, but she'll be in Lancaster. The only other person I know in Askham is Sophie, and I can't face her again. I should never have intruded yesterday. I was incredibly tactless.'

'You speak before you think,' he told her. 'You always did.'

'I know. I did it again just now. I'll never learn that people don't much like being told they've been researched online. They feel invaded. Snooped on. And yet, as Ben says, they persist on putting all their personal details out there for anybody to see.'

'They probably think it's only their friends who are going to have a look.'

'That must be it,' she sighed. 'We could drive around and see if we spot anything, but that seems rather pointless.'

'We need to talk it through logically. You forgot to add that Luke knew Humphrey. Doesn't that mean that Lindsay knew him as well?'

'She did, vaguely, but they weren't close. According to Sophie, she made herself known to them when she first moved to Askham, and that was pretty much it. But when it comes to the point, we know hardly anything about her. Where does she come from? She hasn't always lived here. She said she was related to the Craigs, but I can't remember how. I suppose Moxon's got all that noted down, for what it's worth.'

'When did you see him, did you say?'

'Last night. But we didn't talk much. He was more like his old self, thank goodness – very kind and thoughtful. He's having a pretty horrible time, I think. There doesn't seem to be anything like a proper murder investigation. Ben says there must be something sinister going on at Lowther Castle, but I don't know what sparked that off. It would fit, I suppose – if the local police are knee-deep in something huge, and haven't anybody available to handle the murder, they'd be happy to leave it to Moxon. He is a DI, after all. And they might spare a few uniforms to run errands for him, if necessary.'

'We should drive to Lowther, then,' said Russell decisively. 'It's down this road – no distance at all.'

Unable to find any reason to refuse, Simmy obediently drove the extremely short distance to the castle that appeared to survey everything for miles around. 'It's got good history,' said Russell. 'Drive in.'

As they drove up the avenue towards the castle, Russell related what he knew of the place. Simmy only half-listened, as she focused on the building ahead. 'Hey!' she yelped. 'Am I dreaming or is it just a ruin?'

'Facade and a few outer walls,' her father confirmed. 'Surely you knew that?'

'I did not. I had no idea. It looks so *solid* and powerful and permanent. But it's just a film set. Like those studios that only have shop fronts and nothing behind them. It's a trick. I feel cheated.'

'That's silly.'

She ignored him. 'That's what Ben meant when he said it was misleading. Why didn't he tell me there's nothing here? He said there was something sinister about the place, that it dominated Askham and owned it like something from feudal times. How can it, when it's not even real?'

'The history's real,' Russell persisted. 'The power of the Lowthers has spread all across the land. Politics, industry, sport, arts – you name it, you'll find a Lowther right up there. There's been a castle here for a thousand years nearly. Ben's right. The influence goes much deeper than the mere building.'

'And now it's a Disneyfied tourist destination, with added bikes.' She had noticed a sign describing cycle hire and designated pathways for their use.

'The way of the world,' sighed Russell. 'You can't fight it.'

'But I don't have to like it,' flashed Simmy. She began to turn the car around. 'There's no point in stopping here, is there?'

'At least you've learnt something,' said her father philosophically. 'And I've just read that the Lowther estate is doing wonderful things for nature conservation. They're a force for good, apparently.'

'Something's happening down there,' Simmy suddenly noticed. 'I can see three police cars.' She had turned the car and they were facing back towards the road, which ran around Lowther Park and was quite visible. 'They must be chasing someone. They'll be passing the entrance any second now.'

'That white van, look. Drive down, quick. This is exciting!'

Her father could be very boyish at times, Simmy reflected as she did as he bade her. 'Are we going to join the chase?' she asked.

'Don't see why not. They might be about to catch our murderer. We've got a right to be there, if so.'

His logic was shaky, but Simmy had got caught up in the thrill of the chase. They reached the road a few seconds after the third police car had passed it, and added themselves to the fast-moving procession. 'These roads are too narrow for this kind of thing,' she realised.

'There's a tight bend coming up, if I remember rightly. And then there's the main road.'

Russell Straw's knowledge of the area was prodigious, but Simmy could hardly believe he recalled every twist of every little road. 'How do you know that? When did you last drive round here?' she asked him. 'We didn't come this way on Friday, did we?'

'I just know,' he said.

The car chase was very quickly over. The police vehicle in front of them came to a sudden stop just short of the predicted bend. The road was effectively blocked, and Simmy had no choice but to stop as well. 'Might as well go and see,' said Russell eagerly.

'Look who it is,' said Simmy with a delighted laugh. 'Getting out of the car in front.'

Chapter Twenty

It was DI Moxon, as large as life. He glanced back down the road and immediately identified his beloved Simmy Henderson. She watched his face as this happened: the quick smile, and then a flicker of concern. 'Good God!' said Russell. 'Is that who I think it is?'

'What's going on?' Simmy asked, as they walked along the road beside the stationary cars. Ahead there was already a knot of people, and a white van tilting miserably, its nose against a tree.

'He lost control,' said Moxon. 'That's what generally happens at a time like this. He probably didn't know the road.'

'Who is he?'

Slightly too late, the detective clamped his lips together

and shook his head. Russell chuckled. 'Not for public consumption, right? A sting of some sort? Man in white van.' He looked at Simmy. 'What were you saying about a film set? This might have come straight out of a movie. Where's Michael Caine, then?'

'It's a fraud investigation,' muttered Moxon, unable to sustain his silence. 'Nothing to do with you. See if you can turn round and get away. The road's going to be blocked for quite a while.'

'Fraud? That doesn't sound very exciting.' Russell made a disappointed face. 'Hardly compares with murder.'

Moxon frowned at him. 'You'd be surprised. Have you heard of "courier fraud"? Perfectly ordinary harmless people swindled out of every penny they possess – on an industrial scale. I would have agreed with you until about half an hour ago, but I've learnt a lot since then. These people are far more vile than most of the murderers I've met. They're a scourge, pernicious parasitic scum.'

'And you've caught one of them?'

'Let's hope so,' said Moxon. 'Practically every police officer in Cumbria has been dedicated to this case for weeks now.' He gave a wry laugh. 'And I thought it was all about Russian spies.'

'They might be Russian, though,' Russell suggested. 'Isn't this the sort of thing they're good at?'

'Seems not. All completely home-grown, as I understand it. Nice local accents to reassure their victims.'

A shout from further up the road drew his attention. 'Better go. I wasn't meant to be part of this at all, but I got caught up in it more or less by accident. They had to bring me up to speed on what was going on while we were in the car. I've told you everything I know. Which I very much should not have done.'

'We won't tell anybody,' said Simmy. 'But wait a minute. We've just seen Eldon Franklin and he told us quite a lot.'

Moxon hesitated. 'I can't stop now. Can you send me a text about it? Just the basics?'

Simmy gave him a reproachful look. 'If I must.'

There were more shouts and someone was waving urgently at Moxon.

'Go,' the detective ordered.

They were still in good time for Angie's deadline, so Simmy drove back through Askham slowly, and turned right towards Tirril. 'We can go through Yanworth and hit the main road that way,' said Russell with confidence. 'There are no straight lines up here, but that's a good way to go.' They had gone via Pooley Bridge earlier in the day, which definitely did not involve much in the way of straight lines.

'Askham's really remote, isn't it,' she observed. 'Worse than Hartsop, if anything.'

'It's a little world unto itself,' he agreed. 'Which might make it a clever place from which to base a large-scale fraud operation.'

'I suppose it's all done on computers and phones anyway. No wonder the baddies are so hard to catch. They could be anywhere.'

'You know our old friends the Frasers got swindled out of a quarter of a million quid,' said Russell. 'The bank didn't want to refund it, either. Said they'd done their best to warn them and it was their own stupid fault.'

'I don't remember you saying anything about that. When was it?'

'Last year. They did get it back in the end, after they'd gone to the media about it.'

'What's the bit about couriers, then?'

'I don't know exactly. They send somebody to your door and you give them all your credit cards and the magic numbers that go with them. I suppose it can't be as simple as that.'

'Was that the man in the white van, then?'

'Might have been.'

'But Moxon said it had nothing to do with Pauline Parsons. Just a coincidence.'

'Not even that, really. More like he just walked into this big ongoing operation with his insignificant little murder, and they left him to get on with it.'

Simmy groaned. 'There are so many unanswered questions. Every day brings a whole lot more. Where does Lindsay Wilson fit? How many lies did she tell? What does she *want*?'

'You can look at it in two ways. Either she's perfectly well intentioned, and has told the truth as she sees it. Or she's in cahoots with the killer and everything she says is a lie. She might even be the killer herself, and has concocted some clever alibi.'

'I'd really like to choose the first option. If I could just find her and sit down for a proper talk, I'm sure I could get to the bottom of what she's playing at. She told me such a lot on Saturday, and I still can't remember half of it. She said nobody liked Mrs Parsons. I even forgot that at first. And Moxon hasn't given me a chance to really talk to him.

All he did was to tell me I was being accused, and then threw a few crumbs of reassurance over the next few days. And he did take Bonnie home for me last night. That was very sweet of him.'

'It looks to me as if he's been under a lot of constraint. And now he's managed to get himself caught up in this other business. You could see he wasn't too happy about that.'

'It's unsettling the way the police don't abide by their own rules. I mean – I still think they ought to put a lot more effort into solving a murder than catching a fraudster. The values are all wrong.'

Russell was thinking hard. 'I'm not too sure about that. It's not simple. And if they were right in the middle of a carefully organised sting, they wouldn't want to set it all aside to catch a disgruntled grandson who'd biffed his old nanna, probably not meaning to kill her. From their point of view, it made sense to wheel old Moxon in and let him sort it out, with the help of you and Ben.'

'Except he hasn't made any use of our help, has he?'

'Possibly more than you think. He's probably spoken to Ben, for a start.'

'Oh – yes he has,' Simmy remembered. 'That's how he knew where Bonnie was yesterday. And he has talked to a lot of local people. It's just me he's ignoring.'

'I suspect he thinks that's for your own good.'

'I expect you're right,' she sighed. 'He was obviously horribly shocked to find me being accused of killing somebody. That would never have crossed his mind as a thing that could happen.'

'Nor anybody's. The reason for that is still the crux of the matter, as I see it.'

'We're not actually much further forward, are we?' She made a sound of frustration. 'I need to talk to Ben again. Now, I mean. I suppose I could take Robin to the auction house. It's Friday – people do that sort of thing on Fridays, don't they?'

'Do they?' Russell laughed. 'I'm afraid the world of work is a closed book to me these days. I don't know anybody with a proper normal job.'

'I'll phone Christopher and see what he thinks.'

It was simply arranged. The wife and son of the chief auctioneer would pay a brief visit to his workplace at the end of the lunch hour – which was a casual business anyway. The saleroom was on the outskirts of Keswick, and most people either took a packed lunch from home or bought it from a convenient mobile catering van. There was to be no auction the next day, which meant the workload was not especially onerous. Random people turned up for valuations, the staff arranged the lots for the next week, whilst ensuring that all payments were made for the previous sale. Long before Christopher's arrival it had been established that a regular fortnightly auction was an ideal format. Those who opted for a sale every week worked flat out every day, with a punishing routine of listing, photographing, sending out money, locating missing items, chasing people who took the wrong thing home, with one person perpetually on the computer monitoring everything. Others operated a three-weekly system, which Christopher castigated as just plain lazy.

* * *

263

Simmy and Robin arrived at half past one, having enjoyed a convivial lunch with Russell while Angie went off to her ladies. 'Seems as if she's thrown herself into Threlkeld society,' Simmy remarked.

'She bigs it up,' her father said. 'There are two or three women she actually likes, but I rather suspect the change of pace is unsettling her. She's taking a while to adapt.'

'Really? What about all that lazing around in the morning? And she's always said she wanted a complete abandonment of any sort of routine. The B&B was very constricting in that way.'

'I know. But a person still has to fill the day somehow. I'm sure she'll find a fulfilling project of some kind before long. But I can't quite believe it's going to be the local W.I. or even the Village Fete Committee.'

'No,' Simmy agreed.

The auction room staff consisted mainly of women, all of whom gathered round Robin with exclamations about how much he'd grown and how handsome he was. The baby had initially closely resembled Christopher's father, but as weeks went by he was looking more and more like Christopher himself. He still had the same tightly clustered features, everything close together in the middle of his face, but his colouring was growing lighter, and the shape of his chin was unmistakably identical to Christopher's. Simmy had yet to see anything of herself in him.

Ben hovered behind her, wearing a sling. Quickly, she handed her baby to the nearest woman and turned round to talk to the boy. He looked pale. 'Are you all right?' she asked.

'Not as all right as I should be,' he admitted. 'You see

264

people dashing about with their arm in plaster, as if it was nothing. I don't seem to have any energy at all. And I can't sleep properly.'

'Are you eating?'

'Sort of.'

'How much use are you here? Do you think I ought to take you home?'

'I don't know.'

He was young and wretched and Simmy felt concerned. 'Do you think you ought to see a doctor again? There might be an infection or something.'

'I might try,' came the surprising reply. 'My mother's coming back in the morning. She can take me back to the hospital or something, if I don't feel better.'

Simmy took charge. She found her husband and told him she was taking Ben home, would be gone for an hour and he was holding the baby. 'There's a cup of milk in his bag. He had a big lunch, so he won't be hungry. He might go to sleep in the buggy if someone wheels him about a bit.'

'But why?'

'Ben's not right. I'm taking him home. And I want to talk to him. He's not doing much good here, is he?'

'He was fine this morning.'

'Well, he's not now.' She tried to think through the next few hours. 'Listen – I'm putting the baby seat in your car, just in case I have to go to Windermere or somewhere. I hope I won't have to – but it's all happening out there. I can feel it.'

'We should have got two of those seats,' he said.

'We did get two, but my parents have got the other one. As long as we make sure ours is always with Robin, there's no problem.' This logic had always worked, but transferring the contraption from one car to another was no fun.

Simmy was feeling efficient and purposeful. If Ben could be revived sufficiently to think straight and hear everything she had to tell him, she had a growing sense that the solution to Pauline Parsons' murder was within their grasp. Like one of the more interesting chemical experiments at school, different components were coming together in a pattern that looked inevitable. A picture was forming almost by itself as she reviewed the past twenty-four hours. But she needed Ben to confirm it, as well as to reassure her, because the implications were very disagreeable.

Chapter Twenty-One

The digs were chilly and airless. Ben explained that the sash window was difficult to open and almost impossible to close again. Heating went on in the late afternoon for a few hours; he had agreed that he wouldn't need more than that, expecting to be out at work all day. 'Your mother should have a word with the landlady when she comes tomorrow,' said Simmy. 'Or does the heating go on earlier at weekends?'

'I'm not sure,' said Ben. 'I've usually gone down to Windermere. And the weather hasn't been cold until now.'

She looked round helplessly, wishing there was more she could do to improve his comfort. 'It's all rather bleak,' she concluded. 'You'll have to make better arrangements for yourself than this.'

'I will. I didn't want to commit myself to anything long term until I was sure I wanted to carry on working up here. And it was all thrown into confusion by what happened in the summer.'

'I know. But that was months ago now.'

'Never mind all that. We can have coffee and get down to business. I don't expect you'll be staying long.'

'As long as it takes,' she said firmly. 'You heard what I said to Christopher. We'll probably need your laptop. Get it running while I make the drinks.'

She made two mugs of coffee, using the kettle on a table in the corner. 'Ugh – long-life milk!' she complained. 'How barbaric.'

'It's just for emergencies,' he said carelessly. 'Now – what am I meant to be looking up?'

'Let me bring you up to date first. Did Bonnie phone you last night, after we'd gone to see Sophie? Did Moxon get her home all right?'

'She did but she didn't say much. She felt bad about the way they treated you. It spoilt it for her, rather. And Sophie didn't like it when Moxon came knocking, saying he was there to take Bonnie home. She went very quiet and boot-faced, apparently.'

'What about the girls?'

'What about them?'

'Did Bonnie get a chance to talk to them at all? To get to know them? What was her impression of them?'

'She said they seemed a bit spaced-out, obviously thinking about something else. She felt she'd walked into a situation that had nothing to do with her, and she was pretty much in the way. She was really glad when Moxo came to the rescue.'

'He rescued me as well.'

'But you had a chance to see them – the girls as well as Sophie, right?'

'Briefly. They didn't like me. From what Sophie said, I gather Humphrey had talked me up into some sort of annoying paragon. No wonder she took against me. The girls were just following her lead. Or so I thought. Now I'm wondering whether there's more to it.'

Ben gulped down half the coffee and took his arm out of the sling. 'That's better,' he said. 'This thing makes me feel like an invalid. I'm much more myself without it.'

He did immediately look more energetic. He pulled one of his ubiquitous notepads towards himself and picked up a pen. 'Time for some bullet points,' he said. 'I can see you've got an idea. Let's tackle it logically.'

'Okay,' she said uncertainly. 'Where do we start?'

'Lindsay Wilson,' he said decisively. 'She's the pivotal figure.' He wrote her name in the middle of one page, and on a second sheet he wrote it again, with a blob beside it. 'Then there's the grandson, Eldon. And maybe that builder, Mr Isaacs.' He frowned. 'It's rather a short list.'

'There's a lot more to tell you,' Simmy said. 'I hadn't realised how much you don't know. For a start, Lindsay is in a relationship with Eldon's cousin Luke. She's with him in Tirril.'

'Not missing, then?'

'Seems not – but she'll be in Lancaster today, so we still can't talk to her.'

'What else?'

Simmy's mind went blank. All the conversations she had had through the week scattered to the winds, along with the snippets of information she had been told. 'Can we take it slowly?' she said. 'One person at a time.'

'Okay. Start with Pauline Parsons, then. Has anyone said any more about her?'

'Actually, yes. Eldon told us a bit more this morning. We found him working at Askham Hall.'

'Who's *we*?'

'Me and my dad. We managed to keep him calm and almost friendly, because I told him I didn't believe he killed his nanna. It was only common sense, really, because he seemed to think I'd done it. He repeated what Lindsay had said she'd seen – a woman in a long dark coat leading the old lady up the fell in the fog on Saturday evening.'

'How very gothic! Have you got a long dark coat?'

'I have. He said Lindsay was sure it was me, so her accusation was made in good faith.'

'Utter rubbish. Somebody's lying. What was she doing on the fell herself?' He smacked himself on the cheek. 'Why didn't we think that through from the start? If she was there, watching what was going on, how can she have an alibi? Why don't we all assume it was her all along and the woman in the long coat is pure fiction?'

'She wasn't on the fell – she was going towards it, after a walk down by the church or somewhere. She saw two people, just from the back. That's what Eldon said. We don't know what she told the police about an alibi. Maybe there were people with her. Maybe she went straight to someone's house or a pub or something moments after doing the murder and it works as a clever alibi.'

Ben shook his head. 'The timing is never that precise. They can't know the exact time of death. It could so easily be one big bluff – purely to divert suspicion from herself.'

Simmy closed her eyes, trying to keep hold of the reasoning. 'All right. Let's go through it slowly. Lindsay herself marches Mrs P half a mile or more up to the Cockpit on a foggy evening, hits her over the head and runs back in time to give herself a credible alibi and invent a story about me – or someone in a long dark coat – being with old Mrs P. It could be that it all happened earlier than the time she told Moxon she saw me. So her story was carefully planned to give a false time as well as casting suspicion on someone else. Right?'

'Not bad,' said Ben. 'Quite clever. At the very least it would cause plenty of confusion. It's even possible she killed the old lady in the village and carried the body up the fell. Isn't that what we thought originally?'

'She couldn't do that. She's not strong enough.'

'Well, wheeled her in a pram or something.'

'People would see her either way. There are houses, and you never know when a walker will show up. That's very unlikely to be right.'

'Okay. So the victim was alive until they got to the Cockpit. Let's take that as read. Now then, what more do we know about Mrs Parsons? Anything that might suggest a motive?'

'Lindsay talked about her on Saturday, and you found all that stuff on the computer. Eldon didn't say very much about her personally. She was quite a big character in the village, I think.'

'Yes, we knew that from my searches. We need details.'

Simmy went quiet, forcing herself to think. 'Lindsay did say quite a lot. Something about JWs! That was it. I had no idea what she meant. I think I told you, didn't I?'

'Jehovah's Witness? Really? If you did tell me, I've forgotten.'

'They're the ones who come to your door and try to convert you. Not that I've seen a single one since coming to live up here. We had them now and then in Worcester.'

'We had them once in Helm Road. My dad kept them talking for ages, just for the fun of it. A bit mean, when you think about it, but I expect they enjoyed the novelty.'

'Well Pauline Parsons was one, but only a few of her family have carried it on. Lindsay seemed to think it was all fizzling out. She also said nobody really liked Pauline. I might have told you that already.'

'That's rich grounds for family arguments, all the same. She can't have been happy about her offspring drifting away. They are very strict, I think. No Christmas or birthdays.'

'Sounds pretty bleak. Poor things, being born into that. I often think it's awful the way you can't choose your parents, and can get landed with something that never gives you a chance to have a fulfilling life. Everything's so *random*, isn't it?'

'You can choose to go a different way,' said Ben stoutly. 'We all have that freedom. The Bible itself tells you that.'

'Which has a very ironic feel to it,' she said. 'What

does the Bible think about people who choose to be atheists?'

'I expect they're damned for all eternity – but at least they have that option if they want it.'

They both laughed.

'You look better,' Simmy noticed. 'I was worried.'

He smiled ruefully. 'The fact is, I tried to do too much this morning. Jack was struggling with a big chest and I held the door for him. It knocked my arm a bit, as he went through. It didn't hurt, and the plaster would have protected it, but I panicked. Then I felt silly and carried on trying to prove to myself and everyone else that I was fine. Then I took one of the pills they gave me, just in case it started to ache, and that made me woozy. It was too soon after the last one. I don't know why I take them, because it really doesn't hurt now.'

'Did the hospital tell you to?'

'More or less. But I've decided to stop. They're so keen on medicating everybody. It's very wasteful. I guess I've watched my mother dosing herself with painkillers these past few years until it seems quite normal. And it's not, of course.'

'No,' said Simmy, whose mother never took a pill from one end of the year to the other. 'But I can see how easy they make it. Now, can we talk about Bonnie for a minute?'

'If you like – but why? Have we finished talking about the murder?'

'I think we should try and see if there's a connection. I've wondered all along whether there's some sort of chain leading from Humphrey to Pauline Parsons with links that we've missed. You said days ago that we should ask

"Why now?". Humphrey's funeral feels as if it sparked everything off. That means Sophie is relevant, and she links to Bonnie. Don't you think?'

He tapped his teeth with his pen. 'But wasn't it pure coincidence that Bonnie discovered Sophie this week?'

'Not entirely. Verity forced the issue on Wednesday, whether deliberately or not. She knows people in Askham. She could even be one of the links we've ignored. I'm inclined to think she just wants to feel involved, and grabbed the chance when it came. But somebody might have put her up to it, without her realising.'

He gave her an admiring look. 'That's quite possible. It could even have been Lindsay Wilson. But why?' He groaned. 'Why, why, why? Why did Lindsay accuse you? Why did that Isaacs man show up when he did? Why didn't Moxon tell you much more at the start? Why did Bonnie need to go dashing off to Askham last night? Everybody has annoying secret motives, and that fogs up the whole thing. You don't kill an old woman on the top of a fell just because she's a Jehovah's Witness, or said something annoying at a funeral.'

'She wasn't at the funeral, because she disapproves of Christianity.'

'That might be annoying, I guess. But hardly grounds for murder.'

'Do you think Bonnie has motives she's not telling you?'

'Not really. I think she wants more than she'll admit, even to herself. She phoned me when she got home last night, you know.'

'Yes, you said.'

'She doesn't know what to make of those girls. They

didn't seem too pleased to meet her, which was hurtful.'

'The timing was wrong. Their father just died.'

'Okay. Let's try and construct your chain, then. What about Howard Isaacs? He knows Sophie and the girls, obviously.'

'And he seems to care about their welfare. I don't really think he can be very relevant. I wish you'd met him, so you could judge for yourself.'

'There are remarkably few people left without him. Eldon – and this new Luke person. Various Parsons relations we've never seen. Of course, there's always the real possibility that whoever killed Mrs P is somebody we've never even heard of.'

Simmy pursed her lips. 'I don't think so. It's one of the people we've named in the last twenty minutes. I can't explain why, but I feel sure of that.'

'Well, let's hope it's not Verity, then. However much she irritates Bonnie, your business can't manage without her.'

They laughed, and Ben threw down his pen. 'I need another coffee,' he said.

'There's still a lot I haven't told you. Like seeing Moxon this morning.' She gave a quick account of the brief car chase at Lowther. 'He was trying to explain why the murder hasn't got more police attention, I think. It was lucky we were there.'

'Coincidence.'

'Yes, but not a huge one. Everything comes together in Askham, and Moxon's been there all week. He must have met everybody who lives there by now.' She paused to make more coffee. 'What time is it?' she wondered. 'I didn't bring my watch.'

Ben glanced at the corner of his laptop screen. 'Ten to three.'

'Is it really? We've been doing this for an hour and a half? Amazing. I should rescue Christopher.'

'No rush. He'll enjoy showing off the future Henderson Junior.'

'Like *Dombey and Son*,' Simmy said without conscious thought. 'Does he think Robin will take over the business when he grows up?'

'Probably. Doesn't every man with a business want his son to inherit it?'

'It never occurred to me,' she said.

Ben picked up his pen again. 'We haven't got far,' he complained. 'I've been too much out of it. I don't understand the connections properly. What about this Luke character? Do we know anything at all about him?'

'He lives in Tirril and has a brother called Kieran, if I remember rightly.'

'And a girl cousin with a defective heart.'

'She is actually not his first cousin. Her grandmother – or was it grand*father?* – was one of Pauline's children. I know – the oldest one who died when he was twenty. Apparently, he had time to produce a child. And Sophie's Chloe is friends with the girl. They're probably in the same class at school.'

'Errgghh,' groaned Ben, making Simmy think he was in pain. When she showed concern, he grinned. 'Mental agony,' he explained. 'I'm going to be a failure with this one. I haven't got the least idea who did it, or why – or even when. Everything's so flimsy and unreliable. Just things people say, with not a shred of evidence anywhere.'

'Pity poor Moxon, then.'

'Indeed. He's been handed a very poisoned chalice.'

'I do have one or two ideas,' she said hesitantly. 'But no evidence to back them.'

'Go on.'

'Well, the Jehovah's Witness thing. Don't they refuse medical treatment? Blood transfusion and so forth?'

'That's right.'

'So what if the girl with the bad heart was refused vital treatment – maybe even a transplant – because of her great-grandmother's religion? We don't know who her parents are, do we? I don't remember you finding them on Wednesday. You did say you might have missed a few relations. I think you missed them.'

Ben slumped. 'Darn it! You've put your finger on the only remotely credible motive and we don't know the people most likely to act on it. They weren't anywhere online.'

'Which suggests they've kept up the family faith. I wonder where they live?'

'I vote we leave that to Moxon. Our work is done. Except . . .'

'What?'

'I heard you tell Christopher you might have to go to Windermere. Did you mean it? Could you possibly bear to take me there now?'

She looked closely at him. A boy of nineteen, officially an adult, the age of fighter pilots in the Battle of Britain, who wanted his mother and his girlfriend, and was almost entirely helpless. 'To Helm Road, you mean?'

'Save my mum coming up here tomorrow. I'm not sure

I can face this evening as things are. I've gone all pathetic.'

'Consider it done,' she said. 'Those sisters of yours will love the chance to play nurse.' Ben had three younger sisters, none of whom showed any sign of wanting to play nurse. 'Though maybe not Zoe,' she added.

'Not any of them. But at least the place is warm, and there'll be some food.'

'And the nursing will all be down to Bonnie.'

Chapter Twenty-Two

Moxon was exhausted – *drained*, as he described it to himself – by the drama of the morning. He had blundered into going along on the ludicrous car chase along roads that could not fail to produce some sort of accident. Ushered unceremoniously into the back seat of one of the Penrith police cars, he had clung to the seat belt and wished heartily that he had become an accountant instead of a police officer. When the object of their pursuit had run himself into a ditch, the relief had been huge. Then he had seen, miraculously, Simmy Henderson standing there with her father and the world righted itself again.

He had tried not to disclose any confidential facts about the chase, but he couldn't help himself. It was all so startlingly new and unexpected he couldn't hold it back. If the officer driving the car could be believed, it was all over bar the shouting anyway. The felons had been identified and one of their number apprehended. There would be kudos and publicity and endless months of legal bickering, but the outcome could only be positive. The general assumption that online fraud was virtually impossible to prevent, that the perpetrators were never caught, had been dented at the very least. The vast network of police investigations, painstakingly pursued over almost a year, had paid off. Everybody at Penrith police station was euphoric.

But Moxon still had his odd little murder to concentrate on. Any hope that there might now be some spare officers to assist him looked like being dashed in the short term, and he found himself rather hoping he could come up with a solution all by himself. If there was any kudos going spare, he wanted to bag it for himself.

Simmy had texted him with admirable brevity, as instructed, to the effect that Lindsay Wilson had a boyfriend called Luke living in Tirril, grandson of the murdered woman. 'She's not missing after all,' she concluded, having also mentioned Eldon Franklin as the source of this new information.

'Luke what?' Moxon muttered, knowing he would have to trawl through pages of notes to find the answer. He recalled that there were two brothers, sons of one of Pauline's daughters, but he wasn't at all sure he had ever noted their surname. If they didn't live in Askham, he would not have got round to interviewing them – which now looked very much like an oversight of major significance.

And yet – what was he going to ask, with any hope of a useful response? Lindsay Wilson was bound to stick to her original story. If she was protecting a boyfriend, she wasn't likely to admit it. Simmy had found another connection – another line to add to the flowchart he assumed Ben Harkness had constructed – which by rights should ring bells and offer leads to a new hypothesis. But it did no such thing. It had already become obvious that the villagers were all very much linked together in various ways, which meant that this new detail was sadly unexciting.

Besides, Lindsay worked in Lancaster on Fridays.

The previous evening still lingered vividly in his mind. He had knocked on Sophie Craig's door, and stated his intention of driving Bonnie Lawson home. 'I let Simmy and the baby go,' he added heavily. 'They were getting cold out there.'

Sophie took him into the living room, which felt full of emotional women. Two teenage girls were on a sofa, holding onto each other. The older one was in tears. Bonnie was on a small chair, which made her seem even younger than the other two. She looked at him with palpable relief. 'He's come to take you home,' said Sophie.

'Thanks,' she said to Moxon. Then to Sophie, 'I know I shouldn't have come so soon. I don't know what I was thinking. I guess I wanted to make up for all the lost time – something like that.' She looked at the girls. 'It's so terrible about your dad. I can't imagine how you must feel.' She hesitated, and then burst out, 'But at least you *had* a dad. I never even knew mine.'

'We can show you photos of him, next time you come,' said Sophie. 'And don't feel bad about intruding or anything. It's our fault. We're still not thinking straight.'

'Uncle Howard's going to make sure we're okay, Mum,'

said the younger girl, apparently trying to console her mother. 'He'll see to everything, even Scarlett. She can have that transplant now.'

Nobody gave this much attention, with Bonnie getting up from the chair and Moxon starting towards the door. They were in his car moments later.

'Was that as gruelling as it looked?' he asked, as they approached Pooley Bridge.

'Pretty much. Chloe's the worst. She seems to be close to a breakdown, with the shock of Humphrey's death. You'd think the appearance of a new cousin might be a nice distraction,' she added, bitterly. 'But she hardly took any notice of me at all.'

'You can't really blame her. So who's Uncle Howard?'

'Um – what?'

'Your cousin said just now that Uncle Howard was going to make sure everything was all right. He sounds a bit like a fairy godfather with a magic wand.'

'I don't know,' said Bonnie. 'Maybe Humphrey had a brother.'

Moxon left it there and talked about Ben instead, which suited Bonnie much better. The murder of an old lady on a foggy fell did not seem relevant at that particular moment. At least, so he thought, but Bonnie knew better. 'Ben's quite frustrated about the murder,' she said, after a little while. 'He hasn't spoken to any of the people involved, and only has Simmy to pass on what she knows. I think she forgets to tell him things. And I'm completely out of it.' She sighed. 'I would never have even known Askham existed if it hadn't been for Verity.'

'Oh?'

She explained about the sudden introduction of her forgotten aunt by her colleague in the flower shop. 'She was so pleased with herself,' the girl sighed. 'But I am grateful, really. I've learnt such a lot about my family since then.'

'And you were actually born in Askham?' he queried, as he tried to keep up.

'In that very house, according to Sophie. Not that we got round to that just now. She took against Simmy, you see, and it all got horrible. Sophie's jealous because Humphrey thought Simmy was so wonderful, and stupidly went on about it. Then he died, probably before she could come to see that it was all her imagination.'

'Unfinished business.'

'Exactly. And it's very bad for the girls. Confusing.'

'I got the feeling there was more to it than that.'

'Did you? You were only there for about thirty seconds. How could you?'

'Simmy told me a few things outside, before I went in.'

'I don't think they care at all about the murder, if that's what you mean. They didn't even mention it.'

Moxon kept his thoughts to himself. He had remembered who 'Uncle Howard' was: the man who had approached Moxon himself in the pub that very day. He understood that Chloe's remark might carry quite a lot of significance. He spent the rest of the drive wondering how he might best go about checking his suspicions.

And now he was free to follow up on the 'Uncle Howard' lead, even if he couldn't reach Lindsay Wilson for a while. He could sense that Simmy, Ben and even Christopher were thinking along similar lines – or at least lines that would ideally converge with his and produce a definitive answer. It had happened before, although generally Ben got there first. Howard Isaacs had already transparently stated that he had the welfare of Humphrey Craig's family at heart. Whatever most worried or frightened them, he was ready to tackle. And for Chloe, there was a concern for a person called Scarlett, whose plight might be lessened now – but since when? Since the death of Humphrey or the murder of Pauline Parsons?

There were standard lines of enquiry in most murder cases. You listed the basic questions: why now? who benefits? who was known to be in the relevant place at the relevant time? what sort of attack was it – premeditated or sudden? He had very few reliable answers to any of these crucial elements. Attempts to form a picture of Mrs Parsons' background had thrown up statements as to her roots in the area, her religion, family and activities. Family had dominated, with more than its share of tragedy. The somewhat cool reports of her death in the local newspaper made brief mention of the son who died in an accident, forty-five years before. A neighbour had glancingly mentioned that Pauline had raised the baby grandson left without a father. Thinking over that now, Moxon grasped the similarity with Bonnie's story. Two small fatherless children left with a mother who apparently turned out to be unequal to the responsibility. Moxon had allowed himself to be diverted into musings about the girl and her foster mother, and the sudden change in her life now she'd found an aunt and cousins.

There was plenty of day yet to go. Simmy had cited Eldon Franklin as having located Lindsay Wilson, and

Moxon recalled that the man worked locally, at Askham Hall. He had even spoken to him there briefly on Tuesday, and acquired his phone number. He was Pauline's grandson, acquainted with everybody in the village, a skilled handyman responsible for maintenance of the large handsome property, along with a small team of other men. He featured on a list of potential suspects, for no other reason than proximity and familial connection. But if Lindsay Wilson was telling the truth, then the murderer had been female. The damage to the old lady's head was of a nature to suggest an attacker of limited strength. With minimal zeal, the pathologist had indicated angles and forces consistent with a rather feeble blow from an object such as a walking stick, which by chance collided with the victim's fragile occiput, and probably knocked her over. A large rock lying on the ground had finished the job. The body had been found with its head resting on a sharp point that had symmetrically penetrated the opposite side of the skull and was the final cause of death. The stick was at her side, and was readily identified as the weapon used for the first blow. It had yielded a few blurred fingerprints, all but two from the old woman herself. The others could prove useful in confirming a suspicion, once there was someone to suspect. They were not Simmy Henderson's, which was some small comfort. The killer had been unlucky in the positioning of the lethal rock – or perhaps lucky, depending on the motive. If death had been the purpose, then the blow alone might have been a sad failure. If a mild irritated smack was all that had been intended, then things had indeed turned out very badly for all concerned.

'I would venture to say it was a woman who did it,' said

the pathologist. 'Or possibly an elderly man. Or a young boy.'

All of which led to the necessity of taking Lindsay Wilson's accusation rather more seriously than Moxon would like. 'It wasn't her. It can't have been,' he repeated to anybody in the Penrith station who would listen to him.

'You have to set personal feelings aside,' said Mark – the man who was technically in charge. 'From what I can see, it looks rather bad for her. But I'm leaving it to you to establish a case. Round up some evidence, for God's sake.'

So far, after almost a week, there was no evidence to be had. The forensics were virtually non-existent, eye-witness testimony was limited to one incredible story and two fingerprints that did at least fail to incriminate Simmy. All he could do was carry on talking to people and note down anything that even vaguely resembled a clue. Just the kind of thing Ben, Bonnie and Simmy had been known to do in previous cases.

He phoned Eldon Franklin, who did not respond. 'This is DI Moxon. We spoke on Tuesday. I have a few more things to ask you, so could you please call back when you get this? Thank you.' He recited his number and sighed. There was nothing he especially wanted to ask the man anyway, except perhaps for his cousin Luke's address, which could be found another way quite easily. And to check that he had not upset Simmy at all. There had been mentions of a scene in the pub, earlier in the week, in which Simmy and Christopher had been verbally attacked by this man. Moxon wished he'd known about that when he spoke to Eldon that same afternoon. He would have come over a lot heavier if so. As it was, when Eldon spoke bitterly of the police failing to act on a clear and definite accusation by an actual witness, Moxon had been placating and evasive. 'All in good time,' he had said, or something equally meaningless.

The same logic that Simmy had belatedly grasped – that if Eldon genuinely believed she was the killer, then it couldn't be him – had lurked in Moxon's subconscious, while he had eyed the man with misgivings. Strong, angry, closely related to the victim – he surely had to be on the suspect list himself.

The trouble was that Moxon had known all day what he should really be doing, but he still couldn't bring himself to do it.

Chapter Twenty-Three

'I need to check first with Christopher,' Simmy demurred. 'It'll take me until the end of the day to drive all down there and back. And what about the *dog*?' Until that moment, Cornelia's needs had not once crossed her mind. 'We can't leave her shut in all this long time, poor thing.'

'You never should have got that dog,' said Ben, who was lukewarm about pets in general. Bonnie was the official owner of an ageing Labrador, but had effortlessly delegated his care to Corinne, who loved dogs and had always taken them under her wing just as she did the foster children. 'And you *did* tell Christopher you might be gone all day.'

'He must have forgotten about Cornelia as well. How do people *manage*?' she wailed. 'It's never-ending, keeping all these plates spinning, as somebody said. Your mother did it with *five* children and a job. I'm just hopeless.'

'Calm down. It's my fault. I'm being selfish. We don't have to go now. Why don't we collect the baby and go back to Hartsop to rescue the dog? If you don't mind giving me a bit of supper, maybe one of you could take me down to Windermere later on? I could pay for the fuel,' he offered unconvincingly.

'All right. One thing at a time. Sorry I panicked. Today's been a bit of a strain, one way and another. Actually, the whole week has been like that. I'm worried about Bonnie as well. I want to have a good long talk to her – Moxon too, come to that. Not to mention Lindsay bloody Wilson, who started all this.'

Ben was staring down at the messy diagram he had been constructing, with scribbled notes, arrows and circles. 'You know who we've left out almost completely?' he said slowly. 'Because she doesn't exactly fit anywhere, and yet you could say *she* started it, more than Lindsay Wilson. Or her husband, anyway, by getting himself dead.'

'You mean Sophie?'

He nodded. 'I can't find any credible connections for her, and yet it feels as if she's at the heart of things. Maybe it's only because of Bonnie and I'm muddling everything up together.'

'I know what you mean. Every time I think about her, it's like the opposite of a magnet. I find myself not wanting to go near her again. She was nasty to me last night, but even without that, there's something repellent. Is it just grief, do you think? Am I like those people who cross the road to avoid someone who's been bereaved? The atmosphere in the house was awful. More than just misery, I think. Anger, fear – that sort of thing. Possibly even guilt.'

'All quite normal after a sudden death.'

'I know. And Sophie obviously feels there was a lot of unfinished business between her and Humphrey. I mean – he was such a lovely man. She can't seriously have thought he had fallen for me. She was probably having a midlife crisis or something, and it would all have blown over in no time. So when he died, she was left with all that misplaced jealousy. Poor thing.'

'Just shows how careful you have to be,' said Ben with the wisdom of youth.

Simmy snorted. 'It doesn't work like that. And the girls probably have all the usual teenage dramas going on, without the terrible shock of losing their father. Chloe's sick friend, for one thing.'

Ben went on analysing his flowchart. 'What time do you think Lindsay Wilson gets back from her lecturing?'

'No idea. It's Friday. Probably not late.'

'If I can find an address for her boyfriend in Tirril, do you think we can go there first? It's on the way to Hartsop, and Cornelia can probably last a bit longer. It might take a while, though, not having his surname.'

Simmy heaved a sigh. 'I thought you might say that,' she admitted. 'Although I'm sure we should leave it up to Moxon.'

'When have we ever done that?' said Ben with a twinkle.

Ben phoned Bonnie while they were in the car, and updated her as best he could. 'It's all very vague and muddled,' he complained. 'It would help a lot if you were with us as well.'

Bonnie assured him she wished she was there, too, but sent a message to Simmy that the shop was bustling and things were nicely under control. When Ben told her he was going to shortly be coming to Windermere and would stay the whole weekend, her relief was enough to make Simmy glad of her promise to act as his taxi. 'You'll have to tell me everything that happened at Sophie's last night,' Ben told his girlfriend.

When the call was finished, Simmy ventured to suggest that things might get awkward where Sophie was concerned. 'You'll need to take it carefully,' she warned him. 'If you hint that Sophie might have something to do with the murder, she's going to be upset, isn't she?'

'Is that what we think?'

'I don't know. It might be. Doesn't it feel to you as if that's where it's all heading?'

'Not yet. There could still be lots of Parsons relations we don't know, who hated their old granny. I can't really see why Sophie should be in the spotlight. There isn't anything concrete at all to cast suspicion her way.'

'No, but there are quite a few nasty feelings floating around that I can't make sense of. There's such a lot we don't know. If only Moxon was a bit more forthcoming, we'd be able to make a far better job of figuring it out.'

'Maybe this time he's doing it all by himself and doesn't need our help.'

'More like he thinks he's protecting me. Or that they've told him to keep me out of it – that's probably it. You can't ask a suspect to help with the investigation, can you?'

'I guess not,' sighed Ben. 'Oh – this is Tirril, look.'

'Blink and you'll miss it. It's *tiny*. Just a pub, a garage and a scattering of houses.' She pulled into the side of the road and stopped.

'Luckily, since I couldn't find the address. We can probably stand in the road and shout "Luke!" and he'll hear us.'

'Maybe better to ask them at the pub or the garage,' said Simmy with a smile.

'The pub looks closed, so the garage it is. Stay there – I'll go.'

He climbed out of the car, taking care not to knock his plastered arm. Four minutes later he came back with an ironic expression. 'Spoke too soon,' he said. 'The man there claims never to have heard of anybody called Luke or Lindsay, and said he's not local and doesn't concern himself with people's names or addresses. Maybe if I knew what sort of car he drives . . . and so forth. Hopeless.'

'Bother,' said Simmy. 'Now what?'

'Have you got Eldon's phone number?'

'Ah – yes I have, by a fluke. I actually thought to ask him for it.'

'So call him and get the address. Should have done that before now, silly us.'

She did as he instructed, only to find Eldon's phone was switched off. She did not leave a message. 'Thwarted,' she said.

The car was not completely off the road, but there was not enough traffic for it to cause a nuisance. There were no pedestrians in sight, who might have provided information. 'Now what?' said Ben.

'I'm not giving up, but we can't stay here. What time is it?'

'Four fifteen.'

'Let's park in front of the pub. There might be somebody about.' She drove the short distance and tucked the car to one side of the Queen's Head.

'Oh look – walkers,' said Ben. 'Probably not locals.'

A man and a woman were striding towards them, the man with a pair of binoculars round his neck. 'I've seen them before,' said Simmy, trying to think where. 'Oh – I know! They were up on Askham Fell on Tuesday. Christopher and I took Robin and Cornelia up there for a look. They said they go there a lot to watch birds.'

'Their appearance would confirm that as true,' muttered Ben. 'Do we want to talk to them?'

'Why not? I expect they do live here. They look a bit tired.'

'So would you if you'd walked all the way to the Cockpit and back. Which I bet you they have.'

Simmy got out of the car and smiled at the couple. 'Hello again,' she said. 'Remember me?'

They gave her identical blank stares and the woman shook her head.

'On Tuesday – up near the Cockpit. I was with my husband and baby. And dog. A bouncy black puppy.'

'Ah,' said the man uncertainly. 'We see a lot of people, you know.'

'I remember the puppy,' said the woman. 'What are you doing here?'

'Actually, we're trying to find someone. He's called Luke and he's got a girlfriend called Lindsay. We know they're here in Tirril somewhere.'

'And why do you want them?' asked the man.

Ben had also got out of the car and now interposed himself into the conversation. 'The thing is,' he began, 'we've got good friends in Askham, and Luke's a relation of theirs. They suggested a while ago that he might be interested in some work that's going. It's all rather vague, but we thought while we're here we could see if we could find him and talk it over.'

'Where's your baby?' the woman suddenly asked Simmy, having peered through the rear windows of the car.

'With his dad,' said Simmy easily.

'Your story is very thin,' said the man. 'At the very least you ought to know Luke's surname, if what you say is true.'

'Have you ever even met him?' demanded the woman.

'Actually not,' said Ben. 'But we do know Lindsay. But it's fine. If you don't want to tell us, we'll just come back another day. No harm done. At least – not to us. Luke might be sorry to have missed out on something he would probably have wanted.'

'As far as I can see, he's got plenty of work already. Last I heard he was booked up till next Easter.' It was the man speaking.

So you do know him! Simmy thought. She left Ben to his clever manoeuvrings, confident that he would triumph.

The woman turned to her partner. 'I'm not so sure, Jack. Don't you remember he said those people in Clifton had let him down? The ones who said they wanted five hundred yards of fencing done? He might have some free time, after all.'

'That would be great!' enthused Ben. 'It's my dad, you see. His garden fence blew down and he's got awful trouble with deer eating everything. It's only a day's work, I think.

I was supposed to be doing it with him, but as you see . . .' He waved his plaster in her face.

'Oh well. You can't really miss him if you take a proper look. Go up the road to Sockbridge and he's on the left. He'll most likely be home by now. You'll see his van – it's white with red writing on it.'

'Thanks!' said Ben.

He and Simmy got back into the car, and waited until the walkers moved on. The man had taken a phone out of his pocket and was tapping at it.

'Luke's a fencer and Eldon mends walls,' said Simmy. 'Do you think they work together?'

'Who knows?'

'Might be a family business, although Eldon seemed to be fully employed at Askham.' She frowned and made no attempt to start the car. 'It seems a bit of an unlikely match for Lindsay. I mean, she's a complete intellectual.'

'Careful. You're being classist.'

'I know I am, but you haven't met her. It feels very incongruous. Could she just be hiding here, and not actually his girlfriend at all?'

'Anything's possible,' said Ben. 'Maybe we should go and see.'

'I'm wondering whether we've actually got enough time now. I can't stop worrying about that poor dog. She's been shut in nearly all day. And I can't imagine Christopher's too happy being landed with Robin for all this time.'

'Well, we're not getting anywhere just sitting here, are we?' said Ben impatiently.

Simmy was experiencing a loss of nerve. The unknown

Luke suddenly acquired an aura of danger, at least as powerfully as Eldon had done. If he was intimate with Lindsay, then he was unlikely to have even the slightest positive attitude towards the accused Simmy Henderson. 'He might take the law into his own hands,' she mumbled feebly.

'He probably won't be there, anyway.'

'Those people said he would. It sounded as if they live practically next door.'

'Come *on*, Sim. This isn't like you.'

'Maybe we should phone someone first, to say where we are. Christopher or Moxon or my dad.'

'I can't see what good that'll do. If Luke shoots us both the minute we park outside his house, there won't be much doubt as to our whereabouts, will there?'

'Shut up,' she said. 'You're not helping.'

'So phone someone,' he said resignedly, 'but get *on* with it.'

The desire to go home was strengthening by the minute. 'What are we going to say to them? It's all gone out of my head. I still think we'd do better to talk to Sophie again – if she'd even let me in the house.'

'There's a car coming up fast,' he noted. 'Lucky we got off the road.' As they watched, the car slowed down as it approached them. 'It's seen us,' said Ben, as if they had been hiding.

'It's Moxon,' said Simmy. 'I know that number plate.'

She was right. The detective pulled up alongside them and jumped out of his seat. 'You're still here,' he said, wide-eyed.

'Are we?' said Simmy dopily. 'How do you mean?'

'There was a phone call a few minutes ago, redirected

to me, saying you were interfering in the lives of harmless villagers. I was about a mile away, providentially, and here I am.'

'A phone call?' echoed Ben.

'A public-spirited resident recognised you and thought he should alert us. You are known to be a person of interest to a lot of local people by now. Some of them take it upon themselves to assist the police, even when nobody's asked them to.' He sighed. 'He knew your name, and the girl on the switchboard had been told to refer anything concerning you to me, without delay. She must have reacted remarkably quickly.'

'I'm amazed,' said Ben. 'What about the script with seventeen questions about social security status and time spent at current address?'

'All in your imagination, lad,' said Moxon. 'Once in a while, somebody gets something right, believe it or not.'

'So, what now?' asked Simmy. 'I need to get home to the dog.' Askham and its surrounding neighbours again felt hostile. They did not want her there; sightings of her were reported as if she were an escaped convict.

'Go, then,' said Moxon. 'Do you want me to take Ben home?'

'Careful – it'll get to be a habit. Actually, he's coming with me and then one of us is taking him to Windermere this evening. He can be there all weekend, with plenty of women to tend his needs. He's feeling a bit limp.'

'I am here you know,' said the boy. 'And I stopped feeling limp an hour ago.' He looked at Moxon. 'What are you doing over here, anyway?'

'The same as you, I imagine. Keeping an eye out for Ms

Wilson, thanks to your help.' He smiled at Simmy. 'I admit that Luke Norman had not featured very prominently in our thinking. I never even thought to interview him.'

'He's called Norman?'

'That's right. Son of Irene Norman, one of Pauline's daughters. He's well known in the area as a master fencer. A rare breed, apparently.'

'So you knew that Lindsay wasn't missing after all?'

'Actually no, not until I got your text. You've been very helpful. I'm virtually on my own with this, you know.'

'Except for all the concerned locals keeping track of your suspects for you,' said Ben.

'Right,' said Moxon. He scratched his head. 'Can I ask what your intentions were in coming to find Mr Norman, anyway?'

'We were trying to find Lindsay, really,' said Simmy.

'And then she lost her nerve,' said Ben with an accusing look at Simmy. 'Can't think why. We've spent the whole day, just about, trying to form some sort of hypothesis about the murder. We haven't got far.' He gave Moxon a critical glance. 'You haven't told us anything, so there's a whole lot we don't know.'

'You know about as much as I do. I spend half my time just driving around hoping to hit on something – either in my head or out there in one of these villages. Ludicrous, I admit. I keep on gravitating back to that little car park in Askham, though.'

'You mean Sophie Craig's house,' said Simmy. 'You caught the atmosphere, then?'

'It's a very unhappy little family.'

'Understandably.'

298

'Agreed – but it felt like more than that. Something more complicated.'

'Chloe's friend is dying of heart failure – or something of that sort. Ben found something saying she was waiting for a transplant. I suppose that's terribly stressful.'

'Oh?'

Moxon started to say more, but Simmy interrupted him. 'Except they can't do that if the parents are Jehovah's Witnesses, can they?'

'That was probably only the old woman and she's dead,' said Ben.

All three stared at each other. 'Which would give the family a pretty strong motive to kill her,' the boy went on.

'Chloe practically said that last night,' Moxon remembered.

'They talked about Scarlett when I was there as well,' said Simmy. 'She's Pauline's great-granddaughter. So whose child is she?'

Ben had his notepad on his knee. 'Her father was a very small baby when his father was killed in that tractor accident. The baby was mostly raised by Pauline, I think. Didn't we say that? So that baby's own child would feel much more like her granddaughter – and she might well have had tight control over them all. She'd have enforced the Jehovah's Witness doctrine on them – probably. I'm guessing,' he admitted.

Moxon was also consulting notes. 'Scarlett Parsons is sixteen, lives with both parents near Askham. Brian and Jennifer Parsons. They are all Jehovah's Witnesses. One of the uniforms in Penrith spent a morning listing the whole family for me. That's about all the assistance I could get.

299

I was a bit slow to interview these ones, but I had a word with the father on the phone – just checking out where he and his wife were on Saturday. I didn't know the girl was sick.'

'The parents could have killed Pauline,' mused Ben, 'but it doesn't feel very likely. If they've got this far under her thumb, why change now? Some of the Facebook postings about it go back to the summer – May or June.'

'So we don't really need to talk to Lindsay, after all,' Simmy concluded. 'You need to go and see Scarlett and her parents,' she told Moxon.

'Wait, wait,' begged Ben. 'If Lindsay deliberately named you as the main suspect, did she do it to cover for the real killer? I still think she's the main figure in the whole story.'

Ben and Simmy were still in the car, but with both front doors open. Moxon was standing on Simmy's side, but kept leaning over to address Ben beside her. They made rather a conspicuous group, Simmy realised. Their very indecisiveness must attract attention. The detective must have made himself known to a great many locals over the past days, and Simmy herself was becoming notorious. 'We can't stay here,' she said. 'We have to *do* something.'

'But what?' said Ben. 'We can't all three of us march up to somebody's front door, can we? We're neither fish nor fowl, professional or amateur, like this. We can't expect anyone to open up to us. They'd probably make a formal complaint.'

Moxon grunted an amused agreement. 'You're right. We have to keep to the rules. And we really don't have any evidence against anyone, do we? I suggest we all go home and start again tomorrow. There's a lot to think about and prepare for.'

'You won't let us go with you when you question people, though,' said Ben, stating a fact. 'You'll have to give a detailed account of everything you say and do.'

Simmy lost patience. 'Oh, this is ridiculous. We've wasted the whole day messing about and getting nowhere. The dog's never going to trust us again, Christopher and Robin probably hate each other by now, and I've just drifted about listening to you two make wild guesses. It's a fiasco.'

Ben's phone jingled, which instantly altered the mood. 'Bonnie,' he said before answering the call.

'We're in a little place called Tirril,' he told his girlfriend, and then listened for several seconds. 'No! Why didn't you say before? . . . Yes – we've just worked that out . . . I'm coming down there later on tonight . . . Oh!' and more disjointed responses that Moxon and Simmy shamelessly listened to. Ben told Bonnie they were with him, and then consulted them about the import of Bonnie's words. A plan was formulated between the four of them and both cars moved off.

Chapter Twenty-Four

It was half past nine on Saturday morning when Moxon showed up in Hartsop with Bonnie in the passenger seat and Ben in the back. 'It's so lucky you live in Windermere,' Simmy told Moxon. 'You're much better than a bus. More like a taxi, only free.'

'Not really luck, though, was it? We all started out there, didn't we? We naturally got to know each other after all the things that happened. It was our centre of operations until everyone moved north.'

'I know. I mean – without you, nothing would have worked properly.'

'Don't speak too soon,' said Ben. 'It hasn't worked yet.'

Simmy gave them coffee in the kitchen, looking pale but determined. She had called Tanya Harkness at eight thirty and broken the news that she would be on her own in the shop all morning. 'Or you can just put the Closed sign up,' she offered. Tanya had nobly insisted she would do her best to handle everything and Simmy had suppressed her worries that it might not even be legal to leave a girl of sixteen in charge of a shop.

The previous day had clearly strained her husband's patience almost to breaking point. Cornelia had been thoroughly incontinent, to nobody's surprise, and Robin was damp and exhausted after his time at the auction house. Simmy had not left enough nappies. There was an obvious theme, which Christopher repeatedly pointed out. He was now in the sitting room with both youngsters, trying to recover from feelings of resentment. He had kept Simmy awake for some time explaining how wounding it was to be excluded, taken for granted and treated as a convenience. '*I* wanted to be part of all this as well,' he complained. 'But you charged off without me. It made me feel so useless.'

Simmy had abased herself, apologising and reassuring. 'It was just the way it worked out. It's been wonderful the way you've got so into it all, taking me up to the Cockpit and making so many clever suggestions. I know I did it all wrong yesterday. If it's any consolation, it was mostly boring, embarrassing or frustrating. None of it was fun.'

'And yet you've hatched a plan with the others and left me out completely.'

'That was Ben and Bonnie, not me. It would probably work out just as well if I stayed here with you and let them get on with it.'

'So why don't you?'

'They want to have my car there, just in case. And I'm the only one who can drive it.'

'Just in case what?'

'I don't know, really. I suppose there are a lot of unpredictable elements. Moxon needs some police backup, ideally, but there isn't anybody available. He's in a very tricky situation, actually. Ben pointed that out yesterday. He's got to stick to the rules and be professional, and yet the only help he's getting is from a bunch of amateurs. Lord knows what that'll mean if somebody ever gets charged and taken to court for the murder. The defence people will have a field day.'

Christopher had rolled over to face her. They were both in bed. 'I don't blame you,' he said gently. 'You got dragged into it from the start. All I've wanted is to clear your name and make sure you don't come to any harm. But I do think it's going too far to go all Keystone Kops tomorrow and deliberately walk back into it.'

'I know. I agree, sort of. But there doesn't seem to be any choice. And we need to watch out for Bonnie. I feel towards her the same as you do towards me. She has to be protected.'

'That's the bit I don't get. You haven't explained it to me at all.'

'Because it's all guesswork. If Moxon can't get hold of any proper evidence, the whole case is going to fizzle out and nobody's ever going to be charged with the murder. And that means my name won't ever be entirely cleared. It's all quite logical, really,' she said, aware that she had not answered him at all logically.

'Thanks to young Mr Harkness, of course.'

'Mostly, yes.'

The plan, such as it was, depended on several assumptions, one being that since it was Saturday, people would be at home. It was also quite cold. Angie's predicted blizzard was far from materialising, but there was a nasty wind and the little gang all wore warm coats. Simmy suggested that Christopher might like to light their wood burner later on. 'Keep the home fires burning, eh?' he said.

Robin watched the faces of both parents with interest. He had mostly enjoyed his day at the auction house, with a stream of women all wanting to play with him. Sitting in the same nappy for much too long had been a minor irritation. Now he was expecting to be the centre of attention all over again, which so far had not been the case. His breakfast had been unsatisfactorily hasty, and Cornelia had earned chastisement for jumping up and snatching his bread. When her master had shouted at her, Robin had shared in her chagrin.

Bonnie was quiet and looked as if she hadn't slept. Ben had discarded his sling again, and already his plaster was looking slightly frayed at the lower edge. Moxon was restless and worried. 'This is a terrible idea,' he said – twice. 'What do we think we're doing?'

'We're testing a hypothesis, that's all,' said Ben sturdily.

Bonnie laughed impatiently. 'And if it's right, nobody's going to be happy about it, are they?'

'We have to establish connections,' said Moxon. 'It doesn't hang together until we do that.'

Simmy suddenly giggled. 'We should be including my dad as well. He's sure to find something in *Dombey and Son* that'll explain the whole business.'

Moxon was intent on his notebook and took no notice.

'Just checking my checklist,' he said, and began muttering aloud. 'Phoned Ms Wilson. Got all contact details for Mrs P's relations. List of mourners at the Craig funeral. Results of the post-mortem. Map . . .'

'Is all that on your phone?' Simmy marvelled, seeing no sign that the notebook contained more than a few jottings.

'So they tell me. The nice young constable in Penrith did it for me on Thursday. I'm woefully behind the times with that sort of thing. I've managed perfectly well with a file of paper and an office up to now. I'm not often sent out into the real world like this, miles from my home base.'

'You need a tablet,' said Ben. 'With the phone as backup.'

'Can't we just *go*?' begged Bonnie. 'The suspense is killing me.'

So they went, with Christopher and Robin waving them goodbye from the front door.

'First stop, Lindsay Wilson's house, then?' said Ben, who was riding with Simmy. 'Right?'

'Yes. But we're not going in – that's just Moxon and Bonnie to start with.'

'I've still never seen her. Or Sophie. I feel rather surplus to requirements, actually. I'm surprised Moxo let me come.'

'You're here to support Bonnie. She's liable to get quite upset if things go as we think they will.'

'She'll be fine,' said Ben optimistically.

'We'll park at the bottom of her road facing out, so we can see who goes past.' Which they did, a few yards above the wide opening onto the road that ran through Askham. They could see the shop, and the entrance to the Community Centre, close to the Craig house. Down a hill facing them was the church and Askham Hall, neither of them visible. 'Nobody can come in or out of the village without us seeing them,' said Simmy with satisfaction.

Moxon's empty car was parked right outside Lindsay Wilson's house, a hundred yards further up the road. 'I wonder how they're getting on,' Ben worried, just as his phone trilled. 'We're to go in,' he announced, a few seconds later. 'Come on.'

Simmy found herself shaking with nerves as they approached Lindsay Wilson's front door. Moxon had somehow persuaded Simmy's accuser to be at home and willing to talk – the first item on his checklist – without giving any kind of explanation. In fact, he had not shown any of his workings all week, leaving Simmy and her friends to flounder uselessly on the sidelines. It was quite a surprise that he was including them now.

Bonnie was waiting for them, ushering them into a plainly furnished living room with an encouraging expression. She put her hand on Ben's good arm and murmured, 'I think it's all right.'

Moxon was on a sofa looking fatherly and harmless, a reassuring notepad on his knee. Lindsay Wilson was facing him, her hands clasped together, the picture of shame and self-loathing. 'Oh, here she is,' he greeted Simmy with a smile. 'We'd better run through it all again for her benefit. Just the basics.'

Lindsay turned her face up to Simmy's. 'I'm so dreadfully sorry,' she said. 'I don't know what possessed me – why I ever thought it might be a good idea. I was such a fool, but I couldn't bring myself to change the story. I persuaded myself it wouldn't hurt anybody, because they'd realise it couldn't have been you. Do you see?'

Simmy sat down, and closed her eyes for a moment. She wasn't sure where to start, but one detail took precedence. 'You knew it wasn't me you saw with Mrs Parsons?'

Lindsay put a hand to her brow, and after an encouraging nod from Moxon, launched into something approximating to an explanation. 'I only saw a vague shape in a long coat through the fog. I was coming home from a walk in a bit of a hurry. I'd gone down the road that leads to Helton and then along the footpath that goes back to the church. It sounds straightforward, but I wasn't concentrating and almost got lost. Anyway, I dashed up the road when I got to the church, desperate for a cup of tea. And I was late for a pupil. Plus, just to make everything more complicated, I'd promised to go and feed a cat in a house further up towards the fell.' She looked at Moxon. 'You've already checked all that – the cat and the pupil, I mean.'

The detective merely nodded and then waved for her to continue.

'Okay. Well, it was the weekend so there were quite a few walkers about. When I saw an old woman walking along with somebody much younger ahead of me, I thought it a bit odd, but nothing to worry about. I didn't try to talk to them or anything – they were too far away, anyhow. I wasn't sure it was Pauline, but I had a fair idea. She told me that morning she wanted to go and find the last of the sloes in one of the fields. I thought it was okay because there was somebody with her.' She addressed Simmy. 'I did think it could be you. It looked just like your coat. The one you wore at the funeral.'

'Okay,' said Simmy slowly. 'Then what? When did you go to the police – and what exactly did you tell them?'

'Sunday morning. Coffee time. Luke came banging on my door to tell me his gran was dead. I said I might have seen someone with her the night before and he said I had to report it. When I talked it all over with him, he said it must have been you, because of the coat, and when I did go to the police in Penrith, they somehow made me give your name and it all kicked off from there.'

'And Luke told Eldon and probably other people,' Simmy nodded, with a sigh. 'But how could you *possibly* think I'd do such a thing?'

'I didn't know you. I had absolutely no idea you were that florist who'd helped the police before, along with these two.' She indicated Ben and Bonnie. 'And then this detective inspector showed up, and I realised I was in deep water. I just wanted to escape the whole thing, and get on with my work.'

Ben had been listening with great attention, along with Bonnie. Now he said, 'But if you were there, at the scene at the time she was killed, what's to say *you* didn't kill her?' He looked at Moxon. 'I've wondered that all along.'

'Because I had people waiting for me here at home, and I got back about five minutes after all this I'm telling you, so they can vouch for me. They already have, as it happens.'

Ben persisted, his mind set on a single idea. 'But if this whole story about the person in the coat is invented, then *you* could have marched the old dear up the fell and killed her yourself. There's no certainty about the time she died.'

Moxon cleared his throat. 'We do have some precise timings, as it happens. The spot where the body was found has been shown to be the very place where a group of birdwatchers had been sitting, only about fifteen minutes earlier. They went off towards Ullswater, so they didn't see Mrs Parsons or the person with her. But Ms Wilson's alibi does check out. There's absolutely nothing to disprove her statement.'

Ben was visibly exercising his brain. 'Who were the people waiting here? How many of them?'

Lindsay gave a harsh laugh. 'Believe it or not, one of them was the vicar. I give his daughter some tuition and he'd brought her for a session.'

'How long does it take to walk from here to the Cockpit?' asked Ben.

'I can answer that,' said Simmy quickly, even as she understood that it was barely relevant any longer. 'Christopher and I did it on Tuesday. We left the car further up than here and took Robin in the back carrier. Cornelia was with us. I'd say it took at least twenty minutes. I still don't understand how that old lady could have managed it.'

'It's not particularly difficult or steep,' said Moxon. 'I gather she was used to it.'

'Cornelia,' said Lindsay, with heavy significance. 'That's what did it, you know. Giving that name to your dog.'

'Did what?' asked Simmy.

'Made me stop and talk to you on Saturday. Made me notice you. I'd just written about a thousand words about Cornelia Blimber, and it seemed incredible that I would hear someone say it out loud.'

'But you talked to me on Friday as well. Me and my husband and father. About wakes.'

'That's straight out of Dickens as well. I honestly had no idea who you were.'

310

'Oh,' said Simmy. 'I'm not sure why that matters, except that it makes a lot of our theories look a bit silly.'

There was a pause, nobody saying anything. Simmy glanced at a clock, wondering how much longer they would take to come to the central point.

'So who killed Mrs Parsons?' said Ben loudly. 'It wasn't Simmy, but it might have been a person – apparently female – in a long coat. If you're telling the truth,' he added stubbornly to Lindsay. Simmy gave him an irritated look, trying to convey that Lindsay's truthfulness was no longer the issue.

After the few minutes of relatively robust testimony when speaking to Simmy, Lindsay slumped back into her former attitude. 'I can't say,' she muttered. 'I've learnt my lesson.'

'Lessons!' said Bonnie. 'She teaches my cousin, Chloe. And her friend Scarlett with the heart trouble.. She went to Humphrey's funeral, remember.'

'But Sophie said she hardly knows Lindsay,' said Simmy with a frown.

'It's true,' said Lindsay. 'I haven't had anything much to do with her – but Chloe's another matter. She's been here quite a few times.'

Everyone looked at everyone else, wondering what to make of this news.

'What about the Jehovah's Witnesses?' said Ben. 'Where do they fit in?'

'Pauline was more or less the last of them,' said Lindsay. 'Except her grandson Brian. He's a bit soft in the head, to be honest. Does everything he's told.'

'Scarlett's father,' said Moxon, looking proud of himself.

'What about her mother?'

'Jenny? She's as bad, really. She loves the sense of being special. Always got along famously with the old girl. Believed all the nonsense about Scarlett getting better in God's good time, no need for wicked modern medicine. Mind you, that's all been very much overstated. Scarlett would qualify for a transplant, in theory, but she's not high priority. There's a lot more to the story than you realise.'

'Like what?' asked Ben.

'Like Scarlett being a fantasist, telling Sophie and Humphrey a whole load of garbage about her granny – great-granny to be exact – preventing her from being treated and consigning her to a certain death. When we were discussing *Dombey and Son* the other day, she insisted she was just like Paul, being murdered by his father from sheer stubborn insistence on a stupid idea. She got very carried away with the comparison. I couldn't make her see it was altogether different. At least it meant she'd actually read the book,' she sighed. 'Dickens is badly neglected these days.'

'So it wasn't true?' said Bonnie. 'About the old lady preventing the treatment?'

'Only partly. Scarlett's got a brilliant specialist who's got the sense to tread carefully. She's been prescribing some new medication, and a lot of holistic stuff, which has helped. Brian and Jenny were never going to let Pauline have the final say, anyway. They're not that spineless. But Scarlett turned it all into a wonderful story, making herself the tragic heroine, and the old granny an evil witch. Typical teenager, in fact.'

Bonnie was rigid with realisation. She looked round the room. 'That's it, then,' she said. 'Isn't it?'

'Oh Bonnie!' said Simmy, throwing her arms around the girl. 'And when you've only just found her. It's just so desperately cruel!'

Lindsay reared back in her chair. 'What? What are you saying?' She stared at Bonnie and then Moxon, before bursting into tears. 'I knew you'd work it out in the end. And I know it was all my fault.'

'It's got to have been Sophie, don't you see?' said Ben. 'Getting rid of the old witch so the girl could have her new heart.'

Simmy, Moxon and Bonnie all shook their heads.

'Not Sophie,' said Simmy.

'Chloe,' said Bonnie. 'It was Chloe. She's the same height as Simmy, so Lindsay could easily mistake them...'

'And she's got a coat just like yours,' said Lindsay miserably.

Ben was quick to keep up. 'And she's obsessed with Scarlett. She planned the whole thing, I bet.'

'Helping the old lady to pick sloes up on the fell,' said Simmy. 'Or pretending to.'

Chapter Twenty-Five

Simmy was back with her husband and son well before midday. 'We were wrong about nearly everything,' she said at the start, before giving him the barest summary of the morning's revelations, adding, 'Lindsay Wilson calls Chloe and Scarlett fantasists, but I think there's a touch of that in her character as well. I think she only gradually realised who must have killed Mrs Parsons, when she finally accepted it couldn't have been me. But she didn't say anything to the police. Stupid, really, but she's sorry about it now. Moxon made her cry, lecturing her about impressionable schoolgirls and how she'd encouraged them to believe a lot of nonsense.' She went on to elaborate on the fantasies of schoolgirls.

'So Scarlett Parsons was never in danger of dying? It

sounds quite serious to me. They don't do heart transplants lightly.'

'I rather doubt it was ever even suggested. Just part of the whole imaginary drama. But Chloe believed it. And she saw Mrs Parsons as the whole problem. If she was dead, Scarlett's parents would stop making objections.'

'I still can't credit that she could force a woman of ninety a mile or more up a fellside on a foggy evening.'

'Oh, Lindsay was exaggerating that part, according to Ben. And Mrs Parsons really did want to pick sloes, apparently. Chloe must have offered to help, and just kept her going – talking to her, letting her take her arm – you can just imagine it. And she had it planned all along, how she was going to confront her about Scarlett and maybe force her to give up all the religious stuff about medical intervention. I hate to say it, but I think she knew the only sure way would be if the old lady was dead – or at least made helpless in some way.'

Christopher sighed. 'So how was it done? The actual deed.'

'Moxon didn't say much about that, but Bonnie insisted on knowing the details. Apparently, it was all rather unlucky. The actual blow was pretty feeble, but it must have knocked Pauline down and she hit her head on a stone.'

'Not so unlucky,' he pointed out. 'You remember how many stones there are up there – you'd be very lucky to miss one if you fell over.'

'I feel sorry for poor Moxon. I left him trying to find a Family Liaison Officer and somebody from the Child Protection or whatever they are. It's a terribly delicate business when a child's accused of murder. I could see he was wishing it could all be covered up and forgotten. What good is it going to do to drag her through the courts and ruin her life?'

'If she pleads guilty, there won't be a trial.'

'Well, it's all down to the professionals now.' Simmy hugged her little son to her and tried to imagine the next few days for all the Askham people she had met.

'And your name is redeemed. Not a stain on your character,' said Christopher, aiming for a lighter note.

She gave him a weak smile. 'I don't care about that. All I can think about is how dreadfully sad it is for all of them. Think of poor Sophie! She must be feeling terrible. Lindsay says she believed a lot of what Scarlett said as well.'

'That Scarlett has a lot to answer for.'

'And I expect her entire family will make very sure she knows it,' said Simmy with a dawning flicker of satisfaction.

After lunch Simmy phoned her father and updated him. 'Where does *Dombey and Son* come into it?' he asked. 'Or are you telling me it was a complete irrelevance?'

'It wasn't. I get the impression Lindsay never stopped talking about it to the kids she was tutoring, until Scarlett Parsons saw herself as the wretched Paul, with her great-gran taking the part of Mr Dombey.'

'Hmm,' said Russell. 'Unfortunate business. But I don't think we can blame Dickens, can we?'

'Definitely not,' said Simmy, with a laugh, while at the same time wondering if perhaps they could, just a little bit.

REBECCA TOPE is the author of three bestselling crime series, set in the Cotswolds, Lake District and West Country. She lives on a smallholding in rural Herefordshire, where she enjoys the silence and plants a lot of trees.

rebeccatope.com